"Be ready to leave at first light on the morn."

Slowly, she opened her hands, letting go of his tunic, but unable to remove her hands from his chest. She could feel his heat, and the steady, solid beat of his heart.

"My thanks, Darian," she whispered, looking into his hazel eyes.

His anger, humor, and resignation had fled, replaced by a desire so intense that her woman's places flamed in response. Heaven help her, becoming this man's lover would be no hardship at all.

No matter that he tried her patience, could infuriate her in a heartbeat. No matter that he kept his emotions tightly controlled, gave naught of himself to anyone, not even a hound who adored him.

Heaven help her, if he smiled at her as he had in her vision, demanded a tumble right now in the upstairs bedchamber or a stable's stall, she would relent. . . .

PRAISE FOR SHARI ANTON
AND HER NOVELS

MIDNIGHT MAGIC

"Just the right amount of passion, mysticism, and mythology."
—*Romantic Times BOOKclub Magazine*

Please turn the page for more rave reviews!

AT HER SERVICE

ONCE A BRIDE

THE IDEAL HUSBAND

ALSO BY SHARI ANTON

Midnight Magic

At Her Service

Once a Bride

The Ideal Husband

Twilight Magic

SHARI ANTON

NEW YORK   BOSTON

Cover illustration by Alan Ayers
Cover typography by David Gatti
Book design by L&G McRee

Warner Books
Hachette Book Group USA
1271 Avenue of the Americas
New York, NY 10020
Visit our Web site at www.HachetteBookGroupUSA.com.

Printed in the United States of America

First Printing: December 2006

10 9 8 7 6 5 4 3 2 1

To Mark & Susan Hyzer
who know the full meaning of
for better or for worse.
And are enduring.

Twilight Magic

Chapter One

England, 1145

"Not this morn, Lady Emma. The king has matters of great import to discuss with his counselors, so he will be occupied for the greater part of the day."

Lady Emma de Leon's nails dug into her palms in an effort to control her rising frustration. Shouting at the chamberlain's clerk would do her no good.

Yesterday, another of the chamberlain's clerks had refused her request for an audience with the king, and she'd heard similar excuses on other occasions throughout the past summer. With King Stephen so rarely in residence at Westminster Palace, her opportunities to speak to him had been few and she was determined to gain an audience before he left again.

"On the morrow, perhaps?" Emma asked of the pale little man with the graceful hands and uptilted nose.

He huffed. "A war is being fought, my lady. Events will dictate who will be allowed into the royal presence based on urgent need."

Emma understood all about the damn war. If not for the war's ghastly assault on her family, she wouldn't be forced to plea for royal intervention on her youngest sister's behalf.

In as calm a voice as she could manage, she explained, "A child's fate depends upon a royal decision, and I require only a few moments to make my request. Surely the king can spare a moment for an act of mercy."

"If I yielded to everyone who requested a moment of the king's time, His Majesty would be an old man when all were done."

Emma again tamped down her ire, striving mightily not to strangle the guardian of the royal chamber's door. "I realize the king's time is precious, and if any other person could act on my request, I would not bother him. But no other than King Stephen can make decisions over his ward's fate."

"Is the child in grave danger?"

"Nay, but . . ."

Damn. The clerk's smug smile said she should have lied and told him she feared Nicole in physical danger. But Nicole hadn't complained of beatings or whippings. Instead, the letters stank of amiability and contentment, reeked of resignation.

No plea for deliverance. No entreaty for liberation. If not for the handwriting, Emma would think someone other than Nicole wrote the letters. The girl was either changing or despairing and Emma knew she must procure the girl's release from Bledloe Abbey before the nunnery sucked all the vibrancy and joy of life out of Nicole.

For four months Emma had tried to keep her oath to

Nicole, and four months now seemed far too long to be prevented from keeping that oath.

The clerk waved an irritatingly dismissive hand. "Then the matter is not urgent and does not require the king's immediate attention. Indeed, I suggest you put your request to parchment for the king to consider at his leisure."

"I did, in late summer, but have received no answer. I can only assume my request has been . . . misplaced."

Lost on purpose, no doubt. Shoved aside by the chamberlain's clerks as unimportant. Her deceased father, Sir Hugh de Leon, was considered a traitor, and no one at court felt any obligation to show kindness or mercy to the traitor's daughter.

The clerk's eyes narrowed. "Naught which is overseen by the chamberlain's clerks becomes misplaced. You must have patience, my lady. The king will consider your petition in due time."

With that, he strode down the hallway toward the royal residence, to a doorway leading to the king's chambers, which she could see but wasn't allowed to pass through, leaving her standing alone and with no recourse. Naturally, the guard opened one of the huge oak doors and the clerk swept through without a challenge.

The clerk belonged; she did not.

Tempted to rush the door and force her way in, knowing she might hurt her cause further by such boldness, Emma fled in the opposite direction.

All the way back to the queen's solar, where Emma spent most of her days and nights, she fought the urge to scream and make *someone* listen to her. No one would, however. Not even if she wailed her outrage.

Since her arrival in London, she'd been shunned, considered the undesirable outcast. Emma had known from the moment she'd been informed she was coming to court that she wouldn't be a favorite. However, she had not expected to be treated with malicious contempt—as now, when entering Queen Matilda's sumptuously furnished solar.

Several elegantly garbed women who served as the queen's handmaidens looked up from their embroidery, or loom, or book, to see who had entered. All immediately turned away when they saw who came through the door.

No one of importance, their expressions said. *Only the traitor's daughter,* their malevolence shouted.

Intent on ignoring the hurtful dismissal, Emma plopped down on a bench at the far end of the chamber, near the open window slit through which she heard rain splatter against the palace's thick stone walls. A deep breath helped calm her upset and sort her thoughts, trying not to blame her father or her new brother-by-marriage for placing her in an untenable situation.

On the day of her father's death, King Stephen had knighted Alberic of Chester and gifted him with her father's barony. Then the king had ordered Alberic to marry one of the three de Leon daughters, send another to court, and give the last to the Church.

Alberic's decision on which daughter to marry hadn't surprised Emma. Her younger sister Gwendolyn was by far prettier and more likeable than she was. Nicole, besides being too young for Alberic's taste, had tried to stab him with a dagger. Still, Alberic would allow the girl to return to Camelen, which only proved her brother-by-marriage possessed a generous heart.

Emma had promised Nicole she would petition the king to allow the girl to leave the nunnery and return home. Of late, Emma had considered adding a plea for deliverance of her own, but admitted she didn't particularly want to go home to Camelen. To be dependent upon her slightly younger sister and her brother-by-marriage didn't appeal.

Sweet mercy, she'd been excited when Alberic informed her she was being sent to King Stephen's court at Westminster Palace, and had arrived with hopes of finding a place for herself. Instead, she'd found only misery. 'Struth, she didn't particularly wish to remain at court any more than she wanted to return to Camelen.

For now, however, she must put her own discontent aside and concentrate on freeing Nicole. With her little sister's future settled, Emma could then worry about her own fate.

Not that she had any control over her fate, for that, too, rested in the king's hands. A king whose time was limited and guarded by wretched, uncaring clerks.

People gathering at the doorway signaled the return of Queen Matilda from her daily walk in the garden, accompanied by the flock of men and women who comprised the cream of the queen's court. Everyone in the solar stood, giving the queen the honor due her royal rank. Not until she crossed the room to her ornately carved, armed chair and gave a small hand signal did everyone return to their occupations.

Emma wondered if she should again ask the queen to intervene on her behalf. Matilda, however, showed no more inclination to assist the traitor's daughter than the chamberlain's clerks. Nor were any of the people favored by the royal couple interested in Emma's problems, save one caring soul, who now came toward her.

Lady Julia de Vere, the lovely niece of the earl of Oxford, had come to court years ago to serve as hostage for her uncle's continued support of the king's efforts to hold on to his crown. Though both Emma and Julia were prisoners of the crown—though held gently in the sumptuous prison of Westminster Palace and not the dreary White Tower—Julia de Vere was treated with utmost courtesy and respect by all and sundry. Emma didn't know why Julia didn't consider the traitor's daughter little better than a leper. She was just grateful the woman deigned to be friendly.

She tried hard not to notice how favorably Julia's blond hair compared to her own drab brown, or how much better Julia's bliaut of sapphire silk, shot through with gold thread, fitted into the elegant surroundings than Emma's well-made but now-faded green wool.

Emma accepted the difference in their position at court, even though she outranked the niece of an earl. Being the daughter of a Norman baron placed Emma within the ranks of the nobility, but being the daughter of a Welsh princess boosted her far over Julia. Her high birth was, perhaps, the reason she resided in the palace and not the Tower. However, no one at court felt inclined to acknowledge her station further.

Julia's smile went far to lighten Emma's mood. She took a seat on the bench, careful to spread her skirt to show it to the best advantage.

"How is your head today?" Julia asked. "You are sitting up and seem less pale."

"Better. I appreciate your concern."

"Four days is a long time to spend on pallet in a dark corner with a pounding head. I still contend you should allow a surgeon to examine you."

Julia meant well, and Emma would heed the advice if she didn't already know why the headaches occurred and what she could do to make them cease. However, she considered the cure worse than the agony. She willingly suffered the pain rather than allow cursed, devil-sent visions to overtake her as they had in her childhood. Since discovering how to both evade and fight off the visions, she'd done so—though not with complete success.

If she told Julia of the visions, her friend would be horrified, and Emma didn't wish to lose Julia's friendship. Best to change the subject, an easy task with Julia.

"The surgeon's time would be wasted. How went your walk in the garden?"

"The flowers are fading. Michaelmas is but a fortnight away and with it will come harvest time's chill. You should come with us on the morrow. Each day might be our last opportunity to take the boats into the pond and feed the swans. Were you able to make your request of the chamberlain's clerk?"

Emma suppressed a shiver at the thought of spending the day by the pond and forced herself to continue. "Apparently the king is too busy today to attend to aught not concerning the war. Tomorrow as well. Perhaps I will have better luck the day after."

Julia leaned closer. "I gather you did not offer to bed the clerk."

"Sweet mercy, nay!" Emma said, though she'd been at court long enough not to be entirely shocked at Julia's suggestion.

"Officious, pompous clerks must be bribed into granting favor, either with body or with coin," Julia stated. "If
you have not the coin, then spending a night or two in the
clerk's bed may soften him in your favor."

Emma had already observed that Julia accepted the
practice as a means of getting her way. Her uncle kept her
well supplied with coin, but depending upon what she
wanted and from whom she wanted it, Julia wasn't above
taking a man to her bed, or she sharing his. She was
selective, though, in her bedmates and usually most
discreet.

Indeed, taking a lover seemed common practice. Once
the queen retired to her private bedchamber, a veritable
parade ensued of men coming in and women going out of
the solar. Emma had moved her pallet to a dark corner of
the large chamber to avoid being stepped on or mistaken
for another woman, as much as for a quiet place to endure
her headaches.

"I refuse to offer up my virtue to so mean a little man.
Nor do I have the coin to offer him. And nay, I shall not
take your coin because I have no way to repay you. Allow
me my pride."

"Pride will not open the king's door."

Perhaps not, but to bed the clerk—well, not only did
the pale little man not appeal to her, but even if she offered herself to him, she doubted he would accept. She
wasn't slender and pretty, as were most of the ladies who
lived in the palace, and she would be mortified if she offered the clerk a tumble and he backed away in horror.

Besides, she already *knew* the man to whom she would
give her virginity, and he certainly wasn't one of the
clerks, thank heaven above.

"Then I must find another way into the royal chambers. Perhaps I should slight the clerks and make my request of the chamberlain."

"Tsk. The chamberlain is as hard to gain an audience with as the king. The clerks guard both zealously. 'Struth, Emma, you must somehow bribe one of the clerks or you will never gain a royal audience!"

Emma sighed inwardly. "There must be another way."

"Then you must find a means of entry quickly. I understand the king will be in residence for four more days before he returns to the field."

Four days! Certes, the king couldn't spend all four days in war council, could he?

Well, if she couldn't go through the clerks, or appeal to the chamberlain above them, then she would have to go around them all. Make a direct assault on the royal chambers. Somehow get past the doorway's guards.

Unfortunately, she didn't have any effective weapons in her armory—save one. Bravado.

She would give the king today and tomorrow to meet with his counselors. Early on the morning after, she would be among the throng of courtiers, advisors, and attendants milling outside his chamber door, prepared to sneak, bluff, or push her way inside.

No matter if she lowered her standing at court—which was already so low she didn't see how she could sink further—she would keep her oath to Nicole. Pride and honor, and her own peace of mind, demanded she do no less.

꘎

Darian of Bruges strode through the passageways of the royal residence beside William of Ypres, commander of the Flemish mercenaries, matching his stride to that of his shorter and rounder mentor.

He'd made this trek several times over the past years, and each time Darian felt amazement that he was allowed onto Westminster Palace's grounds, much less into the royal chambers. Of course, there were people who would prefer that a man of his ilk not be allowed in the city of London, much less inside the palace.

Too bad.

King Stephen needed men like Darian if he hoped to win his war against the Empress Maud. Men willing to take risks, capable of accomplishing those tasks that men of refinement were reluctant to undertake. A mercenary skilled in warfare, willing to do whatever necessary to defeat an enemy.

His boot heels clicked against the highly polished plank floors, too loudly for a man accustomed to approaching others too quietly for them to hear before he struck. But then, this morn, his only task was to act as an added set of ears and eyes for his commander.

An easy task, but one few others could perform. Not only did William trust Darian's keenly honed ability to assess his surroundings, but Darian was also a member of a carefully chosen band of mercenaries who knew William's eyesight had begun to fail. King Stephen didn't yet know of the mercenary commander's difficulty, and William planned to keep the problem secret until it interfered with his ability to command troops in battle.

Darian hoped that time might not come for many years yet.

"Do you know why we have been summoned, or who else will be present?" Darian asked.

William shook his head. "The clerk did not say, though I would not be surprised to see Bishop Henry. He did not approve of the plan we decided upon yester noon and I fear he may have convinced the king to change his mind."

Damnation! If the king changed his mind, then Darian wouldn't be leaving London anytime soon, and Edward de Salis, a vile, evil man, would continue to ravage villages and maim and murder more innocents.

The son of a baron, Edward de Salis took advantage of the war's upheaval to add coin to his coffers, uncaring who suffered from his endeavors. Though warned several times to cease, de Salis ignored the king's orders in his pursuit of wealth.

The villain must be stopped. Yesterday, the king had finally given Darian the order to bring the villain to his knees, then send him to hell.

Unfortunately, one of the complaints often heard about King Stephen was his inability to withstand a convincing argument, and Henry, bishop of Winchester, the king's brother, who hadn't approved of King Stephen's decision on de Salis, was quite adept at presenting convincing arguments.

"Bishop Henry might not feel so generous toward de Salis if his villages were being burned and his people harmed."

"Too true. Do you see him?"

They were nearing their destination. Darian's height proved useful as he glanced around at the men and women milling in front of the doors to the antechamber.

"Nay. Nor do I see any of the earls or other advisors present yester noon."

A good sign. If Bishop Henry had, indeed, won King Stephen over, the bishop would surely be present to gloat.

"Perhaps they are already in the king's chambers. Ah, the doors open."

The huge oak doors swung wide. The crowd rushed forward to enter the antechamber. Pushing and shoving ensued, each person trying to gain advantage over their fellows. Their efforts would do them no good. Unless they'd been summoned by the king or paid the clerk a goodly sum beforehand, they would be forced to wait until the clerk deemed them worthy of entry into the royal presence.

One woman had apparently come to that conclusion.

Garbed in a topaz-hued bliaut covering a white chemise, the softly rounded, dark-haired woman actually seemed hesitant to pass into the antechamber. Darian saw her nervousness in the flight of a hand over a gauzy veil that needed no smoothing, her uncertainty in the touch of a finger to the gold circlet that held her shimmering white veil in place. From behind her, he couldn't see her face, but could well imagine the misgivings he might glimpse in her eyes.

When he found himself wondering what color the lady's eyes might be, he pulled his attention back to where it belonged.

He and William edged forward at the back of the crowd, the king's summons guaranteeing they would be among the first admitted to the king's audience chamber. Which suited Darian immensely. He didn't like crowds and found the air in the palace stifling. Better this audience was over quickly so he could get on with more important duties and not have to deal with personages of noble birth, most of whom couldn't be bothered with anything other than their own petty concerns.

The lady in topaz bowed her head and positioned herself close behind two large men who shouldered their way through the middle of the crowd, doing her best to avoid notice by the guards on either side of the door. She slipped into the antechamber without challenge and Darian could almost feel her relief.

She's not supposed to be here.

He admired the lady's boldness, but knew her efforts were for naught. She may have sneaked past the first set of guards, but would never get past the clerk if she wasn't on his list of those who would be allowed to speak with the king. And he highly doubted she was on the clerk's list.

Her problem wasn't his problem. There was nothing he could do to help her, even if he wanted to, which he didn't.

Still, his curiosity prodded him to nudge William and ask softly, "The woman in topaz. Do you know who she is?"

William squinted. "Lady Emma de Leon. Have you heard her tale?"

He'd heard of the woman and her plight.

"Daughter of Sir Hugh de Leon, who had the misfortune of dying while fighting for Empress Maud. King Stephen's ward. Barely tolerated at court." As he was grudgingly tolerated. He brushed aside an unwanted pang of kinship. "Must a royal ward be on the clerk's list for her to speak with the king?"

"Probably. Why?"

"Merely wondering."

Thankfully, William accepted the explanation without comment because Darian truly couldn't explain his curiosity over the king's ward.

Lady Emma glanced furtively from side to side, likely looking for a place to hide, giving him brief glimpses of her profile.

He could see she was a young woman, possessed of creamy, unflawed skin. Her pert nose was offset by a strong jaw, a quality Darian found intriguing.

Though her flowing bliaut hid the exact proportions of her form, the width of her shoulders, the tuck of her waist, and the spread of her hips suggested all of her curves were nicely rounded and well endowed. The hands he'd admired when she'd smoothed her veil were graceful, and her movements might be furtive, but they weren't clumsy.

Lady Emma might not be the most exquisite woman he'd ever seen, but she was certainly lovely and interesting enough for a man to give a second look.

Rather, for a nobleman to give a second look, not a mercenary.

To his chagrin, Darian still wanted to know the color of Lady Emma's eyes, but he didn't have the chance to inspect her more closely. Duty called. Darian followed William to the next doorway, this one guarded by an imperious clerk, as well as two burly soldiers.

The clerk bowed. "Earl William, you are expected."

Darian almost smiled at the clerk's obeisance. Indeed, the king had granted William, a mercenary of noble birth, enough land, rights, and fees to hold the title of earl of

Kent. Accustomed to becoming lost in William's shorter shadow, Darian wasn't surprised when the clerk didn't acknowledge him, merely gave a hand signal to the guard to open the door.

Then the clerk glanced up, and a sly gleam within his eyes sent a shiver down Darian's spine. Something was amiss.

He entered the inner chamber behind William, his senses alert. All seemed calm and normal enough. King Stephen sat in his ornate armed chair, the chamberlain standing beside him, their expressions giving nothing away.

No one else was in the room. Not even a servant.

Still, Darian sensed a threat and for the life of him couldn't figure out why the back of his neck tingled—until he heard shouts coming from the antechamber.

"Make way for the bishop! Stand aside! Make way!"

The bishop had to be Henry, and Darian's conjecture was confirmed when he heard the man's voice.

"Let them in! Let them all into the royal chamber to witness the king's justice!"

"What the devil is Henry about?" William muttered.

Darian didn't know, but whatever the bishop was up to couldn't be good.

Henry, the powerful bishop of Winchester, brother of the king, garbed in the full regalia of his office, burst into the chamber. He hustled toward King Stephen followed by four soldiers bearing a litter.

The room filled up with people. The air grew close and overly warm.

Bishop Henry pointed to a spot on the floor in front of the king. The men lowered the litter.

Darian heard the buzz of voices, was well aware of William uncomfortably shifting his stance, but nothing could tear his gaze from the face of the obviously dead man on the litter.

The face of Edward de Salis, the vile, evil man who yester noon the king had given Darian the order to assassinate. Someone had gotten to de Salis first.

"Darian of Bruges!" Bishop Henry shouted. "I accuse you of murder!"

Chapter Two

Emma marveled at her good luck. She'd been prepared for an encounter with an overbearing clerk when fate intervened, easing her entry to the royal chamber. Of course, she still might have to wrestle with the clerk, but she was closer to her goal and she would allow no one to stop her now.

At the moment she couldn't see what transpired at the front of the chamber. She'd caught a glimpse of Bishop Henry when he'd passed through the antechamber with the litter bearers in his wake. Who the poor man on the litter might be, or how he'd died, she didn't know.

However, the bishop had called out the name of the man he accused of murder. Darian of Bruges.

An unusual name—Darian.

"I did not murder Edward de Salis."

His deep, rich voice rang strong and clear through the chamber, and Emma craned her neck to locate the owner of the powerful voice. But the men she'd used as a shield to get into the chamber were too broad and tall to see around.

No matter. The dead man and his murderer had nothing to do with her. Giddy with anticipation, Emma inched her way forward, certain that once this distraction was over, she could better judge how to approach the king.

"Is this not the man you described to us yesterday as vile and evil?" the bishop asked.

"He is," Darian answered.

"This morn, he was found dead in an alley on Watling Street in Southwark, his throat slit."

"How fortunate for us all." Darian's droll comment drew snickers from a couple of people in the crowd.

She could see the bishop now. In his flowing robes, he stood near where King Stephen sat in an elegantly carved, armed chair and listened intently. She also saw the Flemish mercenary captain, Earl William, a favorite of Queen Matilda's who often visited the queen's solar, step over to the litter to stare down at the dead man.

"You are known for your skill with a dagger, Darian. Have you your dagger with you?" the bishop asked.

"Weapons are not allowed in this chamber. I would not be so witless as to bring one into the royal presence. My dagger is with my belongings in the barracks and I can produce it, if you wish."

Emma squeezed into a small space between two people, inching forward once again.

"You did not sleep in the barracks last night," the bishop stated, his ire becoming palpable. "There are those among your own fellows who will testify they saw naught of you until the dawn. Can you produce trustworthy witnesses to attest to your whereabouts?"

For several heartbeats silence reigned.

"Nay."

After a slight shift Emma saw the accused. While murmurs floated around her, she paid them no heed, aware only of the handsome, sandy-haired, hazel-eyed man garbed all in black.

She almost gasped aloud, her pulse quickening as she recognized Darian of Bruges. Broad of shoulder, narrow in the hip, long and lithe, he stood with his feet spread apart slightly, his arms crossed over his chest, a stance sublimely suited to him.

Amazement mingled with a heady sense of anticipation that weakened her knees. After years of waiting, of comparing all other men to him, the lover of her vision had finally appeared.

Emma closed her eyes and envisioned Darian as clearly as the first time she'd *seen* him. She knew what his upper body looked like without clothing—all taut, sculpted muscle. His lower arms were a sun-touched bronze. Beneath his lowest left rib, he bore a scar. His cheeks dimpled when he smiled, and his smile for her, when holding out his hand in seductive, tantalizing invitation, was glorious.

She hadn't touched his hand in the vision, but had always imagined his touch warm, his grasp firm and sure, his fingers clever and knowledgeable.

True, she'd expected her lover to be Norman or Welsh, akin to her own mixed heritage, but his name implied— Emma's eyes snapped open as reality returned with a hard slap to her senses. Bruges was a town in Flanders, so Darian must be a Flemish mercenary! And he stood accused of murder!

Sweet God in his heaven!

Oh, cruel fate! A mercenary? A murderer?

Surely she would never bed a murderer!

She frantically studied Darian's expression, searching for signs of guilt or innocence. His stoicism gave naught away.

"Sire, consider," the bishop pleaded. "Darian of Bruges is known to hold Edward de Salis in contempt. He cannot produce witnesses to attest to his whereabouts last night. Nor, I believe, can he produce his dagger." The bishop held out his hand to one of the litter bearers. The flash of silver passed between the men's hands. "This dagger was found beside de Salis's body. I believe it belongs to Darian of Bruges."

Darian's eyebrow arched, but he made no move toward the bishop. Neither did he confirm or deny ownership.

Two heartbeats of silence later, Earl William held out his hand. "Give me that."

With a nasty smile the bishop handed the weapon over. "'Twould seem you have less control over your mercenaries than you would have us believe, William."

William tapped the blade against his palm, his eyes narrowing with anger. "I have never known Darian to be less than honest, and I believe his denial of any knowledge of this deed. Whoever killed de Salis has done a fine job of making it appear Darian is guilty."

Bishop Henry waved a dismissive hand. "Spoken as a commander in defense of one of his favorites. I might allow the possibility of his honesty if Darian could produce one trustworthy witness to his whereabouts. But he either cannot, or will not."

All looked again to Darian.

Emma edged her way forward, silently begging him to relent. To prove his innocence by telling the bishop where he'd been last night and with whom.

He simply turned to William and, in that same unwavering tone, stated, "I know not who killed de Salis, or why my dagger is not with my other belongings, but I swear to you, he did not die by my hand."

The denial rang true. Darian hadn't killed de Salis, no matter the bishop's accusations. No matter his inability to provide proof. As Earl William said, someone had betrayed Darian. Surely the king would hear and see the truth.

King Stephen rose from his chair and held out his hand to William, who handed over Darian's dagger. The king flipped it over in his palm, staring down at the weapon—frowning mightily.

A bad omen, that frown.

Dread and anger over her visions flooded through her, and she was once more unprepared and uncertain over *what* she was supposed to do.

Did the visions reveal future events that couldn't be changed, or were they glimpses of possibilities that could be altered?

The confusion had plagued her from an early age. Bewildered and sometimes frightened by seeing odd things in pools of water, she'd told her mother of what she saw. Mother had looked on her with pity, told her to keep the sightings to herself. So Emma had obeyed, told no one, not even her mother.

The pang of grief was sharp, the guilt nearly overwhelming over the one vision she wished she'd possessed the wisdom and courage to reveal. Perhaps if she'd told someone that her mother would die giving birth to Nicole, either her mother or the midwives could have done something to prevent the death.

Or perhaps not. She could well have been accused of causing her mother's death by foretelling it.

And if she hadn't turned coward and foreswore the visions, might she have been able to warn her father of the danger at Wallingford, warned him to be cautious? And despite the warning might he and her brother have died anyway?

Damn. She never invited the visions, didn't want to know what might happen in *anyone's* future because she never knew what was best, as now.

Would Darian come away unscathed if she held her peace, or must she interfere to save his life so her vision of him would come true?

The king now stared at Darian, and Emma wrestled with the dilemma of what to do if Darian refused to save himself from a hangman's noose.

Darian watched the dagger flip in the king's hands, the lion's head on the hilt proclaiming the shining weapon as his own. Someone must have stolen it after he'd returned to the barracks early this morning, stuffed the weapon into his pack, then left to break fast with William before attending this farce of a meeting. The thief would have had ample time, nigh on two hours, to commit the murder and leave Darian's dagger with de Salis's body.

Was that someone a mercenary? He had to believe it probable, though 'twas sickening to realize there might be a traitor in their midst. Darian didn't know who, and hoped he would live long enough to expose the bastard.

But why had Bishop Henry made so public a spectacle over what could have been handled quietly, secretly?

Naturally, any murder in Southwark would come to Bishop Henry's attention. He resided in Winchester Palace in Southwark, and collected rents and fees from the taverns, brothels, and sundry businesses that provided lewd, exciting amusement on the south bank of the Thames.

Henry hadn't approved of the king allowing Darian to dispose of de Salis, and the king couldn't have forgotten that yester noon he'd given permission for an assassination.

Darian knew King Stephen couldn't admit publicly he'd condoned an assassination. If asked, all who'd been present yesterday would deny any involvement in the decision to assassinate de Salis. If Darian were caught, not one of them would come to his aid.

Having accepted the mission, Darian knew he took all the risks, bore all the responsibility, would receive no reward or acclaim beyond his pay.

The king also must realize Darian wouldn't have killed de Salis in so public a place as Watling Street, but in the countryside, quietly and efficiently, making it seem the man had simply disappeared.

The whole thing stank of a conspiracy to frame him.

The king finally stopped flipping the dagger. "You admit this is your dagger?"

"As I said, I have no notion of how it came to be found near the body. The last I saw it was early this morn when I placed it with my other belongings."

"And you cannot produce witnesses to attest to your whereabouts last night?"

Not a *trustworthy* witness. The two men he'd met with would never pass the bishop's test. Honor demanded Darian not utter their names, much less ask them to testify on his behalf.

"I fear not, Sire."

"You give us nothing on which to trust your protest of innocence, Darian."

King Stephen's tone and expression said he wanted to dismiss Bishop Henry's charge, or be given an explanation for the dagger's presence in Southwark, or for someone to come forward on Darian's behalf.

Darian could give him nothing.

"All I offer you is my word of honor—"

Henry huffed. "The word of a Flemish mercenary? You ask too much!"

From the back of the chamber came a shout. "Justice!"

Another voice picked it up, and then another, until soon the word reverberated off the walls in a damning chant, the injustice of their damnation churning his stomach.

Darian considered making an attempt to escape, but even if he could push through the crowd to the door, he considered it cowardly and akin to an admission of guilt.

So he stood his ground, feeling the noose tightening around his neck, choking off his breath.

The king waved the crowd to silence, and the deepening quiet was almost as nerve-wrenching as the chant.

"You give us no recourse, Darian. If this is your dagger, and if, as my brother testifies, it was found beside de

Salis's body, then we must condemn you as guilty. Guards, remove the prisoner and inform the hangman."

Sweat broke out on his brow. Bile rose in his throat.

Guards appeared on either side of him and clamped onto his arms. Thinking reasonably proved taxing.

Certainly Earl William would protest and find a way to stop the hanging. His life surely wasn't meant to end in so unjust and ignoble a fashion.

Then Darian heard footsteps, light but steady across the floor, and he couldn't help but turn toward the sound.

Lady Emma de Leon stood at the forward edge of the crowd, her hands clutching her topaz bliaut. She dipped into a deep curtsy.

"Sire, if I may be allowed to approach?"

The king sighed and gave her a condescending smile. "Lady Emma, now is not the time to speak of your petition. I am aware of your wish to aid your sister and will—"

"You misunderstand my boldness, Sire. What I have to say has naught to do with Nicole, though if you would grant me a moment later to consider my request, I would be forever most grateful." She licked her lips, as if they'd gone dry. "What I must tell you . . . that is, confess . . . well, I believe you do not wish to hang an innocent man."

On the edge of his awareness, Darian saw the king's eyebrow arch upward. Bishop Henry left his post by the litter to stand at King Stephen's side. Even as his instincts distrusted her uninvited and suspect intrusion, Darian noticed the lady's eyes were the deep, soft brown of a doe, and just as wide open and luminous.

But where a doe's eyes shone with innocence, Emma's were veiled. She didn't look at him, intent on the king, who motioned her forward.

So many questions flew through Darian's mind, he couldn't sort them all during the few steps Emma took to stand a respectable distance from the king. He knew, however, that she couldn't possibly know where he'd been last night. No respectable lady would dare visit Southwark after nightfall when whores and drunkards ruled the night. And above all, Emma impressed him as a lady gifted with intelligence.

She might, however, know who had stolen his dagger. A possibility. A damn miracle, even.

"Confessions should be heard in private, my child," the bishop commented, his tone no less condescending than the king's. "I would be most willing to step aside and hear whatever troubles you so deeply."

Darian almost snickered aloud at Henry's obviously self-serving offer.

Emma graciously bowed her head. "I thank you, Lord Bishop, but what I must say should be heard by all in attendance." Then she squared her shoulders, took a long, fortifying breath, and rushed on. "Darian of Bruges is innocent of murder, Sire. He does not tell you of his whereabouts last night because he wishes to protect . . . me."

The implication slowly sank in, and Darian could only stand shocked at what she'd done.

The guards released him abruptly, a welcome occurrence, though he feared the reprieve wouldn't last.

Sweet Jesu, by suggesting they'd been together last night, Lady Emma shed doubt on his guilt, but at a high price to her already tattered reputation.

Why did she lie? For what reason did she interfere? Truly, she had nothing to gain—or did she? She must! No noblewoman would come forward to save a commoner, and a foreign commoner at that, unless she stood to gain . . . something. But what?

Whatever her reason, he couldn't allow her to become entangled in his affairs. Certes, her lie would only make matters worse when the truth came to light.

Darian opened his mouth to refute her; Earl William's hand clamped down hard on his forearm, the order clear. *Hush!* Darian found himself obeying out of sheer habit of following the earl's orders.

The king looked suspicious, as well he should. "Lady Emma, do we understand you correctly? You say you bear witness to Darian's whereabouts last night?"

Emma nodded.

"All night?"

A blush bloomed on her cheekbones as she nodded again.

Murmurs from the crowd weren't complimentary.

Darian leaned toward William, who still held tight to his arm, and whispered, "This is madness. The lady lies."

"So let her."

"This is wrong."

William rolled his eyes. "Wrong or no, she gives you your freedom. God's bones, Darian, allow the lady to have her way!"

Sensible advice, but it irked him to stand there and allow a woman to *save* him from being punished for a crime he didn't commit!

The murmurs grew louder and more damning. Harlot. Whore. Fornicator. Hellfire, the woman didn't deserve their condemnation! And Bishop Henry could well demand she fast for a year as penance. Why the devil did she place herself in such a position?

Bishop Henry, his countenance as dark and threatening as a storm cloud, raised a silencing hand. Not until the crowd quieted did he ask of Emma, "Where?"

To Darian's unwarranted amusement, Lady Emma de Leon insolently raised an eyebrow.

"Does it matter?"

"Answer!"

"The queen's solar."

A gasp rose from the crowd and the bishop puffed up in ire.

"Then we shall send for the queen's handmaidens and ask them to confirm Darian's presence in the solar."

"The queen is frugal with her candles," Emma stated. "Those not asleep would not have seen Darian's face clearly, nor would they pay any heed to his occupying a pallet at the far end of the solar."

Bishop Henry's control slipped as he addressed the king. "Sire, this woman is the daughter of a traitor! Her word cannot be trusted any more than the mercenary's. I say she lies!"

"Why would she lie, Henry?"

Exactly what Darian wondered!

"I know not, but to believe her is to allow a murderer to go free!"

Hands clasped behind his back, his expression thoughtful, King Stephen took two steps toward Emma, bringing them to within arm's reach of each other.

"We are hard-pressed to learn the full truth, my lady. As my brother says, your word is suspect. Is there nothing further you can offer?"

Emma again licked her lips, and for the first time she

glanced at him. Not long enough for him to guess what she was thinking.

In a voice so low Darian strained to hear, she said, "I can tell you of his scars. The one beneath his left ribs is thin and long. The others I would rather not speak of, if I need not."

How the hell did she know?

The bishop didn't give him time to contemplate. "I beseech thee, Sire, to consider how this woman claims to have soiled the sanctity of our beloved queen's solar! She has fornicated with a man not her husband! Punishment under Church law—"

"We are aware of Church law, Henry." The king turned toward his brother. "We are not in a Church court, but a royal one, and while we take a dim view of this morning's revelations, we are inclined to mercy. Darian of Bruges shall marry Lady Emma de Leon and both will leave the court."

Darian's heart leapt to his throat. Marriage! Never. Not to any woman, particularly not to a woman who took advantage of his misfortune to gain . . . something.

The crowd thought the king's proclamation a grand one. Bishop Henry looked stunned. And the woman whose interference had brought them to this pass—her chin drooped to her chest, her eyes closed.

Unable to hold his peace any longer, Darian shook off William's staying hand. "Sire, I cannot say why the lady has invented this tale, but we did not—"

Emma's head snapped up. "Certes we did!"

Determined to ignore her, Darian continued. "We have never known each other in carnal manner. In truth, I have never seen Lady Emma before this morning. There is no reason for us to marry."

Now in high dungeon, Emma crossed her arms. "I agree. No reason whatsoever."

"We do not recall giving either of you a choice!" King Stephen said. "You will pledge to each other with all here as witness. Lady Emma, I will have your consent."

She took a deep breath, her irritation unrelenting. "Only because you so order, Sire."

King Stephen's eyes narrowed. "Darian?"

For the blink of an eye Darian thought to protest once more, but knew damn well that he either married Emma de Leon *now* or suffer a rope slipped around his neck. So be it. Better to live and deal with the mess later.

But not much later. The thought of marriage appealed to him as much as hanging. He wanted no wife, no children, no one to whom he must feel a responsibility. No one to mourn for him or to mourn in return.

He almost choked on his consent.

"If you insist, Sire."

Bishop Henry looked crestfallen. "But, Stephen, what of de Salis? Will you allow his murderer to go unpunished?"

The king glanced down at the dead man at his feet. "Haul him out of here as you hauled him in, Henry. We doubt the happy couple wishes a corpse in attendance as they exchange vows."

He wasn't sure how Lady Emma felt about the presence of a corpse at their wedding, but to Darian it somehow seemed fitting.

Chapter Three

Even the absence of the corpse couldn't help turn what should be a joyous, solemn occasion from a bleak mockery.

Emma knew she'd gone too far, but didn't know what she could have done differently. Had she not spoken out, Darian could now be on his way to the gallows instead of standing beside her before the king, who looked impossibly pleased with himself.

Darian didn't appear to be pleased in the least. He held himself plank stiff, his hands clasped behind his back, frowning mightily, giving all the impression he might prefer the gallows.

Damn. The ungrateful wretch could truly look a bit less put out. She *had* saved his neck from a noose. She saved his life and he didn't appreciate her sacrifice one whit. But then she didn't appear any more pleased with this turn of events, even though it saved her from starving for a year.

She should have remembered that nasty penance before confessing to fornicating with a man not her husband. But she'd been hard-pressed and blurted out the first credible tale that had come into her head.

"Lady Emma, we require your vows."

Was it only four months ago she'd witnessed her sister's wedding, listened to Gwendolyn pledge to Alberic? That hadn't been the happiest of occasions, either, but at least the bride and groom had since come to an understanding and learned to love each other.

Could she and Darian one day come to the same pass? Her vision of him had revealed they would become lovers, but showed her naught of afterward. Uncertainty nagged at her, making her once more wonder if she'd done right to interfere in Darian's affairs.

"Lady Emma?" the king prodded.

"I take Darian of Bruges as my husband," she said before her throat closed up, blocking vows of love and honor and obedience.

Apparently the king didn't notice because he immediately turned his attention to Darian, who sighed before he said, "I take Emma de Leon as my wife."

King Stephen clapped his hands. "We realize the haste prevents the gifting of a ring, but we are sure you can remedy the lack in a trice. Can you not, Darian?"

Reluctantly, Darian nodded.

"We are also certain you are aware that Emma de Leon is a royal ward, and therefore important to us. We will have your assurance she shall be properly sheltered, clothed, and fed by her husband."

Darian rolled his shoulders, as if adjusting them to this new burden. "I shall see to her maintenance."

Once over the amazement that the king would care what happened to her henceforth, Emma had to wonder what Darian considered proper maintenance. She might starve anyway.

"Wonderful! Henry, would you kindly bless their union?"

Bishop Henry's expression clearly stated he would as soon excommunicate her, or worse. His blessing consisted of an angrily waved sign of the cross with no words, more a sign of dismissal than a blessing.

Sweet mercy, she'd thwarted the plans of the most powerful bishop in the kingdom, and had the feeling that her victory might come back to haunt her.

Or Darian.

Had he murdered de Salis? Emma thought not. She believed his fervent protest of innocence, one of the reasons she'd come forward. Had she not believed Darian's stalwart denials, never would she have meddled, not even to ensure her vision came true.

"Go with our blessing," King Stephen intoned, then turned around in dismissal.

Darian grabbed hold of her arm, his grasp firm but not hurtful. The heat from his hand seeped through the sleeve of her topaz gown and sent tingles up her arm.

Though he nudged her toward the door, she wasn't yet ready to leave. Through all that had happened, she hadn't completely forgotten the reason why she'd dared sneak into the king's presence.

"Not yet," she told her new husband. "I must speak with King Stephen about—"

"Have you not done enough harm for one day?"

Emma bristled. "I need only a moment to make my request."

Darian sneered. "I doubt the king is of a mind to listen right now. We have been dismissed. Best we go before he changes his mind."

Emma glanced over her shoulder to see Bishop Henry speaking earnestly to King Stephen, Earl William standing nearby. None of them appeared in the mood to be interrupted—or merciful.

Darian might be right. Approaching King Stephen about Nicole now might not be a good idea. Besides, in order to speak to the king, she would have to shake off Darian's hand, and she doubted she could manage that without calling more undue attention to herself.

The crowd parted to allow them to walk toward the door. Lewd comments accompanied insolent bows. She ignored the rabble, preferring to focus on the man whose stride became quicker as they neared the doorway, making it nigh impossible for her to keep up and maintain a modicum of dignity.

The insufferable wretch! She understood his upset, which she shared. She hadn't planned to marry him, just save his ungrateful hide! At the least he could allow her a measure of deportment!

In the antechamber she flung off all pretense of dignity and jerked her arm from his hold.

"Perhaps I should have allowed Bishop Henry his way!"

His smile twisted with scorn. "I hear that if one pays the hangman well, he will ensure a quick death and hasty burial. Instead, I face a lifetime of suffering. . . . What the

hell were you thinking, woman? What demon possessed
you to conjure up that ludicrous tale?"

Before she could respond, he stepped back two paces
and ran an assessing gaze from her face down to her toes
and back again, a blatant, knee-weakening appraisal of
her attributes.

"Not that I would have minded sharing your pallet last
night," he said. "Had I known you wanted me, I would
have been most pleased to oblige."

Emma knew he meant to give insult, but sweet mercy,
he'd unwittingly given her assurance he found her attrac-
tive, worthy of bedding.

Still, she returned his scorn. "Had I known you were
in need, I would have issued the invitation. You were free
to accept last night, were you not?"

His spine straightened and his eyes narrowed. "I did
not murder de Salis, if that is what you ask."

"So I believed, or I would not have come forward."

"Enough to brazenly lie?"

"Enough to force me to act before the king hanged an
innocent man!"

He tossed his hands in the air. "You do not even know
me. Why risk your own neck?"

She couldn't tell him about her visions or of how long
she'd known of him. He would think she'd gone completely witless, or worse. A witch. A demon. So she told
him part of the truth.

"I might not have if I had remembered the Church's
penance for fornication, or if I thought my selfless act
might be unwelcome and go unappreciated."

He didn't have the courtesy to look abashed. "My
thanks. Now tell me what I am supposed to do with you."

Take me to bed. Become my lover.

She came close to blushing at the wayward bend of her thoughts. One day, he would become her lover, as fate decreed, but not in the next few minutes.

"We are supposed to leave court."

"And go where?"

Earl William clamped a hand on Darian's shoulder, startling them both.

"Go to Kent," William told Darian. "You can stay at Hadone until we deem it safe for you to return."

Darian's mouth twisted in distaste. "Someone killed de Salis with my dagger and I need to find out who." Then his shoulders sagged. "Hellfire. The king still has my dagger."

William wagged a finger. "Let the murder be, for now. Already Henry is trying to convince Stephen that he made a mistake in believing Lady Emma. Neither of you should be in the city if Henry is successful. I will get your dagger back. Both of you gather your belongings and be prepared to leave within the hour."

Then the mercenary captain smiled and bowed to her. "Felicitations on your marriage, Lady Emma."

Stunned, Emma couldn't think of a thing to say except, "My thanks."

Chuckling, William headed back toward the royal chamber, leaving Emma alone in the antechamber with Darian.

"Kent!" he complained. "How am I supposed to catch a murderer if I am exiled to Kent?"

He wasn't the only one who preferred not to go to Kent.

"I shall not be able to speak with the king about my

sister from there, either. Sweet Jesu, how am I to explain to Nicole that I have failed her? What a mess!"

He raised an eyebrow. "You will remember who got us into this mess."

She raised her chin. This unpleasant turn of events was *not* all her fault. "Perhaps next time you will keep better track of your belongings so you cannot be accused of murder!"

He leaned forward, so close she caught his musky scent. "Perhaps next time you will do me the favor of not meddling in my affairs. And just how did you know I have a scar under my ribs?"

Emma bit her bottom lip. She'd interfered and knew of his scar from a vision. She didn't dare tell him how clearly she'd seen, and admired, more than his scar.

"I guessed. All men who wield weapons bear scars somewhere, and I doubted the bishop would force you to remove your clothing to prove it."

"You guessed?"

"Had I told him you have a scar on your right thigh, would I have been correct?"

He backed away, his eyes widening in horrified disbelief. "Aye."

"Then my guesses are not too off the mark, are they? If we are to leave within the hour, had we best not prepare? We shall need a cart for my trunks."

Her change of subject brought a frown to his face. "How many trunks?"

"Two."

"Must you take them both?"

"For certes, I cannot leave anything here. If I send for

them later, I might not get anything back, maybe not even the trunks."

"Should they not be safe in the queen's solar?"

"As safe as was your dagger in the barracks."

Darian traversed the long, narrow room lined with pallets the mercenaries closest to William occupied as their barracks when at Westminster.

Marc, Philip, and Armand, all men he'd trusted, sat cross-legged on the plank floor at the end of the room, tossing dice. Had one of these men betrayed him? The very thought made him ill.

Damn, he wished he didn't have to leave, but William had ordered him to go to Hadone, so go he would.

Where Emma de Leon required two trunks to hold her belongings, Darian needed but one leather satchel to contain all his worldly goods. He picked it up from where it sat on the pallet he'd been using, the same satchel from which someone had filched his dagger this morn.

He flipped it open to see if aught else had been disturbed.

He rummaged under a spare tunic to find a small pack containing his shaving knife and an ivory comb. A large, heavy sack of coins felt no lighter than before. 'Twas all he owned and aspired to nothing more. What a man owned could be taken away from him, as his father had been robbed of his family, property, and life. As Darian's dagger had been taken this morning.

From behind him he could hear the other mercenaries approach.

"Heard rumors, Darian. What happened?" Marc asked.

"Rumors already?"

"The men loading de Salis into a cart possessed loose tongues. Is it true?"

"What did you hear?"

"That the watch found your dagger near de Salis's body, and Bishop Henry hauled both the corpse and dagger before the king and accused you of murder. That the woman who you were with last night came forward and the king was forcing you to marry her. Quite eventful for so early in the day."

News traveled quickly at court, and Darian wasn't sure which bothered him more, being unjustly accused of murder or being forced to marry Emma de Leon.

Married. Ye gods.

Surely Emma disliked being forced into marriage as much as he. Was it possible to have the vows declared illegal, obtain an annulment? A bright thought on a dreary morn. He'd have to speak to her about an annulment and would have plenty of time to do so in Kent.

He almost groaned aloud. He did *not* want to go to Kent. Unfortunately, William's reasons were sound.

"I did not kill de Salis. Someone must have taken my dagger from my pack this morn. Did any of you see anyone rummage through my satchel?"

Philip shook his head. "I was not here. Thomas and I slept in the stables to watch over the horses. I came in but a few moments ago."

"I heard you come in," Marc said. "Once I realized who it was, I went back to sleep."

Armand confessed, "I did as Marc—woke briefly, then

went back to sleep. Are you sure you did not misplace your dagger?"

All mercenaries were light sleepers. Their profession demanded they be alert, even in the comparative safety of the barracks. Even in his sleep Darian knew which men came and went from the sound of their footsteps and didn't doubt his fellow mercenaries possessed the same ability.

"I did not misplace it. I put my dagger in my satchel this morning before meeting with William. Someone took it out and then used it to kill de Salis—or at the least handed it over to Bishop Henry."

That possibility gave Darian pause. Perhaps the dagger hadn't been used to murder de Salis, only handed over to make it appear Darian had committed the murder.

Which would mean the bishop might be more involved than simply seeking justice for a murdered man who deserved no justice. But that made no sense. Why would Henry become involved in the murder of a man whom he'd staunchly objected to being assassinated the day before?

"No one enters the barracks except those who belong here," Marc insisted; then his eyes narrowed. "Are you saying one of our own stole your dagger and killed de Salis?"

Darian still felt ill. Marc was right. No one entered the barracks except the men the earl considered his personal band among the many bands of mercenaries he commanded. These were the men to whom the earl gave special privileges and entrusted with challenging, sometimes perilous duties.

All men Darian had trusted—until today. One of them

had to have stolen his dagger. "If not one of our own, then who?"

Philip puffed with indignation. "You are mistaken, Darian."

"Am I? We all know when we each come and go. Were an outsider to enter the barracks, neither Marc nor Armand would so quickly fall back into slumber, would they?" Darian suddenly wished he'd paid better heed to which men had been on their pallets when he'd entered the barracks. In his haste he'd not noticed, nor had reason to notice. "Anyone who heard me enter could have waited until I left, taken my dagger, and walked out without question or suspicion."

Marc rubbed his chin. "We would be alert to those entering but not going out, I grant you. But tell me why, Darian. We have all been together for an age, guarded each other's backs. I know of no dissention among us, do you?"

Armand rocked back on his heels, grinning. "Well, there is that matter between Julian and Lyle over a sweet little doxy in Southwark. And if I remember aright, Perrin still owes Darian twenty pence from a wager over a—"

"Stop it!" Philip snapped. "Perrin would not steal Darian's dagger. 'Twould only add to his debt. And irritation over a lost wager is not dissention."

Marc nodded. "True. But if not one of us, then—"

"*Not* one of us!" Philip insisted. "And I resent Darian's accusation and demand he withdraw—"

"Enough!" William strode into their midst—and not a one of them had heard him coming. "Darian, out. The rest of you, I will speak with later."

Philip flung a hand in the air. "My lord, you cannot truly believe one of us would betray Darian!"

"I am not sure what to believe, and until the puzzle is solved, everyone is suspect."

Darian walked out of the now-silent barracks beside William and headed across the busy palace yard for the stables, both to fetch his horse and arrange for a cart to carry Lady Emma and her two trunks.

"I sent the stable boy to the kitchens for a packet of food for the journey," William said. "When you get to Hadone, give my regards to Gar and Maura and pat the hounds on the head for me."

William made the journey sound like a pleasure trip, not being forced into exile.

"I do not like this, William. 'Twould be best if I stay in London."

"Your duty now is to remain out of the bishop's reach and take care of Lady Emma. Get your horse while I arrange for a cart."

Readying his horse didn't take long. The stable boy showed up with a packet of food and the carter with his ox and cart. All was ready except for his tardy wife.

So where the devil was Lady Emma?

❧

"A mercenary?" Julia de Vere exclaimed in horror. "Oh, Emma, had you told me you wished to take a lover I could have helped you choose from among several suitable men! How could you sink so low?"

Emma pulled her cloak from the trunk Julia had

helped her pack, her ire rising at the one person at court whom she would miss.

"Earl William is also a mercenary. Would you be wroth with me had I taken him as a lover?"

"William comes from noble blood. Your new husband does not! Truly, Emma, you cannot think to go off to the wilds of Kent with a man you barely know. This Darian might be dangerous! Only think of how he might harm you."

The harm was already done, and Emma didn't worry for her physical well-being. Other concerns took the fore. Right now, she worried that if Darian were forced to wait too long, he might leave without her. The man was angry, and in her experience angry men lacked patience.

"The king ordered us to leave court, Julia. Go I must." Emma managed a small smile. "You need have no concern for my well-being."

Julia sighed. "You cannot be certain."

Not certain, but hopeful. True, mercenaries were soldiers for hire, and such men could be unmerciful and violent. She had to trust that this particular mercenary could also be gentle and giving, as she'd sensed of him in her vision. Besides, he was under royal orders.

"Darian is also charged to ensure I am well cared for; so if I have a complaint, I have recourse."

"But certes, you must be offended. The daughter of a baron should not be forced to marry a Flemish peasant. Were your parents still alive, the king would never dare such an insult. You do intend to have this situation put to rights, do you not? Many of the nobles will not like what has happened to you, even if you are in disgrace. Noble blood is noble blood, after all."

During the past four months, no noble except Julia had noted Emma's rank. "I have seen little evidence they respect my noble blood."

"Still, should you apply for an annulment, they may rally behind you."

Annulment? Was that possible? Perhaps. But on what grounds? Certes, they'd given their consent before a large crowd, presided over by the king and blessed by a bishop.

The vision had shown her she and Darian would become lovers, so they would consummate the marriage. An annulment might not be possible.

So did the vision mean they had been destined for more? Were they meant to be man and wife?

Emma's ire over her visions rose once more. 'Twas useless to wish she knew if they were glimpses into a certain future or merely possibilities along life's path.

Her musings ended when two large footmen entered the solar. She raised her hand until they saw her and began to move her way. All was ready to go, with only one thing left to do.

"Julia, might I ask a boon? In late summer I gave a petition to one of the chamberlain's clerks. Would you do me the great favor of finding out if one of them still has it, and if it will be presented to the king anytime soon?"

"I can try. Where do I send a message?"

Emma had to think for a moment. "I believe the earl called the place Hadone."

"That makes sense. Earl William builds a castle there." Julia caught her up in a hug, which Emma gratefully returned. "Have a care."

"Fare thee well." Emma laughed so she wouldn't cry.

"By the by, I do not require you to sleep with a clerk. A simple inquiry into the petition's whereabouts will do."

Julia gave her a saucy smile. "Why bother with a clerk? Perhaps I will entice the chamberlain!"

Emma followed the footmen who carried her trunks, not at all sorry she was leaving Westminster Palace behind, her worst regret having miserably failed Nicole.

How was she to explain to a ten-year-old girl that she'd put a mercenary's life above her sister's—all because of a vision of a naked chest and a glorious smile.

And now she was headed for Kent, and the king would soon be on his way back to the siege at Wallingford, and only God knew when their paths might cross again.

Chapter Four

Darian shifted in the saddle, envying the man who rode past him at swift pace. Were he alone, he could easily reach Hadone by nightfall. But he wasn't alone, and the cart couldn't go any faster than the ox's stride allowed.

Nor could he banish the mist that wet his cloak and face. And no matter how much he hated leaving Westminster, he knew William was right about staying out of Bishop Henry's reach for a time.

Still, he didn't like being banished or allowing de Salis's murderer to remain free.

Not that he minded Edward de Salis no longer lived. The man had been evil, a purveyor of death and destruction, a boil in need of lancing, and deserved death for the atrocities he'd committed. For the people burned out of their villages, for those who'd died by sword or starvation, Darian would have ensured the villainy halted if someone hadn't slit de Salis's throat first.

However, being accused of murder in so public a fashion for something he didn't do gnawed at his innards. Knowing he could do nothing about it for the nonce didn't sit well, either, and the need for a diversion turned his head to look back at the cart.

The ox plodded through the mud at a steady if agonizingly slow pace. Emma sat beside the driver on the hard plank seat, huddled in her hooded cloak.

Smart woman to have thought of tossing on her cloak.

Witless woman for involving herself in his affairs.

Had she not come forward and lied outrageously, she wouldn't now be out in this miserable weather but enjoying the queen's warm, dry solar.

Oh, he'd heard her explanation for meddling, but still couldn't fathom why a woman of her rank would take the side of a commoner. All because she'd believed in his innocence? He wouldn't have been the first innocent man to be convicted and hanged. Why a noblewoman would care if justice was served was beyond him.

Discovering her reasoning might not matter so much if her audacity hadn't led to their marriage.

Marriage! Lord have mercy—marriage to a woman who required two trunks to haul around her possessions. Hardly the ideal wife for a mercenary who traveled without encumbrances.

Like many of his fellow mercenaries, Darian preferred his lone existence, wanting responsibility for no one but himself. All too well he knew the grief of losing loved ones. Resolved to never again suffer such overwhelming pain, he'd foresworn becoming entangled with any woman, wanting no family. No ties.

The mist turned to rain and his stomach grumbled.

Time for a rest.

Darian watched for a wide spot in the road with enough space for the cart to pull to the side and not get stuck. As luck would have it, his cloak was soaked clear through before he found such a place.

He'd no more than dismounted when Emma rushed past him, headed for the cover of the trees . . . and beyond. Guessing at the reason for her haste, he gave her privacy, wondering why she hadn't told him of her discomfort earlier.

"Nasty day," the carter said, pulling what looked like bread from a crate under his seat.

"Could be better." Darian fetched similar victuals from the satchel strapped behind his saddle. "Have you drink?"

The carter smiled and held out his hand. After a few moments he sipped from his palm. "Rain is good for somethin' leastwise."

Amused, Darian shook his head and pulled out a wineskin, preferring heftier drink.

A rustle of leaves and snapping twigs announced Emma's return. She glanced at both him and the carter, then made her way to a log sheltered by a huge oak and sat down.

"Not hungry?"

She shrugged, loosening droplets to slither down her cloak. "Not particularly."

But the look she gave his bread told him differently. The thought occurred to him that she wasn't eating because she hadn't brought any food along and was too proud to ask for a morsel of his.

Of course, he hadn't remembered to bring food, either.

William had sent the stable boy to the kitchens. Still, it seemed to Darian a woman would prepare better.

"Did you bring nothing along?"

"You did not give me much time to prepare."

"So you chose to bring all your fripperies instead of food."

Her eyes narrowed in indignation. "I will neither faint away nor starve. Tonight will be soon enough for me, at whatever inn you choose to spend the night."

Her expectations were rather high. She assumed they would halt for the night in a town large enough to sport an inn. If the weather worsened and the roads became streams, they might not be so fortunate.

And she had been rushed.

And the king had extracted his vow to take care of her. So he would while Lady Emma was still his wife. Which wouldn't be for long, he hoped.

He fetched another chunk of coarse bread and handed it to her. "Best you have something now. Supper could be a long way off."

At first he thought she might refuse, but she took the bread and nibbled on it.

He watched her eat, admiring her straight, white teeth behind her lush lips. Her tongue darted to the corner of her sensually curved mouth to recover a stray crumb.

In danger of becoming overly intrigued by her quick, pink tongue, Darian sat beside her on the log, careful to sit only close enough to permit a quiet exchange.

"We agree this marriage is a farce. How do we obtain an annulment?"

She stared at him as if coming to a decision before finally answering, "I believe we must present our case to a bishop, but which one might be best, I do not know. Nor am I sure of what reasons we could use. Unfortunately, if we petition for an annulment, the king and Bishop Henry are sure to learn of it. Neither will be pleased and may try to hinder our efforts."

She had a point. They couldn't act too soon. But the time would come when they'd be free of one another and he could return to the life he preferred. But what of Emma?

A solution of what to do with Emma suddenly hit him, making him wonder why he didn't think of it sooner.

"Perhaps you should go home and wait there until all is settled."

"To Camelen?" After a pause she shook her head. "That was my father's home, and now belongs to my sister's husband. 'Tis not truly my home anymore. Besides, I should rather be closer to London. I have yet to petition the king to release my youngest sister from Bledloe Abbey." She shook her head harder. "Nay, I cannot go far. Kent is far enough."

Which meant he was saddled with her for the foreseeable future. He thought to ask why her sister needed release from a nunnery, but decided it wasn't any of his affair.

Too bad he couldn't send her home, though. Not that her company would be overly hard to bear. Emma was easy on the eyes. She didn't complain or make insistent demands—or hadn't as yet. She impressed him as a woman who took what fate tossed her way and then dealt with it in a quick, effective manner.

She was also easy to talk to, not an unpleasant companion with whom to share exile. An exile that would last too long, no matter if it were but for a few days. Except he shouldn't have to suffer her company at all. Shouldn't be noticing any of the lady's finer qualities.

'Twas Emma's fault he'd been exiled when he need to be in London. The longer he was away, the longer a murderer went free.

He rose. "The cart driver appears ready to continue. Let us hope the weather does not worsen."

Despite the protection and warmth of a beaver cloak, Emma was both chilled and wet by the time they reached the Curly Goose. She was hungry, too. Stupid not to have thought about bringing provisions for the road.

But then, she really hadn't had time to visit the palace kitchen to beg for bread and cheese, worried that Darian might leave without her if she didn't hurry. Upon arriving outside of the stables, hard on the heels of the footmen carrying her trunks, she'd looked for signs of his impatience and, to her amazement, found none.

Oh, he'd been upset. What man wouldn't be after all that had occurred? The murder accusation. Gaining a wife he didn't want. Being exiled to Kent. Except for a couple of unkind remarks, he'd not proven himself intolerant.

So things could be worse. Much worse.

As she sat by the fire in the inn's common room, a bowl of thick stew in her lap and a mug of hearty ale on the plank floor at her feet, she recalled the few moments when events could have taken a cruel turn.

She hadn't realized they must ford a river, and she'd

almost panicked the moment she realized they were about to cross water. A *lot* of water.

She'd thanked heaven and all of its inhabitants for sending the rain, not heavy enough to make the fording dangerous but enough to create ripples on the surface. Still, she'd taken no chances, pulling the cloak's hood tighter to cover her closed eyes, preventing any possibility of being lulled into fixation.

She was drawn to water. To look at a puddle or pond too long and become enthralled brought on the visions that caused her pain, both physically and emotionally.

She'd learned as a child to close her eyes when doing something so ordinary as bathing or dipping her hands in a washbasin. Those effective actions prevented the visions and spared her the pain.

The last thing she needed on this journey was to struggle with an oncoming vision and suffer the resulting headache.

"More ale, milady?"

Emma smiled at the fair-haired, apron-wrapped innkeeper, who held a pitcher. Since their arrival he had done everything he could to make her comfortable. He'd recognized her nobility immediately, even before she'd removed her cloak to reveal her finely made bliaut. He'd even given up his private bedchamber for her use, the inn lacking private rooms to let.

"I thank you, but no more. I compliment you on both your brew and victuals."

He beamed and bowed before he turned to Darian, who sat nearby, cross-legged on the floor, his stew gone, staring into the flames. The wavering light caressed his face, flickered over his features, played along his rugged jawline, and deepened the shadows around his eyes.

She'd thought him lost in thought until noticing his brief, barely discernable reactions to noise. The man knew immediately whenever anyone came into or left the room, knew precisely where everyone was located. To all, he might seem preoccupied and vulnerable. He was neither.

"What about you? Want more?"

The change in the innkeeper's demeanor was immediate and telling. He'd assumed her noble and that Darian was merely her escort. Nearly true, but she wondered how Darian felt about being relegated to the upstairs room lined with pallets, not offered any special accommodation.

Darian raised his mug for the innkeeper to fill, not saying a word, not even of thanks. Not until the innkeeper returned to his place behind the plank counter did Darian speak.

"'Ware how you smile at the man or he may forget he gave up his bed and pay you a visit."

Emma bit back a retort that *some* man should share her bed tonight. This was her wedding night, after all.

Her appetite suddenly vanished. Sadness washed through her and nearly brought forth tears. Sweet mercy, she'd been married this morn and nothing about the day was worthy of celebration.

She put her bowl on the floor and picked up her ale.

"You should finish that," he said of the stew. "You will need your strength. Tomorrow will be a long day, no matter the weather."

Most likely. Except she was no longer hungry, and

when she finished eating, Darian would expect her to retire and she would rather not. Her gown was finally dry-
ing, and the warmth of the hearth felt good.

If she went to bed now, she would only reflect on what
a wedding day should be like. Feasting. Dancing. Well-
wishers. A marriage bed.

Her vision of Darian wouldn't come to pass tonight.
He was in far too surly a mood for a glorious smile, and
she was far too irritated with him to attempt to coax him
into a less churlish state of mind.

"How far do we go tomorrow?"

"All the way to Hadone, which should take most of the
day at ox pace. Weary of traveling already?"

She bristled at his tone. He seemed to believe her weak
and fastidious when she'd made a resolute effort to be
neither.

"I shall manage. I merely wish to know so I can prepare." A continuance of this conversation would raise her
ire. A change of subject was in order. "Have you any in-
sight into who de Salis's murderer might be?"

He finally looked up at her, revealing anger and frustration. "Not as yet. What irks me is that the murderer
might be someone I trusted. If one of the mercenaries has
turned against me, I did not see signs of betrayal. I will
solve the puzzle, however, and when I do, that person is
going to feel the noose he tried to put around *my* neck."

Emma almost shuddered at his vehement certainty,
glad she wasn't the current target of Darian's wrath.

She remembered Julia's warning that Darian could be
dangerous. At the moment he certainly seemed capable of
taking another man's life. He was a mercenary, after all,
a soldier whose business was war.

But she'd known many soldiers in her lifetime, including her father and brother. Both had been capable of taking other men's lives, but both had also been honorable, at times kindhearted men.

Was Darian capable of compassion?

Sweet mercy, she'd meddled at court because she'd once envisioned him wearing little more than a glorious smile, and her original dilemma returned to haunt her.

Had she been wrong to interfere? They'd done naught but snap and snarl at each other since meeting. Right now, she couldn't imagine him softening enough toward her to become her lover.

By acting on no more than her vision, she might be guilty of changing his life's path for the worse—a betrayal of sorts.

At the moment Darian of Bruges didn't strike her as a forgiving man.

Chapter Five

They'd headed out at first light, and because the day was fine and the road dry and not crowded, Darian spotted Hadone at twilight.

He marveled at the progress made since his last visit, nigh on two months ago. The masons had finished much of the thick outer wall built of Kentish ragstone. Only a portion of eastern wall of pike-tipped timber remained of the old palisade.

The work progressed ahead of William's expectations. Even now, during the supper hour, the sharp ring of chisel and hammer against stone echoed over the countryside.

Darian doubted the masons worked so diligently out of pride or duty, but because Gar drove them hard. The steward of Hadone wasn't above taking harsh measures when his needs weren't met or wishes unfulfilled.

Much like his overlord, William of Ypres.

But where Earl William could show mercy, Darian knew Gar nearly incapable of compassion. Where William gave rewards to those who served him well, Gar considered the courtesy unnecessary, except when it came to himself.

Naturally, the drawbridge over the deep ditch surrounding the castle—not yet filled with water—had been raised for the night. For a moment Darian considered camping in the woods rather than risk an argument with Gar over lowering the plank bridge and opening the gate.

But then, over the next few days, he and Gar were likely to spar over one thing or another—especially if Gar took it into his head that Darian wasn't a guest, but a servant.

"Hail on the wall!" he shouted at the guard on the wall walk near the gatehouse. "Darian of Bruges requests entry at the behest of Earl William."

"Who is that with you?"

"Lady Emma de Leon, who I assure you is no threat."

The guard turned around and shouted down into the bailey below, no doubt sending someone to the keep to seek permission from Gar.

Darian glanced over at Lady Emma, who'd borne the entire journey with admirable stoicism. Not usual for a lady, at least not the ladies of his acquaintance, which he admitted weren't many. Still, he remembered last summer's flight from London when William had insisted Queen Matilda flee the city before it was captured by the enemy. Her life had been endangered, and she hadn't fled this far into Kent, and yet she'd chided William over her discomfort.

Not so Emma. She must surely be stiff and sore from bouncing on the cart's unyielding seat, and likely hungry from lack of food since nooning. At the moment, she was looking up, inspecting the wall and gate, waiting patiently for someone to lower the drawbridge.

A second man appeared on the wall walk. The light was now so dim Darian couldn't say for certain who the man was—though from the man's height and silvery hair, he surmised that Gar had come to see for himself.

"Were it not for the lady I would tell you to come back on the morn," Gar declared from above.

If not for the lady, Gar might refuse to let him in at all, which would suit Darian fine. But there were William's orders to consider, so Darian strove to keep his tone amicable. "Were it not for the lady's sake, I would not request admittance at this late hour."

Soon chains rattled and winches groaned as the drawbridge began to lower and the iron gate to rise.

"I gather you and Gar are not on the best of terms," Emma commented.

"We have no great liking for each other. Gar would prefer that all the Flemish in England be sent back to Flanders."

Her eyebrow arched. "Even Earl William?"

"Especially Earl William. The notion of a man of Flanders being named an English earl doesn't sit well with Gar."

"Then why does William keep him as his steward?"

A question Darian had once asked of William after Gar had ordered a peasant whipped for mixing a batch of mortar too thin.

"As long as Gar continues to efficiently oversee the defense of Hadone and the building projects, William sees no reason to replace him. The man is a reliable steward and William considers that a boon."

The drawbridge thudded to the ground. He nudged his horse forward and the carter snapped his whip.

Darian led them across the bailey. Here, too, were changes. The pile of rough stone had been moved to near the uncompleted section of wall, where masons and laborers applied chisel and hammer to smooth those stones to be raised on early morn. More shelters, built of timber and roofed with thatch, abutted the new wall. Flickering candlelight seeped from the closed shutters of most of them.

Just as Earl William wanted, people were settling here, a new town forming.

When Darian reached the keep's stairway, where Gar now stood with a group of servants and stable lads, he dismounted and tossed the reins to one of the lads. Before he could turn around to aid Emma from the cart, Gar rushed by and held up a hand, which Emma courteously accepted.

"I welcome thee to Hadone, Lady Emma."

Emma descended with as much grace and dignity as was possible when climbing down from a cart. "My thanks, Gar. Your hospitality is greatly appreciated."

"'Tis not right that a lady should be forced to endure the rigors of the road in such rough company. I hope your journey was not overly harsh."

Emma's eyes narrowed as she withdrew her hand from Gar's. "Darian did all he could to make the journey pleasant. Our English weather, however, did not cooperate with him."

"Earl William will be pleased to hear of Darian's diligence. Come, food and drink await. While we eat, you can tell me why the earl sends you to Hadone."

Emma's gaze settled on Darian. "I believe the tale best left to my husband."

Gar looked around for a noble male he might have missed seeing before he reasoned out the identity of Emma's husband. Distaste twisted Gar's mouth.

Darian could almost hear the steward's disapproving thoughts. A noble lady married to a lowly mercenary? Unacceptable. Unforgivable. Unimaginable!

"You?" was all Gar asked.

"Dreadful, is it not?" he responded, for once agreeing with Gar. "I would not feel too outraged on Lady Emma's behalf, however. The marriage will be short-lived, so she will not suffer unduly."

Gar arched an eyebrow. "You will seek an annulment?"

"With all due haste. Neither the lady nor I wish to be bound to each other any longer than we must." He waved a dismissive hand. "However, I have more formidable problems to solve first. I fear we must impose on your hospitality for several days. Pray see Lady Emma made comfortable."

Servants passed by carrying Emma's trunks. The carter tugged on the ox's lead rope and headed for the stable. A stable lad had already led away Darian's horse. Intending to retrieve his satchel, Darian took several steps before Emma appeared in his path.

Her wide eyes revealed apprehension. "Where are you going?"

Where the devil did she think he was bound at this time of night, and why should it matter to her? He need not answer to her for his whereabouts, so why did he feel it necessary to answer?

"Merely to the stables to retrieve my belongings."

"Oh. Well, then, I will leave you to your errand and await you in the hall."

Her relief was so apparent Darian had to wonder why she seemed so nervous. Gar might not be one of his favorite people, but the steward would treat Emma with the respect and courtesy due her. But perhaps she didn't know that. From the rumors he'd heard bandied about at Westminster, she hadn't been treated with much courtesy of late—not at court, and not from him.

An unwarranted prick of guilt prodded him into giving her the reassurance she seemed to need.

"You have naught to fear here at Hadone. We are safe. You will be treated well. Go eat. I will be in anon."

She nodded slightly and glanced at where Gar waited for her. "What shall I tell him?"

"Of what happened at court? Might as well tell him the truth. Neither of us has aught to hide."

She pursed her lips. "Nay, only a regret or two."

She might, he didn't. "I learned long ago that regret serves no purpose. One simply deals with what fate tosses one's way and hopes all comes out right in the end."

Looking into Emma's upturned face, still seeing uneasiness, for the first time in a very long time, he hoped the end came out right for another person other than himself as well.

A hope he had no business harboring. What happened to Emma shouldn't concern him. Their fates weren't entwined. He'd do well to save his concern for his own well-being, keep his nose well and clear of other people's problems.

Only that way would he survive.

❧

Emma tilted her head, watching Darian stalk off toward the stables.

"He has upset you," Gar stated. "I fear Darian can be difficult. You should not take his lack of manners or hurtful comments to heart."

She was beginning to understand why Darian disliked Gar, and to her chagrin, she found herself coming to Darian's defense. "He said nothing hurtful. Why did you assume he did?"

"That is his nature, and your distress is most apparent. Mayhap a cup of wine will ease you somewhat."

A cup of wine would ease her thirst, but not her worry over whether Darian would still be at Hadone when she awoke on the morn.

He certainly didn't want to be here, and all during their journey the feeling had strengthened that he came to Hadone only because he'd told William he would see her safely delivered to the castle.

What would she do if he abandoned her to rush off to find de Salis's murderer? The erroneous charge must be uppermost in his mind, nagging at him, eventually pushing him to take action. How soon? Would he even come in to supper as he'd said?

Perhaps she did need a cup of wine, so she allowed Gar to lead her up the steep stairway to the keep's second floor and through the large oak doors that opened into the great hall.

A cold, damp hall, despite the fire in the hearth and several lit torches. No rushes softened the floor. Though three magnificent wolfhounds lounged by the fire, no hunting birds perched in the high rafters. No adornments graced the walls.

At Camelen her father had hung weapons and tapestries to tease the eye and arouse the imagination. At Hadone one was greeted with unembellished gray stone. Still, Hadone's hall was akin in shape and size to Camelen's, bringing a lump to her throat, which she quickly swallowed.

No dais had been built to support a high table for the lord and his favorites. The men who gathered for supper crowded around two trestle tables in the middle of the room, and silence descended as they began noticing the stranger in their midst.

Master craftsmen, she guessed, from the quality of their garb and other revealing clues. The thin man with sawdust sprinkled in his dark hair was likely the master carpenter. Another bore gray dust on his tunic. The master mason? The hulk of a man at the far end of the table could be none other than the blacksmith. The rest would be of their rank, though she couldn't be sure of their crafts.

Emma kept her chin up, her expression passive. Darian was convinced she would be treated with consideration, but then, these people hadn't yet heard why she'd come to Hadone. Once they found out what she'd confessed in court, and that she'd been forced to marry a mercenary because of her imprudence, many wouldn't be inclined to friendliness.

Not that she would make friends among the craftsmen. Her rank set her above them, and she wouldn't be here long enough for the barrier to lower.

Of more import to Emma was the only other woman in the room. Young and pretty, she stood near the stairway, obviously giving orders to the servants who bore Emma's trunks. No veil covered the woman's raven-black braid. Her brown gown might be simple and devoid of embroidery, but the fit was excellent and the wool of fine weave. When finished with the servants, smiling softly, the woman hurried toward the doorway.

"Lady Emma, my daughter, Maura," Gar said, the fondness in his voice impossible to mistake.

Maura dipped into a curtsy. "My lady. I bid thee welcome to Hadone. I took the liberty of having your trunks sent up to my bedchamber, and ordered the serving wench to bring two more trenchers from the kitchen. You and Darian will join us at table, of course."

Maura's smile was so genuine Emma couldn't help smiling, too. Perhaps being exiled at Hadone wouldn't be too bad.

Emma removed her cloak; Maura took it and handed it off to a servant.

"I thank you, Maura. I would be honored to join you, as will Darian, I am sure."

"Wonderful." She looked to her father. "So where is he? Not staying away because he argued with you, I hope."

"Oh, nay," Gar answered in a casual tone that wasn't casual at all. "He will be in shortly, I imagine. I should think he would wish to dine with his wife."

Maura's smile slipped, and then her eyes widened slightly as she caught Gar's meaning.

"You and Darian are wed?"

Emma took a steadying breath, having hoped to avoid

explanations so soon. And what was keeping Darian? He knew these people and should be here to tell the tale. He'd said to tell the truth, but sweet Jesu, how much of it?

"Aye. We were wed yester morn. I know it is unusual for a lady to wed a mercenary—"

"Outright unheard of," Gar interrupted.

She contained her irritation for the sake of harmony, not knowing how long she would have to endure the steward's arrogance. "The tale is rather confusing. If you do not mind, I would prefer Darian relate it."

Maura fairly beamed. "Oh, this is intriguing. But come, you must be weary and hungry. Sit and eat and we shall await Darian with eager ears."

As they approached the nearest table, all of the men stood. Gar took his seat at the head, and Maura waved a hand at where Emma should sit, on Gar's left. A trencher already sat on the table, the gravy having seeped into the almost white bread.

This was Maura's place and trencher, certainly.

Emma bit her lip to keep from declining the seat so Maura could finish her meal in her accustomed seat. But as the steward's daughter, Maura knew the rules of hospitality, which she'd already followed when giving up her bed. So Emma gingerly sat on the bench, acknowledging the men's bows with a nod as if she were some important personage, which she wasn't.

Maura then waved her hands. "Move down, all of you. We have guests."

The hulk at the end of the table didn't resume his seat. In a voice so quiet Emma strained to hear, claiming he had finished his meal, he begged leave of Gar.

With permission granted, Maura pouted. "I did not mean to rush you, Master Smith."

"I rush myself, Maura. I have chisels to sharpen and trowels to straighten before the morning work begins."

The men on the other side of the table accommodated Maura, who dragged her trencher over to her new seat. The men on Emma's side slid down, leaving plenty of room for Darian.

As host, Gar felt obligated to make introductions. She'd guessed right about the master mason and carpenter. Then came the forester and bailiff, and, to her surprise, the falconer.

"Do you like the hunt, my lady?" Gar asked.

"I have not hunted in an age." She again searched the rafters. "Have you hawks?"

"Earl William decided he preferred no feathers in his meals, so we built a mews. On the morrow, pray go have a look. The earl spared no expense for his hawks and falcons."

Gar's pride said he approved.

At the edge of her vision, Emma caught sight of a lad with goblet and flagon in hand. The sound of more footsteps behind her meant her food had arrived and made her stomach growl.

To cover her noticeably loud appreciation for the upcoming meal, she continued the conversation. "I noticed the dogs by the hearth. Wolfhounds, are they not?"

Again more pride.

"They are. Great hunters, and excellent guard dogs, too. We turn them loose in the bailey at night. Since the darkness hampers their ability to tell friend from foe, everyone remains inside their quarters." He leaned forward with a conspiratorial wink. "Keeps everyone in their place."

Apparently Gar put great importance on keeping everyone in their place, which she'd already witnessed when the steward spoke to Darian. Was that why Darian took so long to come into the hall, because he didn't want to deal with Gar?

One of the servants reached around her to serve the meal, and Emma looked down expecting to see a trencher. To her utter horror, there sat a washbasin, the water clear, the surface still and shining.

Caught off guard, Emma watched as her reflection wavered in the small but perilous pool of water. The water turned bloodred, and chilled her to the bone.

Terrified of what horrors might be revealed, Emma plunged her hands into the water basin and clamped her eyes shut. The entrancement broke, preventing the vision.

As always happened when she halted a vision, pain immediately pierced the base of her skull and spread swiftly upward and outward to encompass her entire head.

"My lady, is aught amiss?"

Emma couldn't answer Maura, the pain too new and sharp to allow speech just yet.

Gar shouted an order at someone to fetch Darian, a hint of panic in his voice. As she took her hands from the water and placed fingers at her temples, she hoped everyone would just remain calm and Darian wouldn't appear until the sharp pain subsided into the wretched ache with which she'd learned how to deal.

This wasn't how she'd wanted to begin her stay at Hadone. Not with a headache that could force her to bed and darkness for several days. They would all think her weak, fragile, sickly.

Damn visions! Why must they make her life so miserable? What had she done to deserve their intrusion? Why was she so flawed?

On the verge of tears, Emma fought to control her emotions until the sharpness gave way to a throbbing ache. Careful not to look down at the washbasin, she opened her eyes to encounter Maura's distressed concern.

Emma grasped hold of the first explanation for her distress that came to mind. "I beg your pardon, Maura, Gar. The journey must have been more trying than I thought. 'Tis merely a headache, but I think it best if I go up and lie down."

"Want you aught to eat first?"

The thought of food churned her stomach. If she didn't escape the hall soon, she might embarrass herself further.

"Nay, not now. Perhaps later."

Eager to escape the stares of everyone in the hall, Emma rose from the bench. Too fast, too soon. She swayed.

Someone clasped her upper arms.

"I have you. Easy."

Darian held her upright, his strong hands a counter to her dizziness. She leaned back for further relief and fell backward into his equally strong arms.

Chapter Six

Darian's arms enfolded her, and though revealing her weakness wasn't wise, Emma couldn't help but lean back and lay her head on his solid shoulder.

Within moments her dizziness began to slowly subside, an unusual but welcome treat. She credited her speed in halting the vision for the rare luxury. Too often the water held her captive for longer spells. The longer the entrancement, the more difficult to break it, the more painful the headache.

His heat seeped through her garments, warming her clear through, including places where she shouldn't be affected when in the throes of a headache.

Darian held her firmly but gently, as if she were fragile. Emma knew she was as durable as steel, but then, even steel succumbed to fire. If she remained unmoving, pressed against Darian, she might never be cold again.

"What happened?" His voice was soft, almost a whisper.

She dare not speak the truth, fearing Darian would be horrified, think her possessed of demons and let go. Surely she'd fall, and she'd embarrassed herself enough for the nonce.

"Headache. Came on so swiftly."

"Let us get you into a bed."

Oh aye, let's!

Ye gods! How could she have amorous thoughts *now*? The dizziness had eased, but her eyesight was still blurred and sensitive to light.

Maura came around the table. "This way. Up the stairs."

Distrustful of her balance, but well aware she should lie down as soon as possible, she tried easing away from Darian. He held fast.

"I need to follow Maura," she said.

"You are not steady enough for the stairs."

She'd done far more than climb stairs when enduring the throbbing in her head.

"I can manage."

He actually chuckled. "So you have told me before. Manage or not, you are not climbing those stairs."

How he accomplished the feat Emma didn't know, but next thing she realized, Darian had picked her up and, with her cradled in his arms, was heading for the stairway.

"Wrap your arms around my neck."

She didn't even think to disobey.

'Struth, she should be mortified. Pride demanded she protest his heavy-handed ordering her about and carrying her around. She did neither. That he lifted her as if she weighed no more than a feather—and she knew her weight more likened to a boulder—astounded her to silence.

She hadn't been carried since childhood, and even then not often. Her parents hadn't believed in coddling, had insisted their children endure stoically whatever hardships came their way.

If this was spoiling, sweet mercy, she could too easily become accustomed to the spoiling.

Darian didn't even breathe hard going up the stairs. Amazing. But more astounding was the scent she caught when he turned to head down the passageway.

Mingled with the scents of horse and leather and wool was an aroma that made her nose twitch. Not floral or herbal. Not sweet, but not sour. The dark, dusky scent hinted of something wild and dangerous. Of power and vigor.

Of Darian.

How odd his unique aroma, now intense in her nose and memory, didn't set her stomach to churning as pungent scents sometimes did when she was in the grip of a headache.

Darian paused while Maura opened the bedchamber door and Emma shifted to whisper in his ear.

"Pray put me down. I give you my oath I will not fall."

He turned his head slightly, his intriguing hazel eyes narrowing.

"I do not like the look of your eyes. They shine strangely."

Shine strangely? What might that mean? If her eyes had ever shone strangely on a headache's onset, no one had mentioned it.

"Strange how?"

"Like pools of still, clear water."

Pools of still, clear water were her enemy and she didn't like the comparison.

"My eyes are brown. The water should be muddy."

He shook his head. "Clear and sharp, their color brilliant and shiny, as if you can see things no one else can."

The observation veered too close to the truth for comfort. She turned her face into his shoulder to hide her eyes, so he could see no more, guess too much.

"Darian, you may put her down now." Maura's voice drifted into Emma's hearing from some far-off place. "While you help her into bed, I will brew a potion of feverfew and willow bark."

Emma knew whatever potion Maura brewed wouldn't ease the pain, but she wasn't about to stop Maura from leaving the bedchamber.

Darian slowly crossed the floor. Emma felt more than saw Maura rush out the door.

For the first time in her life, she was alone in a bedchamber with a man, one she knew would become her lover. A wave of intense longing and need washed through her, her vision of him as clear as the day he'd first come to her.

Would he make love to her today? Now?

He halted by the bedside. "You are still in great pain?"

His voice was low and husky. If she told him no, he might well climb into the bed with her. But the dull throb at the base of her skull warned her to resist the temptation, no matter that she tingled all over. She dare not trust the headache to go away anytime soon, not to flare into pain so agonizing it hurt to lay her head on a bolster.

"Not so great. You will recall I told you that you need not carry me."

"So you said." Her senses reeled when he unexpectedly kissed her forehead, his warm, full lips so soothing she nearly moaned aloud with pleasure. "No idea what brought on the headache?"

She knew exactly, but couldn't tell him, so answered with the shrug of a shoulder, wishing he would kiss her again.

"Perhaps rest and the potion will cure you quickly."

"Perhaps."

Except right now she wasn't interested in any potion. With brazenness she hadn't known herself capable of, Emma unclasped her hands from around his neck and cupped the sides of his face. "Some cures cannot be found in a brew of herbs."

Then Darian's eyes changed color, darkening with what could only be desire. So clearly did she see his want of her that she trembled.

The corner of his mouth quirked upward just before he granted her wish and kissed her again.

Oh, mercy, his lips were warm, and the pressure of his mouth wonderful. And just when those delightful tingles sparked with renewed fervor and her hopes of a bed partner began to rise, Darian broke the kiss and swiftly set her down on the bed.

"If we continue this folly, we may rip asunder all hope for an annulment," he stated before spinning around and leaving the chamber.

Emma groaned and she snuggled into the bed, a spot low in her belly aflame and yearning.

Damn, her head hurt, but her thoughts weren't as muddled as usual, and she clearly understood Darian's comment. He might want her, but he also wanted an annulment. Apparently he believed not consummating the marriage the best way to go about it.

Lack of consummation wasn't the only grounds for an annulment, and if her vision came true, it certainly wouldn't be the reason for *their* annulment.

Of the several visions she'd suffered before learning to halt them as they formed, only three had come true: her brother's fall from a horse, a fire in one of Camelen's storage barns, and her mother's death.

There were others, of places and events that as yet made no sense to her, but she assumed would appear in time. Like the set of tall oak doors with a huge, finely carved rose set into the center of each panel that had intrigued her for nigh on two years now, but hadn't appeared as yet. 'Struth, she truly didn't want to know what she'd been about to see in the bloody water in the washbasin. Some horrible event, no doubt.

She'd never purposely swayed events to suit her visions, until yester morn when she meddled in Darian's affairs.

Darian might want her, but he was resisting. Would she ever see his glorious smile, ever experience the pleasure his kiss promised?

After that kiss, this was the one vision she *wanted* to come true.

Darian took another long swallow of ale to ease his dry throat. Gar had insisted on hearing why the earl had sent him to Hadone, and Maura had hung on his every word.

The tale hadn't been complete, of course. No one at Hadone need know about the king's giving the order for de Salis's assassination, or the names of the informants he'd spent most of the night with, or how he now mistrusted his fellow mercenaries.

"So William sent us here to stay out of sight for a time. I expect I will hear news from him shortly."

At least he hoped so. Being exiled to Hadone was bad enough. But being exiled with Emma—ye gods.

He should have taken Emma at her word and allowed her to walk up the stairs. From the moment he'd picked her up, his body had suffered the tortures of the damned. Wanting what it couldn't have. Desiring the forbidden. He hadn't been sweating from merely the exertion of carrying Emma up the stairs.

He shouldn't have given in to her obvious invitation to kiss her. An extraordinary melding of mouths. He'd come frighteningly close to joining Emma in the bed. Only knowing she hurt had stopped him. Had she been well, they would likely be scuffling in the bed, limbs entangled—consummating the marriage neither of them had expected or wanted.

Gar shook his head like a father at a child who'd misbehaved. "So where were you that you could not produce witnesses?"

Darian almost didn't answer. Gar's attitude of superiority irked him, and keeping peace with Earl William's steward might prove the most difficult part of staying at Hadone.

"Southwark. Bishop Henry would not have considered the men I was with trustworthy."

"Out getting drunk with the cutthroats and thieves. Had you naught better to do?"

Those cutthroats and thieves sometimes provided useful information. Unfortunately, he'd learned nothing from Hubert or Gib that night to make what had followed worth the time or price of several tankards of bad ale.

"What I do on my own time is of concern only to me."

"Except when your heathen ways almost get you hanged."

"I did not kill de Salis."

"Then who did?"

He wished he knew. "Whoever stole my dagger, most likely."

The hall grew quiet again. The hour was late, and servants, craftsmen, and laborers alike had taken to their pallets. He should have, too, but the ale had gone down smoothly while answering Maura and Gar's questions. And parts of him were too restless to allow slumber.

To quiet those parts he needed a female. Problem was, the only female his parts yearned for was Emma. Not good.

"I do not understand," Maura said. "Why would a lady damage her reputation for . . . someone she does not know?"

For the likes of you, he heard.

Darian didn't understand, either. He wasn't satisfied that she'd meddled to save an innocent man from hanging. Noblewomen did not concern themselves with a commoner's affairs.

"She told me she believed I did not commit the murder and could not stand by and see an innocent man hang."

Gar scoffed. "Lady Emma saved your neck and now you will repay her with an annulment? How generous of you."

His ire pricked, Darian leaned forward. "Better an annulment than being forced together for life. Lady Emma wants this marriage no more than I do. I should think freeing her of me the better repayment."

Maura glanced over at the pallet on the floor near the hearth he'd requested for himself. "So you two have not, uhm, consummated the union?"

"Nor will we. Leaving her virginity intact may be the best way to ensure an annulment."

Gar pinned him with a censorious stare. "How do you know for certain she is a virgin?"

Darian inwardly shuddered. He'd assumed Emma a virgin. Lord knew she kissed like one, all sweetness and innocence. Oh, she'd set him aflame, too easily, but experience told him she had little if any familiarity with kissing, much less coupling.

Still, she'd confessed to taking him to her pallet in the queen's solar, so could easily have done so with another man. He might believe Emma innocent of fornication, but he certainly shouldn't count on it.

"If she is not a virgin, then we shall have to find another way to end this travesty of a marriage," he finally answered Gar. "The marriage was forced. Neither of us wants it."

Which brought him back to why he and she were in this muddle to begin with. Emma might believe him innocent of de Salis's murder, but to further blacken the de Leon name to save him still seemed extreme.

He couldn't think of any other motive, however. If she'd truly come forward out of conviction and compassion, well, that had to be the nicest thing anyone had done for him in years.

But no matter the reason for her act of mercy, he refused to be beholden to her. Or even like her overmuch.

Best he not like anyone overmuch. Losing someone he cared for hurt like the devil, and he wasn't about to suffer that agony ever again.

Chapter Seven

With an earthenware mug in hand, Emma eased down the stairs, amazed at how well she felt this morn. The headache had already dulled to a nagging ache at the back of her skull. Usually, the headaches required two days or more to ease, and Emma rejoiced at this one's lack of tenacity.

Nearly all of Hadone's residents had already broken their fast. Only one of the trestle tables remained in the middle of the hall, where Darian sat with Maura. They appeared to be conversing companionably, a feat she and Darian hadn't yet accomplished.

Not surprising, she supposed, because they were doomed to be at odds until their circumstances changed. Emma didn't know which problem Darian was more anxious to have settled—their annulment or de Salis's murder.

One of the huge, shaggy wolfhounds she'd noticed yester eve rested its head on Darian's thigh. With a contented smile, he scratched the hound behind the ears. The hound sat statue still, eyes closed, most satisfied with the quality stroke of Darian's fingers.

Jealousy niggled at her even as she acknowledged the senselessness of envying how easily he talked to Maura or the attention he gave the hound.

She'd fallen asleep last night with the sensation of floating in Darian's arms, with the taste of him lingering on her lips. Their kiss had thoroughly aroused her and should have kept her awake half of the night. Instead, she'd slept so soundly she hadn't heard Maura enter the room to deliver the cup of herbs mixed with ale or to lie down on the pallet placed under the room's single window. 'Struth, Emma hadn't heard a sound until this morn when a crowing cock greeted the sunrise, pulling her and Maura from slumber.

Maura had arisen and dressed to begin her day. Emma had fallen back asleep, not yet able to rouse sufficiently to get out of bed. The added sleep had done wonders, giving her the strength to leave the bedchamber behind.

As Emma took the few steps to reach the table, Darian's hand stilled on top of the hound's massive head. He looked up, and his smile faded.

He stared at her for a moment. "Your eyes yet shine. Should you be out of bed?"

Maura spun around to have a look, too. "Ah, but her ladyship is not so pale." She pointed at the mug. "Would you care for another?"

Though the potion would do no good, Emma saw no reason to be ungracious or ungrateful for Maura's thoughtful offer.

"My head no longer feels about to split open, so I need

not stay abed." She handed Maura the mug she'd not emptied until a few minutes ago. "My thanks for the potion, Maura. Another would be welcome."

"Bread and cheese?" Maura asked.

"The bread only." She gave Maura a conspirator's smile. "Best not to tax my stomach too soon."

"As you say, milady. I will be back anon."

Maura hurried off to fetch the victuals; Emma took the vacated seat across from Darian. He still stared at her hard, and Emma fought the urge to turn away.

Did he truly see a shine in her eyes? Certes, she saw things other people did not, and his comment of last eve still bothered her. However, he couldn't possibly know how close he came to the truth. More like, he viewed her as feeble and waited for her to stumble.

Irked that he judged her as a weakling, but determined to make an attempt at companionability, Emma sought a distraction by reaching over to run a finger along the hound's nose.

"Gar's hound?"

"William's. Are you certain you should not remain abed?"

Darian didn't distract easily. Sweet mercy, did he believe all women fragile beings or just her?

"Remaining abed will not banish the pain. I have learned that if I move slowly and attempt nothing too taxing, I do better by being up and about. 'Struth, I suffered one all through my father's and brother's vigil and burial without stumbling or collapsing."

Though she'd stayed close to her sister Gwendolyn for support. Darian need not know that, however.

He hesitated before he said, "Then you have suffered

these sudden headaches before. How long have they plagued you?"

Too long. "Half my life. They come on quickly and leave when they will."

"I knew a man whose aching head could send him to bed for days. He discovered he could not drink more than one goblet of red wine in a sitting. Do you know what causes yours?"

The lie she'd told for years came easily to her lips. "Nay. Does the hound have a name?"

Again he smiled down at the hound. "This is Rose. The others are Daisy and Lily."

Which made *her* smile. "Somehow I cannot envision the earl standing out in the field calling to his . . . flowers. Whatever possessed him to name them thus?"

"William deserves no less for allowing Maura to name his hunting dogs, particularly since the bitches are ferocious in the field. I have seen Rose bring down a lordly buck all on her own."

"Impressive."

He nodded, ruffling the hound's fur, causing the bitch's head to rise and lean into the more vigorous rubbing. "One cannot always judge by a name, or title, or rank. Not with man or beast."

How well she knew. Ladies were accorded courtesy; traitor's daughters were not. Neither were mercenaries.

"William could have renamed his hounds."

"Perhaps, but he decided their names did not matter so long as they performed in the field." He stood abruptly. The wolfhound looked up at him excitedly, her long tail whipping back and forth.

"Outside" was all the command necessary to send Rose racing to the door.

"Going hunting?"

"Merely for a run. Only William and Gar are allowed to hunt with them."

Emma watched him leave, supposing she should be pleased they hadn't argued. But then, their talk had been short because he'd left so abruptly. Because of the hound? Or because he simply couldn't wait to be rid of her?

"Rose should be Darian's." Maura's terse statement startled Emma from her melancholy musings.

"Oh?"

Maura held out the cup, which Emma took. "I mixed the herbs with broth instead of ale this time. Kinder to the stomach."

"My thanks. Darian said the wolfhounds belong to William."

Maura eased onto the bench opposite Emma. "They do, but only because Darian refused to accept Rose as his own. Two summers ago, Darian rescued the hounds as pups from an unappreciative owner. Rose chose Darian as her master from the start, and one has only to see the two of them together to know who possesses Rose's loyalty and affection."

She sighed, sorrow mingling with anger. "William insisted Darian should own Rose, but he refused. Stubborn man."

Emma could understand why having a hound underfoot might not be the best of situations for a mercenary.

"A mercenary's life is an unsettled one. Perhaps he fears he could not properly care for her."

"To claim Rose as his own would be no burden. Darian could leave her here, as William leaves the other two hounds. Certes, my father might extract a stipend for her food, but Darian could well afford the payment. He does not spend his pay on fancy rings or other fripperies, as do some of the other mercenaries. I swan, the only costly thing Darian owns is his dagger, which he highly prizes."

Emma well remembered Darian's forlorn expression in the antechamber when he'd feared he wouldn't get the dagger back from the king. What Darian owned, he obviously prized—and all he owned fit in one small satchel.

Did Darian hoard his coin, or did he merely shun possessions?

Maura placed her hands on the table and pushed herself upright. "Time I saw to my duties. Are you in need of aught before I go?"

For only one need could Maura be of aid. "I should very much like to be of help to you while I am here. Is there some task or chore you are willing to trust me with?"

Maura looked horrified. "You are a guest, my lady. And you are ill and should rest!"

"I promise to rest when the need arises, but I also dislike the thought of becoming a burden. Pray, Maura, surely there is something I can do to help the time pass more quickly, keep my hands from idleness."

Maura hesitated, then smiled softly. "Perhaps there is. Are you feeling well enough for a walk out to the kitchen?"

⌒

Darian heaved the stick as far as he could throw it. Rose trembled with anticipation, but sat beside him as commanded. The stick landed near the kitchen door. With a small hand signal, he turned the wolfhound loose, admiring her gait and speed.

Then he saw Emma and Maura about to step into the hound's path. Intent on the stick, Rose wouldn't see the women until too late to veer around them.

"Halt!"

The hound's big paws dug into the ground, spewing dust as she skidded to a stop barely an arm's length from Maura and Emma. Emma halted so abruptly she spilled some of the headache potion from her mug. All around him sound and movement ceased, the buzz of the bailey reduced to silence.

He'd intended to stop one hound from barreling into two women and managed to bring several people to a halt. Amazing.

And embarrassing. Darian wasn't one to draw attention to himself. The accomplishment of his missions, and sometimes his survival, depended upon his stealth. Now everyone looked at him with wide-eyed wonder over the force of his shouted command.

Feeling a bit sheepish, Darian headed for the hound, allowing everyone to figure out on their own what had happened and then go back to what they'd been about. Fortunately, it didn't take long until only Maura, Emma, and Rose remained still as statues.

"I beg pardon, ladies. The command was meant for Rose. I should have been more attentive to possible hindrances before I tossed the stick."

"No harm done," Emma said softly, then took the step

necessary to reach Rose, whose head was level with her waist. Without hesitation, she touched the dog for the second time, laying her palm alongside the hound's powerful jaw.

"My compliments, Rose, on your superb obedience. Had we crossed paths, I have no doubt you would have won the day!"

Rose accepted the compliment as her due, her head tilting up with pride. And, damn, but he would swear the dog smiled. Emma smiled back, and after a brief scratch that closed Rose's eyes in ecstasy, the woman continued on to the kitchen with Maura.

Darian watched Emma enter the building from which wafted the aroma of the roasting meats being readied for nooning, wishing Emma had put her palm alongside *his* jaw, run her fingers through his hair instead of the hound's.

'Struth, he deserved thanks for saving Emma from a rough tumble in the dirt, did he not? Yet Rose received the reward of Emma's touch.

But he deserved no reward, especially not the prize he was again envisioning and knew better than to entertain.

For too long last night he'd squirmed on his pallet, seeing the shine in Emma's eyes, discomfited by the feeling she'd peered into his thoughts and comprehended his desire mere moments before he'd kissed her.

And even the discomfit hadn't halted the ache in his loins, reminding him he had every right to share Emma's bed, urging him to claim a husband's rights. Foolish, to be sure. Emma might be his wife, but she wasn't truly his for the claiming, and only a beast would make demands on a woman in so much pain.

She still hurt this morn, but not as much. Perhaps being up and about would do her good and by this eve she would feel well enough to . . . Nay, he couldn't have her tonight, either.

Kissing Emma had been a grave error, one he wouldn't repeat. Nor should he pay heed to the lovely curve of her body or the melodic tone of her voice. Or admire how affectionately she'd touched an animal that could rip off her arm if it sensed a threat or smelled fear. Courageous or foolhardy?

He hadn't decided when he picked up the stick. "Let us find something else to do before we come near to maiming anyone else."

Rose loped beside him across the bailey to the quickly diminishing pile of stone. Since today was warm and dry, several layers of stone could be laid—but not too many or the mortar would squish out from between the lower layers from too much weight above.

Gar and the master mason stood near the wall, overseeing the men who hauled up finished stones with a series of ropes and pulleys. Darian foreswore Gar's company, preferring to watch the stonemasons carve the rough stone that the hewers had sent in from the nearby quarry.

With hammer and mallet, chisel and file, they smoothed the blocks to precise measurements. In some the masons carved out notches. When put together with a similar grouping of stones, the notches formed arrow slits.

The men looked like ghosts, gray from the ever-present dust. A couple had tied rags over their lower faces to keep most of the grit out of their noses and mouths.

A bit farther off others shoveled sand and lime into a trough, then added water to make the mortar. Everywhere laborers scurried about, hauling stones or the wood for framing, or carrying buckets of mortar. Hard work. Demanding work. Something to keep them busy and earn their coin. At day's end they could point to the wall with pride in their accomplishment.

His own achievements weren't so solid and visible. When he did his job well, no one was the wiser. He garnered no accolades, expected no praise.

Darian took a long breath, wishing he were back in London doing his duty—ferreting out who had stolen his dagger yester morn and perhaps killed de Salis with it.

"Darian!"

He looked at where the shout had come from. The wall. Gar, as usual, didn't look happy.

"What?"

"If you have naught better to do than pamper that hound, take a ride out to the quarry and inform them we run low on stone."

Playing lackey for Gar didn't sit well. Unfortunately, Darian had naught better to do.

❧

"Oh, gracious me," Emma commented as she beheld the kitchen.

Maura chuckled. "William of Ypres withheld not a pence in its building. He knew we must feed an army's worth of workers, so provided the means."

Emma didn't doubt Maura's word. Two hearths dominated the room, and she would swear the larger one big enough to hold a whole beef. Right now, a spitted sheep roasted in the smaller hearth, a young girl in charge of turning the crank.

Sinks lined one wall, with drains on the floor beneath them, a wondrous improvement over hauling around splashing buckets.

At large, heavy tables, girls chopped turnips and wild onions destined for the ever-bubbling soup kettle. Bunches of pungent herbs hung from the rafters. Pots of all sizes and utensils of all shapes decorated the walls.

"If William went to this much expense on the kitchen, why did he not build a covered walkway from here to the keep? If the servants did not have to carry the platters across an open bailey, the food would arrive at table warm!"

"Father says that is in the building plan, but must wait until after the wall is finished."

The wistfulness in Maura's voice made Emma smile. "Aye, I suppose the castle's defense must come first. I must say, I am impressed with Hadone, even unfinished. How long has it been in the building?"

"Nigh on four years now. When my father and I came here, there was naught but a small, timber manor house and a few huts. I thought then that four years sounded a horrifically long time to build a castle. But now?" She shrugged. "Hard to believe all will be done in a few months. By summer, Father says, if spring is not too wet."

All might be wonderfully wrought, but Emma felt uneasy in this new castle. Everything seemed too clean, too cold. Hadone might be well built, but it lacked . . . character and history. Like Camelen.

A pang of longing brought her up short. She might see

her old home again, but not for a long while, and longing for the comfort of Camelen wouldn't make the time go faster. Work would.

"So what task did you wish me to do?"

"First I want you to meet Cook."

Cook turned out to be a small, thin woman with a no-nonsense way with the servants and a magic touch with food, if one judged from the pastry offered for Maura and Emma to sample.

Emma wasn't hungry, but the apple and almond filling, tucked into a warm biscuit, was simply too tempting to refuse. She gave thanks that her stomach didn't protest. But then, how could it when gifted with such a delicacy?

She washed it down with the remains of the headache potion, handed the mug over to a scullery maid, then followed Maura out of the kitchen.

Despite her intention not to, she glanced around for Darian, only to see him riding out the gate, Rose running by his side.

Near panic urged her to call out his name, order him to halt. Thankfully, common sense held her tongue. Darian might be riding out the gate, but he wouldn't be gone long. Were he leaving, his satchel would be sitting behind the saddle, and he wouldn't allow the wolfhound to accompany him.

Maura's keys jingled as she selected one on the large ring she wore at her waist. "If you are willing, I should like you to check our food supplies. As you might imagine, we consume more food in a season than I once thought existed in the entire kingdom."

Insuring adequate supplies was a steward's responsibility.

"Does your father not keep accounts?"

"Aye, but my father's time is heavily occupied by the building, so some of the accounts have fallen to me these past two years. I am rather confident of my numbers; however, with harvest and slaughtering soon to begin, and winter not far behind, knowing precisely what we have on hand will allow me to better decide necessary purchases."

Neither had William spared his coin on the storage rooms in the keep's undercroft. One contained an armory of spears and lances, bows and shields, maces and swords. In another were stacked barrels of salted fish. Yet a third and fourth were stocked with huge rounds of cheese; sacks of wheat, oats, and barley; waist-high jars of oil and smaller jars of honey. A huge cask contained wine; smaller barrels held ale.

"Some of the wheat and rye is stored nearer to the baker's ovens," Maura commented. "I am aware we need salt before butchering takes place."

To preserve the meat. No castle in the kingdom could survive winter without a goodly supply of salted pork and fish. At Camelen, Gwendolyn would be making similar preparations to feed many people over the course of months.

Earl William's castle must have cost him a pretty pence, and she had to wonder how much of his coin came from the rents and fees granted him with the earldom and how much from his mercenary activities—from looting and plunder.

Not that it was any of her concern or affair, but it made her wonder if Darian, too, earned a pretty pence as Maura had hinted. And if he did, what did he spend it on if not personal possessions?

Could he have a home somewhere, perhaps relatives to support that Maura wasn't aware of? Was that where he spent winter, when fighting in the kingdom generally ceased because of the weather, with parents or siblings?

With a hitch in her heart, Emma wondered where she would spend the winter. Here at Hadone? Back at Westminster Palace? Home at Camelen? Or at some as yet unknown place?

Her future wasn't entirely hers to decide. Would she still be married and subject to Darian's decisions, or would they have obtained an annulment, which would place her back under King Stephen's wardship?

And worrying about it now would be a useless waste.

Emma suspected Maura knew the whereabouts of every sack of oats and jar of honey. Making a listing of the supplies likely wasn't necessary. However, to sit around and do nothing with her hands would drive her witless.

Perhaps, when done with the meaningless task, she would ask Maura about any stitching that needed doing. Embroidery had always been one of her favorite cold-weather pastimes.

She had to keep busy until she and Darian were more settled. Problem was, she had a feeling Darian wouldn't settle easily. Especially with de Salis's murderer still on the loose.

Chapter Eight

A cry of "Riders!" drew Darian up to the wall walk. Though 'twas nigh on supper, the light fading fast, he had no trouble identifying the group of four men thundering toward the castle.

"The earl!" Darian called to the gatekeepers, who immediately set chains and winches to motion to allow their lord's entry.

As they neared, Darian more clearly saw William of Ypres in the lead. With him were Armand and Marc—who, Darian imagined, might still be angry over the heated words they'd exchanged in the barracks the other morning—and Thomas, the eldest of the mercenaries, both in years and time in William's service.

King Stephen was supposed to have left for Wallingford this morn. Earl William should have accompanied the king. Either there'd been a delay, or William bore news he wanted to deliver himself.

Good or bad?

Darian dashed for the stable and arrived as William dismounted. "What news?"

"None of it good. What in the devil's name did you do to vex Bishop Henry?"

As far as Darian knew, the bishop didn't need a reason for vexation at a Flemish mercenary. He disliked the whole lot of them, and loathed William in particular for rising so high in King Stephen's esteem and court. "Naught that I know of."

The other mercenaries gathered around, all looking grim.

William huffed. "Well, the bishop is so vexed with you the mere mention of your name disturbs the king's peace. And mine. How does Lady Emma?"

To his chagrin, Darian realized he knew precisely the state of the lady's health.

Despite her aching head, she'd insisted on being of use to Maura instead of lying about as might be expected of a noblewoman. Too often he'd admired the gentle sway of her hips as she'd flitted between the kitchen and hall and undercroft, smiling at everyone from Maura down to the scullery maids. And each time she'd come into view, he'd checked her eyes for their degree of shine—almost gone now.

"Lady Emma suffered an aching head last eve, but is mostly recovered. She is in the hall, helping Maura ready for supper. Why do you ask?"

"I will discuss that with Lady Emma. You have more important things to worry over. Your neck is still far from safe." William dusted the road grime from his tunic and glanced around at the swarm of stable boys holding horse's reins and servants waiting to unload the men's belongings. "I need an ale. We will speak of the matter later, when not so many ears are able to overhear."

Gar, who'd been at the work site all day, must have seen the earl's arrival, too. The steward and the master craftsmen joined the group of mercenaries as they reached the outer stairway to the keep.

Knowing he would get no more answers until William considered himself settled, Darian had no choice but to follow along behind the earl and steward and wait, likely until after supper.

In the hall Emma and Maura came forward to greet the earl and, after noting the clarity of Emma's doe-brown eyes and suffering a moment of unwarranted relief at her recovery, Darian deliberately focused on the earl. He crossed his arms and called on his patience as a host of pleasantries passed between William and the women.

From beside him Armand nudged his arm and whispered, "How goes married life?"

A natural question, but Armand's teasing tone made Darian uneasy. "We are married in name only."

Armand's eyebrows rose in surprise. "Name only? Then you have not consummated . . ." He glanced at Emma. "She may not be the most beautiful woman in the kingdom, but Lady Emma is far from repulsive. I should think bedding her might be pleasant enough."

Darian took immediate umbrage on Emma's behalf, but held his tongue. Armand's preference in bed partners leaned toward short, bird-boned women, where Darian liked a woman he didn't fear breaking or crushing. A woman of substance, like Emma.

That Darian thought Emma one of the most beautiful

women in the kingdom made no difference. Bedding her wasn't permissible.

"We intend to seek an annulment, so no bed sport."

"Not even once, out of curiosity?"

Not that he wasn't curious. Not that he hadn't been tempted!

Lady Emma's softly rounded curves invited a man's hands to stroke and caress. Her lush mouth begged for kisses. Temptation reared up and seized him nearly every time he saw her. He'd fought her allure all damn day, including now as she smiled at the earl. The woman truly possessed a lovely smile, which she rarely turned his way.

"Nay, not even once."

Armand's smile turned wry. "'Tis little wonder you are so surly. What say you to an ale or two before we must take our seats?"

Normally, he would have matched Armand mug for mug, but Darian decided he needed a clear head, and didn't want to get too far away from William in case the man deigned to reveal his news.

"Perhaps later."

"Now I know you are not yourself." Armand nodded toward Marc and Thomas. "Should you decide to join us, we will attempt to tolerate your company."

The three mercenaries moved as one toward the ale keg at the back of the hall, enjoying a chuckle—likely at his expense. He didn't want to think about what ribald remarks his fellow mercenaries bandied about over Darian's ill-fated, sexless marriage.

Naturally, Maura seated everyone according to rank, with the earl at the head of the table, Emma at his left hand, and Gar on his right. Only because Darian was married to Emma was he allowed to sit at the high table, when he truly should be seated with the other mercenaries. Where he belonged. Where he would be seated on his next visit to Hadone because by then, 'twas to be hoped, he would no longer be a noblewoman's husband.

He eased onto the bench beside Emma, too aware of her rank for comfort, too drawn by her scent to excuse himself from what was sure to be an unsettling next hour.

Wine was poured, and as was the custom at Hadone, supper consisted of a bowl of stew, chunks of brown bread, and slices of mellow cheese. Through most of the meal, William spoke with Gar and the master craftsmen about the building project's progress.

Darian held his peace, unable to contribute anything of import to the conversation, fighting the urge to lean closer to Emma and ask her to confirm that she'd fully recovered.

He'd almost given in to the impulse when the earl turned his attention to Emma.

"Have you been treated well?" William asked.

"I have no cause for complaint, my lord. Your hospitality is excellent."

William grinned. "What think you of my new castle?"

Darian rolled his eyes; Emma merely smiled at the bid for compliments.

"I am impressed at how much has been accomplished in so short a time. I spent part of the morn in your kitchen and in the undercroft, and I most admire your modern thinking. Having sinks so close at hand must make Cook's tasks much more bearable."

Sinks. They were talking about *sinks*! And because of

those silly sinks, William so puffed up with pride he strained his tunic's seams. Ye gods.

Darian stopped listening, concentrating on the delicious little apple pastries, doing his best to ignore the tantalizing scent of the woman next to him, determined to take little notice of how her creamy white hands delicately tore chunks of near-white bread from the loaf, or the grace with which she scooped up chunks of stew and spooned them past her lush lips.

Then the earl asked Emma a question about the great hall at Camelen, her birthplace.

She answered, "My father chose to decorate Camelen's hall with weapons, but my sister has removed several. In her last message to me, Gwendolyn said one of the tapestries she had commissioned from a weaver in Shrewsbury was almost finished. By now, it should occupy the space where a group of lances once hung." She glanced around. "I see several places where a tapestry might be placed to warm your hall."

William gave Emma an apologetic smile. "Your mention of your sister reminds me of a task I should have taken care of earlier. Forgive me, my lady, for not immediately handing over your letters—one from Lady Julia, and another received at court from your sister. They are in my packs upstairs. I shall send a servant to fetch them."

Smiling hugely, Emma put her hand on the arm William had raised to summon a servant. "No need, my lord. I would not be so discourteous as to read them during supper. They can wait. Do you know from which sister?"

"Gwendolyn, I believe. Your other sister, Nicole, is the one you wish to speak to the king about, is she not?"

Emma nodded. "Nicole resides at Bledloe Abbey by king's order. I had hoped to have her freed of the place and back home at Camelen by now."

Darian heard how much she loved and missed her sisters. Did she also still mourn her dead father and brother? No mention had been made of her mother, so he assumed the woman no longer lived. Did she miss all of her family as much as he missed his?

He swallowed the lump that swelled in his throat, chiding himself for allowing an unexpected attack of grief. A long swig of ale eased his throat but a little.

He'd tucked away memories of his family long ago, unable to bear recalling the day his parents and siblings perished, of the blood and fire and horrific carnage. His hand shook as he put down the mug and again took refuge in his vow to avenge the deaths he hadn't been able to prevent.

The man responsible for burning a small village in Flanders had died before Darian could seek direct revenge, so he did the next best thing—in the name of justice, he rid the world of men who murdered innocents for sport.

Men like Edward de Salis.

Except someone had already slain de Salis and sought to put a noose around Darian's neck in the process.

William patted Emma's hand. "I realize helping your sister is important to you, but first we must free you and Darian from this unfortunate turn of events."

"Of course," she said, but he heard her impatience at the delay. Emma would rather attend to her sister's problem than her own, put her own well-being behind that of someone she loved. A noble and unselfish sentiment.

A foolish sentiment.

One must always take care of one's own neck first before someone took advantage of said exposed neck.

He no longer had a family or home because the villagers near Bruges hadn't done enough to protect themselves. Having escaped the carnage by luck only, blessed with William's patronage, Darian had made his own way in the world, never forgetting that important lesson. With the exception of being accused of de Salis's murder, he'd done a good job of taking care of himself thus far. And would again when the murderer was caught.

The earl rose from his seat, signaling the end of supper. As the servants cleared away the bowls and refuse, everyone walked away to attend late-afternoon chores or see to evening duties.

William walked Emma over to the stairs, her hand resting on his arm, her head bent toward him to better hear whatever he was saying.

Lady Emma should marry the earl. Or some other man of his rank and wealth.

Darian ignored a burst of revulsion, wishing the idea hadn't popped into his head upon realizing how comfortable Emma and the earl were with each other. They might be years apart in age, but age made no difference in noble marriages. The two of them had far more in common than he and Emma.

When the two of them drifted up the stairs—and he knew William would only fetch Emma's letters, naught else—Darian reined in his unwarranted jealousy, turned around, and nearly tripped over a wolfhound.

Rose must have been sitting behind him all through supper, awaiting a tidbit he'd never tossed her way.

But there were no tidbits left on the table. And the responsibility for feeding the hound wasn't his.

He left her there and stalked off to fetch the ale he'd refused earlier and join the other mercenaries—where he belonged.

The chamberlain claims he never set eyes on your petition. I fear you must write another.

Emma rolled the parchment and laid it beside her on the bed, hoping Julia de Vere hadn't considered it necessary to bed the chamberlain for such unsatisfactory information.

Damn. She shouldn't have to compose another petition for Nicole's release from the abbey, but write it she would. Surely, parchment and quill and ink might be found somewhere in this castle. And perhaps the earl would agree to take the petition back to London when he returned.

And perhaps—heaven be merciful—perhaps Earl William might be willing to present it directly to King Stephen, thus bypass the odious clerks and an unhelpful chamberlain altogether.

Emma liked Earl William. He'd been attentive and friendly all through supper. She truly appreciated his efforts to be hospitable, unlike Darian, who'd been very quiet, almost brooding.

Had something the earl said irritated him? Or was he upset at being seated next to her?

The latter seemed more likely.

He'd spoken not a word to her after her near mishap

with Rose in the yard this morn, and he'd done his best to avoid her all the rest of the day. At supper he'd held himself aloof, taking no part in the conversations. Not that she expected Darian to be interested in tapestries and sinks, but she sensed they could have been talking of battles and he wouldn't have voiced an opinion.

Why was he so distant today when he'd been so gallant and kind last eve? Certes, if their kiss last eve was any indication, his defenses against their attraction weren't as high or as strong as he wished. If by his silence he strove to bolster his fortifications, then he'd built them too high. 'Struth, he'd pulled inward so far he'd even ignored Rose!

The hound shouldn't be made to suffer because Darian happened to be in a bad mood.

Maura had the right of it. That wolfhound should belong to Darian. Only look at how swiftly the hound obeyed him this morn. The command in his voice had halted Emma, too, as well as everyone around him. Not all men possessed a voice of command. Darian should be giving orders, not merely following them.

Ferocious on the hunt or in battle, a wolfhound could also be the most loving and devoted of companions. The poor thing had sat behind Darian all through supper, awaiting a tidbit or kind word and received neither.

Why Darian shunned the hound's freely given, affectionate loyalty was beyond her.

Emma shoved thoughts of Darian and the wolfhound aside as she picked up Gwendolyn's letter, which she'd already read once. The second reading proved as exciting and disturbing as the first.

She still wanted to dance for joy over Gwendolyn's

happiness in her marriage and at being with child, and nearly wept over her sister's concern about Nicole. Apparently Gwendolyn had noticed the oddity in Nicole's letters, too. Nicole was changing and Gwendolyn didn't like the change, either.

The resignation in the girl's letters broke Emma's heart. She had to get to Nicole and find out how a strongheaded, outspoken girl of ten could turn submissive in four short months.

Bledloe Abbey was three hard days of riding away. She was no longer subject to the king's will and she considered herself free to travel. Except Darian was now her husband, so she supposed she needed his permission. She also lacked the funds or means to get to the abbey.

Emma rolled up Gwen's letter and rose from the edge of the bed. The large room gave her space to pace.

Would the earl give her aid? Perhaps, but then she would be even deeper in his debt, and would rather not be. Gar might be persuaded to provide her with a horse, or cart and driver, perhaps even guards. But that would put her in Gar's debt, and she liked that even less.

Could she convince Darian to take her? Would that not be the most sensible solution? But since he preferred to avoid her, would he refuse her? And how bound did he feel to obey William's order to remain at Hadone?

In frustration she plopped back down on the bed.

Sweet mercy, at times like these she wished she could stare into a bowl of water or a garden pond and see what she wished to see. Then she would know if Nicole simply matured at a pace her sisters didn't credit as possible, or if sadness or fear battered at the girl too hard.

She might be able to tell Gwendolyn to plan for a son

or daughter. She might know if Darian would be cleared of the murder charge.

But mostly, she longed to peer into the future and see what became of her and Darian. She had to believe they would become lovers, but then what? How long would he remain her husband before he obtained an annulment—if he could obtain one? And if the Church approved the annulment, what would become of her then?

Emma shook her head at her foolishness. To allow the visions meant accepting the good with the bad, and the bad could be horrific. If she allowed the visions and saw Gwendolyn die in childbirth as their mother had, she would be devastated. Nor did she want to know what vision had been forming in the bloody-hued water in the washbasin on the night of her arrival at Hadone.

Of the visions she'd endured before learning how to halt them, several had come to pass, her mother's death the most heart-wrenching.

But a few remained a mystery. Like the identity of a little girl playing in a meadow blooming with spring flowers, whom Emma hadn't yet met. A tall door made of oak into which was carved a beautiful rose. A rolled-up parchment tied with a scarlet ribbon, beside which sat a gold pendant in the shape of a clover.

There were others, but none of them had remained sharp in her memory except these—besides the one of Darian, of course. That vision had been the clearest of all, and taken her several years to understand.

Emma suspected some visions retained substance because within each she sensed both great sorrow and unbridled joy. What she didn't know was whether the sorrow or the joy would dominate.

Would the joy and pleasure of making love with Darian lead to the greatest sorrow she would ever know? And had she somehow ensured the sorrow when she'd interfered with events to obtain the joy the vision promised?

And none of this mattered at the moment. Nicole had never appeared in one of her visions, so Emma couldn't knowingly change the course of the girl's life because of them. Observations and decisions would be made based on facts and feelings, not an image in a bowl of water.

The door opened and Maura entered the chamber much earlier than Emma had expected to see her. She shut the door and leaned against it, obviously disturbed.

Something was dreadfully wrong.

"Maura?"

Maura took a deep breath before saying, "I could not help but overhear the mercenaries talk when I passed by their table. They spoke of you."

Emma felt an ill wind brush against her face. "One would think they would have better things to do than gossip."

Maura raised her chin. "Is it true your father and brother were traitors to the crown?"

Emma inwardly sighed. She'd been confronted before on the subject, and as at court she refused to beg pardon or excuse her family's stance in the war between Empress Maud and King Stephen.

"My father and brother fought for a cause they strongly believed in. Both considered Empress Maud the rightful successor to the crown. If you deem that traitorous, so be it."

Maura's countenance turned stormy. "Here at Hadone we are loyal to the earl of Kent, and so to King Stephen.

How can you expect us to shelter a traitor? Why did you not hie yourself off to Bristol, where you belong?"

Emma's defenses heightened to counter the attack. "Believe me, given the chance, I might have gone to Robert of Gloucester's stronghold and placed myself in the empress's service. Becoming a ward of the king and going to his court was not by my choice. Coming here was not my decision, but one made by Earl William and obeyed by Darian. If you wish to argue that decision, pray argue with the one who made it."

Maura looked around the bedchamber. Her bedchamber, which she'd so graciously shared. "You may continue to use the chamber for the remainder of your visit. I will sleep elsewhere."

Maura spun around and left the room, leaving Emma with an aching heart, having believed she and Maura were becoming friends.

Perhaps she should have softened her words. Maybe she should have tried to convince Maura that the war between the empress and king shouldn't affect their budding friendship.

And maybe Maura would have rejected any plea for understanding and left the room anyway. The steward's daughter hadn't been the first and likely wouldn't be the last to blame Emma for her father's actions and subsequent downfall.

A journey to Bledloe Abbey sounded better than before, for her own sake, as well as Nicole's.

Chapter Nine

William of Ypres, earl of Kent, commanded several hundred men, all of whom considered life as a mercenary a fine way to earn a decent wage.

Darian served William for other reasons, as did Marc, Armand, and Thomas. They were among the dozen men who did the earl's bidding out of loyalty as much as for their pay. All were Flemish and indebted to William for life or limb or sustenance. Until two days ago, Darian would have wagered a considerable sum that each of them would willingly lay down his life for the earl's—and for each other.

Now Darian wasn't sure which men in the band he could trust at his back and which not.

William entrusted this choice group with the command of troops in battle and with the secret of his failing eyesight. To suspect one of the band of stealing his dagger felt strange and impossible, but Darian could think of no other way the dagger could end up near de Salis's dead body, and then in Bishop Henry's hands.

That one of the band could have killed de Salis with the intention of placing the blame on Darian made his stomach coil. Could the murderer be one of the three men with whom he now shared ale?

He dearly hoped not.

"William travels with a small guard," Darian commented. "I am surprised Julian and Edgar do not accompany you."

"They command the troops who guard the king on his way back to Wallingford," Marc explained. "If all went as planned, they left this morn. A blessing, certes. The bands were becoming restless. Had the king not moved soon, we feared trouble."

Grunts of agreement sounded around the table. No fighting meant no pay, no loot, and too much time for restless men to create mischief.

Armand smiled. "If we leave on the morn, we should overtake the troops long before they reach Wallingford. I swan, sitting on siege is a dull business. A pity the king allows no looting of the countryside. The men all itch to take the castle, and a fine day of justice and recompense that will be."

Wallingford, the stronghold of Brian fitz Count, a staunch supporter of Empress Maud, had been under siege for months. And if Darian remembered court gossip aright, Emma de Leon's father and brother had lost their lives outside that castle's walls.

A pang of sympathy for the woman wasn't surprising. He knew how much losing loved ones hurt.

"Any progress at Wallingford?" Darian asked.

Thomas, rotund, gray-haired and grizzled, shook his head. "Neither side has moved so much as a gnat's breath. Wallingford is so well supplied they can last out a year or more. The walls are too high and strong to scale or bring down. All the king's forces have managed to do is surround the place and cut off communication with Maud and Earl Robert." Thomas wagged a finger. "Were the king to ask me, I would advise him to give up this futile siege and march on Bristol."

Marc snickered. "Bristol is twice as strongly fortified as Wallingford. Besides, were the king to take Bristol, then the war would end and we would all be out of work."

Thomas shrugged. "Not such a bad thing. I would not mind settling into a cottage somewhere, perhaps here in Kent, with a plump wife to share my bed and cook my meals."

Darian inwardly shivered at the thought. While the others teased Thomas about going soft, Darian saw the earl come down the stairway. William came straight toward the table and took a seat on the bench next to Armand. The teasing stopped when the earl cleared his throat.

"Have you told Darian about Philip and Perrin?" he asked.

"We thought it best you explain, my lord," Marc answered.

Darian braced for William's bad news.

The earl crossed his arms on the table. "Not only is Bishop Henry vexed with you, but Philip took umbrage at your suspicion that one of the mercenaries stole your dagger. He decided someone must make inquiry into how an outsider could breach the barracks. He declares it possible, but not probable."

Darian considered that good news. "Possible" meant that someone other than one of the mercenaries could have stolen his dagger. "Why not probable?"

"Because each time Philip tried to sneak in while others were sleeping, at least one and betimes all the men awoke. Most everyone's senses are too finely honed to allow intrusion."

Either that or the mercenaries' alertness had heightened after learning the barracks had been visited by someone who shouldn't be there.

The earl continued, "I do not dismiss the possibility that one of the band might have stolen your dagger. However, I refuse to accuse anyone of a misdeed without proof." William leaned forward. "Where were you that night?"

Darian didn't have to ask which night, but he hesitated to answer, unsure of whom to trust, despite William's disinclination to believe any of the mercenaries guilty. One of the men sitting around the table could be his enemy. And the longer he remained silent, more of them realized mistrust held his tongue.

William waved a dismissive hand. "All of these men, and Philip, know what happened during the audience with the king and that you did not spend the night with Lady Emma. So who did you spend the night with?"

He wished he'd spent the night in one of Southwark's many brothels. At least he would have been doing something pleasurable.

"I was in Southwark. Hubert and Gib sent a message they had information for me, so I met them. They told me about rumors of the earl of Chester's wish to invade Wales—nothing new. By the time we were done, London Bridge was closed and I had to await the morn to get back into the city. So I bought them a few more mugs of ale to pass the time."

"Why did you not say so to Bishop Henry?"

"Henry demanded *trustworthy* witnesses. Can you imagine those two passing the bishop's test? Most likely, Henry would have hanged both of them right beside me."

William rubbed his chin. "Likely. Still, Philip guessed rightly at your whereabouts and has been making quiet inquiries among our many informants around London. Perhaps he will succeed in learning who truly killed de Salis."

Philip's involvement bothered Darian. "I should be the one making inquiries, not Philip. He puts himself in danger on my account and I prefer he did not."

Also, if Philip were involved in de Salis's death, he might not be working too hard on Darian's behalf.

William shrugged. "I do not worry over Philip's safety. He has proven time and again he can take care of himself."

"Still, I would prefer to hunt this murderer myself."

William shook his head. "Best you remain here. If you go into Southwark in particular, Bishop Henry will learn of it. 'Twould be senseless to risk being captured and chained in the deepest cell of White Tower."

Darian nearly cringed at the thought of those dark, dank, rat-infested cells, but ire proved a strong deterrent against any such weakness. "I also can take care of myself."

"Perhaps, but Philip does not present so tempting a target. Leave it be, Darian. Allow Philip to find out what he can before we decide on further action."

Too desperate to escape Hadone for his own mind's peace, Darian leaned forward. "Then at the least allow me to accompany you to Wallingford."

"Nay. Best you keep out of King Stephen's reach, too. If you are not within his sight, he will have no reason to question his unusual decision in court. You are safe at Hadone. I already have one man missing, and should hate to have another."

Darian didn't have to guess who. "Perrin."

"We assume he is again hiding from someone to whom he lost a wager. I do wish he would stay away from the cockfights."

Not Perrin. The man's gambling debts were legendary. He owed every member of the band at least a few pence. 'Twas not the first time he'd run afoul of someone who insisted he pay up, nor the first time he'd disappeared.

The timing of this disappearance, however, made Darian uneasy. "I know most of Perrin's hideaways. I could—"

"Nay! Philip also searches for Perrin. *You* stay here!"

Then William turned away, a dismissal as sharp and clear as a slap across the face.

So he was supposed to sit on his arse at Hadone, endure Gar's distaste, and wrestle with his attraction to his wife while another man roamed Southwark in search of both Perrin and de Salis's murderer, was he?

Darian looked down the road of days ahead and judged them unendurable.

And all could be cured by a journey to London.

While the others considered the subject closed by

William's direct order and returned to discussing the war, Darian sipped at his ale and tried to hush his instincts.

His gut told him to leave Hadone, that he could do more for his cause in London. While searching for both Perrin and the murderer, he could also explore ways of obtaining an annulment, a task nigh on as important as capturing the murderer.

Lust for a woman wasn't new to him, but never before had he fought his urges so hard. But then, never before had he shared such close quarters for days on end with his desire's target. And knowing he possessed a husband's rights, that he could take her if he wished to, made the fight harder.

Ending his marriage to Emma was of utmost importance, and he must do so before the sight or scent of his wife overcame his good senses. He had to be rid of her before he weakened.

William surely wouldn't mind if Lady Emma resided for a time at Hadone. Gar and Maura would ensure their guest taken care of, as they'd done for the past two days.

Emma would be safe—especially from him. He could leave on the morn after William and the mercenaries departed to join the king, and none would be the wiser that he disobeyed the earl.

The disloyalty of such an action clawed at his insides, but God's truth, he resented William's reasoning. He *could* take care of himself, and leaving his fate in Philip's hands stank of William's mistrust and his own cowardice.

Sweet Jesu. For the first time since William had dragged a scrawny, terrified boy out of the carnage of a burned-out village, fed and clothed him, given him a purpose in life, Darian considered disobeying the earl's orders.

❧

Emma wished the earl would hurry along so she could ask him for a favor, then approach Darian with her proposal to go to Bledloe Abbey.

But nearly everyone had come out to the bailey to see William off, and the earl took his own good time saying fare thee well, much to the chagrin of the already-mounted mercenaries.

Darian certainly wasn't happy about being left behind. Grim-faced, he stood beside her with his arms crossed and feet spread, doing his best not to look forlorn.

William said his farewells to Gar, and then to Maura, who not only had abandoned the bedchamber but hadn't said one word to Emma while they'd broken fast. Emma hadn't tried to speak to Maura, either, fearing a rebuff she wasn't prepared to deal with just yet.

When the earl finally stood before her, Emma couldn't bring herself to wish him good fortune in the venture at Wallingford. She might not be as ardent in Maud's support as her father, but she did consider the woman's cause just.

"Good journey, my lord. May God see you safely to road's end."

William smiled. "Your graciousness does you credit, my lady. Have you any message for Lady Julia?"

The question surprised her. "Did I misunderstand? I thought you bound for Wallingford, not London."

"I go through London to ensure the king and my troops have left."

"Then if you happen to see Lady Julia, pray give her my thanks for her efforts on my behalf. If I might be so bold, I would ask a boon of you, my lord." She held out the rolled-up parchment she'd worked on until the wee hours of the morn. "Would you be so kind as to present this petition to King Stephen?"

Much to her relief, he took the scroll. "Nothing would make me happier than to be of service to a beautiful woman."

Emma felt her cheeks grow warm. No wonder this Flemish noble had become a favorite of Queen Matilda's and risen so high in King Stephen's court. Not only did he command troops with authority and success, he made free with compliments, even when undeserved.

More important, he'd accepted the scroll without question or condition, and she was sure he would carry through. Another of his known qualities—William of Ypres kept his word. Finally, her request on Nicole's behalf would reach King Stephen.

"My gratitude, Earl William."

Then he gave Darian an affable buff on the arm. "All will come right in the end."

"I am sure you are correct. Good journey, my lord."

Darian didn't sound convinced, and absently reached down to pat Rose's head. The wolfhound pressed against his leg, apparently pleased that the object of her loyalty wasn't leaving her behind.

With the earl on his way, people scattered to carry on with their morning tasks. With long, purposeful strides, Darian headed in the direction of the stable.

Emma hurried to catch up. "A moment of your time, Darian. I have a boon to ask of you, too."

He slowed, but didn't stop. "What might that be?"

"I wish to journey to Bledloe Abbey to visit my sister, and I hoped you could be prevailed upon to take me."

He stopped, his grim expression worsening with a deepening frown. "You know we are under the earl's order to remain at Hadone."

"So I assumed."

"Yet you ask me to ignore that order."

"I ask you because until we obtain an annulment, you are my husband and I am obliged to seek your permission for such a journey." The realization had struck in the wee hours, at first setting her teeth on edge—until she'd realized the obligation might work in her favor. "As I see it, a husband might feel it his duty, even his sacred obligation, to accompany his wife on a long journey to protect her against the dangers of the road."

"Pray tell me why I would consider doing either."

"Because you do not wish to remain at Hadone any longer than you must, just as I would rather not."

"I thought you were getting on well enough, particularly with Maura."

"I was until last eve. Apparently your fellow mercenaries are prone to gossip. She heard them speak about my father and then came up to wish me to Bristol. Maura now considers me the enemy and I doubt any words of mine will sway her to accept otherwise."

"Like at court."

Her heart beat a bit faster on remembering those horrible remarks and intolerable looks.

"Most of them could not bear my presence. I fear once

people begin noticing Maura's distaste of me, all will follow her lead."

He stared hard at her for a moment, then took a long breath.

"I understand. However, I cannot oblige you."

Damn. She'd known Darian might balk at disobeying the earl's orders, but she truly preferred making the journey in his company than going alone or in the company of guards she didn't know. Not that she knew Darian well, but better his company than another's.

"Did the earl order you to remain at Hadone or merely to stay away from London?"

"Both!" His answer was both sharp and final.

Resigned, Emma asked, "Do you object to my asking Gar to provide a horse or cart and an escort?"

"Where is Bledloe Abbey?"

"South of Oxford."

He shook his head emphatically. "So is Wallingford. The roads there are far too dangerous. You should remain here."

She couldn't do that. She needed to see Nicole. "I should be safe enough with guards."

"Nay!"

The forceful refusal pricked her ire. "I did you the courtesy of asking you to accompany me. If you do not wish to, I see no reason why I cannot make other arrangements!"

"Did you not hear? 'Tis not safe to travel the roads near Oxford!"

"Are you saying Hadone's guards are unfit?"

"Nay. They are well trained. However, 'tis foolish to put yourself in unnecessary danger!"

Emma tossed a hand in the air. "This journey *is* necessary. Nicole is a mere child, shut up in a nunnery where she loathed to go, and right now she needs assurance that I have not forgotten or *abandoned* her!"

An odd look came over him, and then was gone before she could grasp its meaning. And she was far too angry with him in that moment to decipher that unusual, swiftly banished show of his emotions.

"And what care you about my safety anyway?" she continued. "You intend to end this marriage as soon as it can be arranged. Were I to lose my life, you would be spared a good deal of trouble!"

He firmly grabbed her upper arms. "Never believe I wish you harm. We may not be a contently wed couple, but I would not wish you an injury, much less death. If I could take you to Bledloe, I would, but I cannot. Stay here. Be safe. When I return, we can—"

He closed his mouth abruptly, indicating he'd said too much, so he wasn't merely making a trip to the quarry, which she'd understood he did on occasion. There was only one place she knew of where Darian would rather be.

"You are going to London, are you not?"

He looked around to see who might be nearby before he answered. "As my wife you are obliged to keep my secrets."

So now he found the marriage convenient, when it suited his purposes. The wretch.

"Only if you take me with you."

"The streets of London are more dangerous than the roads to Bledloe Abbey."

"I trust you to keep me safe." And she did, she realized, or she wouldn't have asked for his escort to begin with. Urgently, she continued, "We can go to London. You can do whatever you must do. Then we can go on to Bledloe."

He looked about to refuse again. She clenched fistfuls of his tunic.

"I beseech thee, Darian. Do not leave me here with naught to keep me occupied and no friendly person to talk to. I will go raving mad. I give you my oath to obey you without question. Perhaps I can even help. I swear, if you go without me, you will never have your annulment, because I will not be of sound mind when asked for my consent."

An absurd threat and he knew it, for the corner of his mouth twitched in humor.

"What would I do with you?"

"I know not, and I care not, so long as you do not leave me behind."

Heaven above, she sounded desperate. Perhaps she was—and her desperation seemed to have a convincing effect on Darian.

He sighed. "You will not be able to take many of your belongings, only what you can carry on your person."

Relief nearly buckled her knees. "Allow me to fetch my cloak and we can leave right now. You will have no regrets, I swear."

"I already do. We cannot leave so soon that we may catch up to William. Be ready to leave at first light on the morn."

Slowly, she opened her hands, letting go of his tunic, but unable to remove her hands from his chest. She could feel his heat, and the steady, solid beat of his heart.

"My thanks, Darian," she whispered, looking into his hazel eyes.

His anger, humor, and resignation had fled, replaced by a desire so intense that her woman's places flamed in response. Heaven help her, becoming this man's lover would be no hardship at all.

No matter that he tried her patience, could infuriate her in a heartbeat. No matter that he kept his emotions tightly controlled, gave naught of himself to anyone, not even a hound who adored him.

Heaven help her, if he smiled at her as he had in her vision, demanded a tumble right now in the upstairs bedchamber or a stable's stall, she would relent.

He made no such demand. Instead, his grip on her arms eased. "Do not give thanks so quickly. Perhaps you are the one who will have regrets."

Chapter Ten

Darian breathed deeply of the crisp, morning air, savoring it for a long time before releasing it.

Behind him, riding pillion, Emma laughed lightly. "I know how you feel."

"Do you, now?"

"You feel as if you have been set free. The heavy weight on your shoulders has lifted, and the chains around your chest are melting away. You can breathe again and you relish the scent of freedom."

A poetic notion, but she had the right of it. And there was only one way she could have known.

"You feel it, too?"

"The moment we passed over Hadone's drawbridge. Your chains must be heavier than mine because they did not melt as quickly."

Or he'd been burdened with an additional chain— Emma's hands resting lightly at his waist, a warm, constant reminder of her presence.

They'd bid Gar—who wasn't unhappy to see them leave—fare thee well at sunrise and had been riding for over an hour with the morning sun at their backs. It had taken Darian all this time to become accustomed to the heat of Emma's hands—and to stop debating the wisdom of allowing her to accompany him.

As she'd done on the trip to Hadone, Emma made no complaint now. Riding pillion couldn't be comfortable. Though they didn't travel as quickly as he could alone— he always knew by her grip on his tunic if he rode too fast for her peace of mind—they would make London by nightfall. Then he needed to find a decent inn where he could safely leave Emma while he visited Southwark.

He probably should have sneaked out of Hadone without her, but every time he decided to leave her there, he remembered her distress when she spoke of her little sister. Her anguish over the well-being of a younger sibling had overshadowed all.

"Tell me about Nicole."

Emma was silent for a moment before answering. "She is now ten. Our mother died giving birth to her, and Gwendolyn and I did our best to raise her." A deep sigh teased his ears, her breath warm on the back of his neck. "We were children mothering a child. Not the best of situations. I fear we spoiled Nicole beyond bearing, allowed her liberties our mother did not allow us. She grew headstrong and outspoken."

"Like you?"

She huffed. "I am neither."

If Emma believed she was demure and soft-spoken, she was mistaken. Deciding they might argue if he disagreed, and he loathed to argue on such a lovely morn, Darian stayed silent and she continued.

"After my father and brother died, the king gave Camelen to Alberic of Chester. When Nicole learned Alberic slew our brother, she sought revenge with a dagger, and was most upset when Alberic avoided injury. I do not condone her actions, but I must admit she was the only one of us to act swiftly and decisively on our feelings."

He whistled low. "And the nuns at Bledloe Abbey allowed her into their cloister?"

"As King Stephen ordered, Alberic married Gwendolyn, sent me to court, and gave Nicole to the Church. I know of few abbesses who would disregard the king's orders—or the hefty fee he paid for her admittance." Her hands again tightened on his tunic, though not due to the horse's speed. "Nicole has changed so much that I must learn why. Do you have family in Flanders?"

He almost refused to answer, but she'd been so open about hers, 'twould be churlish to say naught.

"No longer. I lost them all many years ago."

"All?"

Everyone he'd loved, all in one unspeakable day. A day he strove not to remember too often. "Mother, father, and four siblings."

"Illness?"

"War."

"How horrible for you! You could not have been very old. Were you there?"

Her genuine sympathy touched his heart, and more, he could feel the wish to comfort in the slight movement of her hands.

As a man he didn't need her compassion, and he saw

no sense in her feeling sorry for the child he'd been so long ago.

"I was working in the fields when Bruges was attacked. I did not see them die, only had to deal with the grief and their burials."

He'd required years to bury his guilt for not dying beside his loved ones. The grief was bearable now, but he doubted the sorrow would ever fully vanish.

He thought Emma's silence meant she felt remorse for asking about his family, but apparently she'd been mulling over what he'd revealed.

"I remember my father speaking of a war in Flanders, when Charles the Good died without an heir of his body."

"Much like when King Henry died leaving no son. So now his nephew Stephen and his daughter, Maud, wrestle for the throne."

"William of Ypres was a contender for Charles's throne, was he not?"

"An unsuccessful contender, but a kind one. His forces helped put out the fires another man started; then he bid me join his band. I have been with him ever since."

"As a mercenary. I had wondered . . ."

He had to smile. "Wondered how a man takes up such a life? A soldier's life is not a bad one and the work is steady. Some lord or another is always in need of men-at-arms. At the moment the king pays for our services. When the war ends, well, for as long as men crave power and wealth, there will always be the need for mercenaries."

"I hope you do not mind if I wish all disputes were henceforth settled by peaceful means and so end the need for mercenaries."

His smile widened. "So long as you realize your wish is futile, you may engage in fantasy all you like. Do you need to stop, stretch your legs?"

"If you are ready to stop."

"You need only tell me when you are uncomfortable and require a rest."

"Have you ever ridden pillion? I do not believe comfort is possible."

Darian pulled off the road and wound through the woods until he reached the stream he'd heard bubbling. He tossed a leg over the horse's head to dismount, then reached up to aid Emma's descent.

She took hold of his hands and slid off with such grace one would think her practiced in the art.

And there he stood, her hands in his, staring into the most lovely doe-brown eyes he'd ever seen. A man could drown in those deep, dark pools, escape his cares and worries, and become lost.

She tilted her head and wet her bottom lip. The flicker of pink tongue along her full, lush mouth sent his senses and imagination reeling.

He knew the taste of Emma's mouth. Their one kiss had lingered on his lips for hours afterward, ruining his sleep, wishing he hadn't retreated from the bedchamber.

He could kiss Emma now, and kiss her thoroughly, and she would let him.

And more. If he read her expression right, she would allow him liberties without hesitation, just as she might have the night before last. He could have her here, now, in the grass by the stream.

His loins stirred, urging him to take what he should not

have, yearning for forbidden fruit. The temptation proved irresistible.

Darian leaned forward. Emma closed her eyes. Their breath mingled.

A rustling in the brush snapped his instincts to alertness, all thoughts fleeing except those of survival and protection. He dropped Emma's hands and spun toward the sound while reaching for the dagger in his boot.

He never drew the dagger. Stunned by what he saw, he straightened up as Rose plopped down on her haunches a few feet away, looking damn pleased with herself.

"Sweet mercy," Emma commented, a smile in her voice. "She must have escaped shortly after we left. I wonder how she managed to get out."

He, too, wondered how Rose had slipped out the gate. More important, did anyone know she'd gone missing? Had Gar sent anyone to fetch her back? Not likely. Anyone riding at a quick pace would have overtaken him by now.

Hands on hips, he addressed the hound. "Did I not send you back to the keep to stay with Maura?"

Rose stood and took a few steps toward him, her head lowered in submission. She knew she'd disobeyed him and awaited a scolding—which she damn well deserved.

"You must go back. I cannot take you with me."

The hound whined pitifully.

Emma touched his arm. "You cannot send her back alone. She might become lost."

He raised an eyebrow, taking unwarranted umbrage on the wolfhound's behalf. "You think Rose cannot find her way back to Hadone? Along a road where her own scent is yet fresh?"

Emma relented. "Perhaps she can, but trouble might find her. What if she were somehow captured by brigands, or if a well-meaning soul approached her and she felt threatened and attacked someone she ought not?"

Both were unlikely to happen. Surely Emma knew that.

He tossed a hand in the air. "If we take her back, then we waste an entire morning."

"Then allow her to come with us. 'Tis obvious that is what she wants."

He could hardly credit what he heard. "You would give in to the whim of a hound?"

Emma held out a hand, and Rose, no doubt sensing a champion, went straight to Emma.

"Her escape from Hadone is no whim. Someone must have turned her loose. I would wager Maura had a hand in it. She feels the hound belongs with you, and it is you who denies the hound her rightful place."

Hellfire. Maura must have told Emma about William's offer of ownership. Then, as now, the wolfhound wasn't a gift he could accept. The hound should have a home, and a mercenary's home could be a tent near a battlefield, a barracks in a castle, or the hard ground beneath the stars.

And, aye, Maura could well have turned the hound loose to force him into accepting her. Which he couldn't do.

"Rose's rightful place is at Hadone. She does not belong to me, but to Earl William."

Emma said naught, just gave him a look that said he was wrong and shouldn't bother to deny it.

"We cannot take her with us."

"Certes, we can. She would be no trouble whatever. Truth to tell, she might prove useful. Think of her as a fellow soldier, one you can trust to guard your back. Would that not be an advantage when roaming about Southwark?"

Rose leaned against Emma, looking up at him with pleading brown eyes. It wasn't fair that he must deal with two willful females united against him. Not that they could overpower him if he set his resolve.

Except on further contemplation, Emma's argument made sense, though not in the way she thought. Rose would make an excellent guard, not for him, but for Emma. He could leave Emma in any inn for any length of time and not worry over her safety. If ordered to *guard*, Rose would tear the hand off anyone who dared touch Emma.

For that reason alone, a short while later, Darian led his own horse through the Kentish countryside, with Emma settled comfortably in the saddle, a wolfhound trotting merrily beside him.

"Ye cannot keep that big beast in here," the innkeeper stated firmly. "Tie it up outside. I will not have it scaring my patrons."

Emma opened her mouth to protest; Darian beat her to it.

"You want her tied outside? You do it. And then do not complain to me if she howls all night."

The innkeeper's nose scrunched in annoyance, glaring at Rose, who sat at Emma's side in the common room of his slovenly kept establishment. Those few patrons who sat at ale-stained tables, which wobbled on an uneven plank floor, stayed seated, likely deciding they had best stay well clear of the hound. Emma could hardly blame them. Rose *was* a big beast.

"Then ye will have to pay for the private room and take her up with you."

Private meant costly. Darian pulled a leather purse from the folds of his cloak and began placing coins on the wide wooden plank that served as the inn's bar.

"We shall take the room. We also require stew, bread, and ale, and board for my horse. Is there a brazier in the room?"

The innkeeper nodded.

"Have it lit, with a bucket of charcoal placed beside it."

Grunting, the innkeeper scooped up the coins. "Have a seat. I will have yer food brought out while I see to the room. Be sure ye keep that beast close."

"She is likely better behaved than most of your patrons. She will cause no trouble."

"Best not, or I will toss ye all out."

No, he wouldn't, Emma knew. Darian had paid more coin for their board and bread than the innkeeper likely earned in a month or more.

They took a table at the far end of the room. Emma settled precariously on an unstable stool near the hearth's fire, the crack and hiss of burning wood as comforting as the heat.

Darian eased onto the stool next to her; Rose plopped down at their feet. Having earlier caught and devoured her own supper of hare, the wolfhound seemed ready for sleep.

For that matter, so did Darian. He'd walked most of the way, insisting she ride in the saddle. Misplaced gallantry, to her way of thinking, but arguing had proved futile until late in the day. He'd ridden the last few leagues only to ensure they arrived in London before nightfall.

"My apologies for the poor lodgings," he said. "I fear the stew and ale will be thin, the bread brown and coarse, and the bed uncomfortable."

She'd already assumed as much. "Perhaps on the morrow we can find better, but for now, we have shelter and it is all I require."

Indeed, the meal proved as scanty as they'd feared, and by the time the innkeeper announced the room readied, Emma's thoughts had turned to the comfort of the bed and who would sleep in it.

The room stank of dust and mold. The mattress bore visible lumps. The glow coming from the claw-footed brazier provided meager light.

The door's latch snapped closed and Darian threw the bolt, shutting the three of them away for what might prove to be a restless night.

Rose sprawled at the foot of the bed, her eyes closing even before she arranged her legs to her satisfaction.

Soon all Emma could hear was her deepened breathing, feel her heartbeat quickening. For the second time she was private with Darian in a room with a bed, and this time she didn't suffer a headache.

She eased off her cloak, warmed more from her now-racing, wanton thoughts than the heat from the brazier.

Would tonight be the night her vision of Darian came true? Would he wear that glorious smile and naught else, holding out his hand in invitation?

Heaven help her, but she hoped so, if only to prove she'd done right to interfere so boldly in his life. That she'd not made a mistake to put her own affairs aside, for a time, to save Darian from hanging.

If her vision didn't come to pass, then all she'd done had been for naught and she could hardly bear the thought.

And she wanted the kiss she'd been denied this morn when Rose had joined them. Their lips had been a breath apart, so close and too far away. Not that Emma minded Rose's appearance, just wished the hound had waited a few minutes longer.

As she turned to hang her cloak over Darian's on the single peg by the door, he stepped past her, crossed the room, and opened the shutters. With hands gripping the window's sill, he leaned forward to stare down at the road below.

Was he, too, affected by the closeness of the air? Did his skin also tingle over the prospect of sharing the bed? That he wanted her wasn't in question. She'd seen his desire and responded to it too many times to have doubts.

"A quiet night," he commented from the window. "We should not be disturbed unduly."

"That is good."

"You take the bed. I can sleep on the floor."

Not if I have my way.

Emboldened, she crossed the small room to stand beside him and peer down onto the street. Few souls braved the dark road. Those who did walked quickly, seeking shelter and safety.

"You are not going out tonight then?"

"I probably should. We are not far from the docks. But today's journey was long and tiring."

She chose not to remind him that his weariness was his own fault for walking instead of riding with her.

"Perhaps you should take the bed. You need sleep more than I." She pressed a hand to his forearm, feeling the muscles beneath his sleeve tighten. "Or we could share the bed."

He peered down at her. "If we share the bed, we will not sleep."

"Perhaps not."

"Then we do not share a bed."

"Because of the annulment?"

"Just so."

Did he try to protect her, or himself?

"An unconsummated marriage is not the only permitted reason for an annulment—or a divorce." She couldn't help but smile at one of the reasons that came to mind. "I could always claim you are unable to satisfactorily perform your husbandly duties."

Unamused, he raised an eyebrow. "That would be a lie."

"As big as my lie when declaring to the king we had become lovers? Most will scoff at any claim that I am still a virgin. The bishop might well burn such a petition without giving it any consideration whatever."

She ran her hand up his sleeve toward his shoulder, wishing she were touching skin and not wool. "Certes, we shall end the marriage, but that does not mean we cannot enjoy each other while it lasts."

"I refuse to bed you just to prove myself capable of fornication."

She almost winced at the ugly word, but knew he used it apurpose to shock her. He hadn't moved, not so much as the twitch of a muscle. His hands yet gripped the sill, his knuckles white.

Perhaps she'd gone too far. Or not far enough.

"Then shall I assume you no longer desire me?"

"You know that is not true." Faster than she'd thought possible, he grabbed hold of her and pulled their bodies firmly together. "Can you feel how much I want you?"

The part of him that made him male had hardened and the proof of his desire, pressed so near to her yearning woman's places, thrilled and emboldened her further.

"My father once owned a stallion that went randy at the scent of a mare. But put to the test, he could not carry through. Can you?"

Dear God, what had made her think of that? And to say such a thing! But she couldn't be wholly sorry, for Darian's eyes darkened wonderfully.

"Why are you intent on seducing me?"

"Is that what I am doing? Am I succeeding?"

He shook his head in disbelief. "I assumed you were a virgin, but did not know you that much of an innocent. Aye, you are seducing me. Beware, Emma. A man can resist only so long. You may succeed and later regret your victory."

"I regret no victories, only failures."

"Why me? Why a man so unsuited to you?"

Time for truth, but only in part.

"Because you are the one man in this kingdom who I have ever wanted to be the stallion to my mare. You are the one man I have yearned to look upon naked and then spread my legs for. I know not why you, but fate has thrown us together and I fear 'twould be worse than a sin to deny fate."

As an answer, his mouth took hers in a punishing kiss. Surely her lips would be bruised, but she didn't care. And oddly enough, the deeper the kiss, the gentler it felt, and oh, so right.

Eagerly she kissed him back, hoping he knew she liked how his mouth moved over hers, that she wanted more.

Enfolded in a warm, knee-melting embrace, Emma thrilled to Darian's barely leashed passion, to the wildness in his harsh breathing and rapid heartbeat.

His need swept through her, fanning the flame low in her belly. The yearning ache she'd become familiar with whenever he was near now fairly screamed for easing. Relief only Darian could give her.

Somewhere in the far reaches of what remained of her senses not centered on Darian, she heard the window shutters close. Then his long-fingered, strong hands pushed her back to put a mere inch between them, breaking their string of kisses and leaving her bereft.

"Emma, we should not. . . . Oh, hell."

Not the most romantic of surrenders, but again she did not care. She would have Darian tonight, and naught else mattered.

She ran fingertips along his troubled brow, down over his pursed lips. "Our coming together cannot be wrong. An indulgence, certes, but not wrong. We want each other, Darian. Say you will not deny me."

"You told the king we shared a pallet, so now you wish to fornicate in truth."

Again his crudity startled her, but aye, to have him inside her was exactly what she wanted.

"Did you not tell me you would be pleased to oblige had I made my want known?"

He let go of her. "Disrobe and get into bed."

Unsettled by his curtness, she watched him tug off his tunic, then his shirt, baring his chest. He appeared as he had in her vision. A wide, hairless chest with a long, thin scar beneath his left ribs. Except he wasn't smiling.

"Well?" he asked. "Do you reconsider?"

Emma shook her head and, with unsteady hands, reached for the ties on the back of her bliaut. She allowed the garment to slide off into a puddle at her feet, her trepidation rising. Darian wanted her, but he disliked the idea of bedding her.

Perhaps she'd truly pushed him too hard. She'd been appallingly bold, nigh on demanding. She'd just begun to regret her behavior when her chemise hit the floor and bared near all of her to his gaze. He stared hard, his expression softening into appreciation.

She'd never thought of her body as enticing, certainly not comely enough to enthral a man. Her breasts were a bit heavy, the tips too dark. Her hips were too wide and her thighs and rump overly thick. Apparently Darian didn't see any of her flaws. His inspection went on forever, and she saw not one whit of disapproval.

Feeling both nervous and powerful, she stepped away from her garments. Clad in hose and boots, she slowly crossed to the bed, perched on the edge of the mattress, and proceeded to remove her boots.

"Leave on your hose," he ordered, his voice rough.

"As you wish."

The heady sense of confidence overcame the nervousness. She scooted back a bit, placed her hands on the bed, leaned back, and ever so slightly spread her legs.

The effect was all she could hope for. His nostrils flared, this time captivated by the reddish brown hair between her legs.

"Your turn," she said softly.

In a flash he disposed of boots, breeches, and hose, allowing her to look upon what she hadn't seen in her vision. The man was nothing short of magnificent. Tautly muscled, perfectly formed, and . . . big.

She almost closed her legs. They parted wider on their own, her body sure of what it wanted despite her sudden doubt over the harmonious mesh of male to female.

He moved toward her. "You know what I am about to do."

She swallowed hard, her confidence slipping. "I do."

Darian loomed above her. "Lie down."

Emma obeyed, striving to lie still. Then he placed his hand at her woman's entrance—the intimate touch so unexpected and arousing, she rose off the mattress with a sharp cry.

"Sweet mercy," he whispered harshly, then sighed and climbed onto the mattress to lie beside her. "Come here, sweetling."

Emma quickly snuggled against him, noting the change in tone between "mercy" and "sweetling," an endearment she hadn't expected and rather liked. "Is aught amiss?"

"Not with you. Truth to tell, you are so damn perfect the likes of me should not be allowed within your presence."

Because he was a mercenary and she a noble? Lord knew she was far from perfect! Perhaps the difference in their rank bothered him more than it should, but she sensed a deeper reason for the diffident if misguided statement. But he gave her no time to deduce his meaning. He might be reluctant to bed her; but, sweet heaven above, he wasn't allowing misgivings to stop him.

He kissed her until her wits scattered, allowing her to feel only the glide of his hands over her tingling skin. Gently, he pet her breasts until she swore they swelled to invite further ministration. Less gently, he cupped her rump and pulled her tightly against his hard, full sex, thrusting in steady, firm strokes against her belly, a foretelling of what was to come.

Skin to skin, breast to chest, legs entwined, she delighted in the wanton sensations. Heedless of all but his powerful passion, of her uncontrollable craving for Darian, she whispered his name in a plea.

"Not yet," he said. "For days now I have wanted to feel your skin beneath my hands, measure the swell of your curves. I will have my fill of you first."

"Have mercy."

The wretch dared to chuckle. "You showed me no mercy, so should expect none in return. Patience, Emma. Allow me to make love to you as you deserve. All will be better for it in the end, you will see."

He slid downward and drew a taut, tingling nipple into his mouth. The exquisite torture was so appealing she let him have his way, the pleasure too wondrous to demand he cease suckling at first one nipple, then the other.

His lack of mercy didn't stop there, his hand seeking and then finding the entry to her core. As before, she rose up at his touch, unable to remain unmoving under the gentle assault of his fingers. Her heart thudded in her chest. She could barely draw a breath. The craving grew unbearable.

"Darian, please. Oh, please."

This time he showed mercy. Finally, he covered her, his weight a welcome burden. At long last he placed the tip of his penis where his fingers had played. Ever so slowly he eased inward, filling her, halting his progress but once. Then he plunged, and a sharp pain signaled the demise of her maidenhead.

She gasped and tightened those inner muscles around the part of him so wonderfully invading her body. He hissed, his breath no steadier or less harsh than hers.

The short-lived pain faded. Her tenseness eased. With the same slow, steady thrusts he'd used earlier, Darian flung her heavenward. Higher and ever higher she flew, until she burst apart in a frenzy of pleasure. Then Darian moaned low, burrowed deep, and the pounding she felt within told her he had found his pleasure, too.

Ecstasy. Rapture. Bliss.

No word could describe what she felt, except perhaps joy. So deep a joy she nearly cried from the wonder.

She raked her fingers through his long, sandy hair, then ran her palms along his broad shoulders which glistened with sweat. The thought occurred to her that he'd shown himself no mercy, either. Darian could have plunged into her much earlier to satisfy his own needs. Instead, he took the time to pleasure her, to show her how coupling between a man and woman didn't compare to that of a stallion and mare.

And for a short while, perhaps a mere few weeks, this incredible man was her husband, her lover.

He'd become her lover, but not the lover of her vision. Truth to tell, that didn't bother her overmuch because that meant they would couple again.

He rose up on his elbows, staring down at her with a tender expression, but no smile graced his mouth.

"Was it what you expected?" he asked.

"'Twas all I had envisioned," she assured him.

And it had been—in only one way less, but in others so very much more.

Chapter Eleven

A nxious to be away, Darian grabbed his cloak from the peg. "Rose stays here with you. I am not sure how long I will be gone."

Emma tossed a hand in the air. "You allowed the hound to accompany us so she could guard your back on the docks. I shall bolt the door behind you, so I have no need of her."

The woman could be stubborn, and convincing—only look at how he'd surrendered to her reasoning and abundant charms last night. This morning, he was determined to stand his ground.

"I did not allow Rose to come with us to guard me, but you! Rose stays here."

Emma crossed her arms over her breasts, bunching the chemise she'd put on before eating the bread and cheese he'd brought up after taking the hound out for a necessary walk. Emma's thin, white gown hid none of her ample, lovely attributes, and even now, after a tempestuous, pleasure-filled night, her curves tempted him to return to bed and banish the irritation on her pursed lips.

Which was why he must leave the room before his wits took flight again.

"I need no guard," she stated.

"Nor I, particularly in daylight. If you have need of aught, inform the innkeeper and I will settle with him later. I will also inquire about other inns where you might be more comfortable."

She glanced at the bed, where they'd spent little time sleeping last night. "I do not remember being discomfited."

He hadn't lacked for comfort, either, too captivated by Emma to notice the lumps in the mattress or the heat from the brazier dying. Not until very early this morn, when the enthrallment lifted, had the enormity of what they'd done hit him hard.

"Tonight you sleep alone, whether in that bed or another. What I allowed to happen last night cannot happen again." He pointed at the wolfhound. "Guard."

Then he was out the door and down the stairs before he again allowed his enchantment with Emma to overcome his resolve, leading to another wondrous bout in her bed.

If he must, tonight he'd sleep in the large upstairs room lined with pallets among the other male patrons, as he should have done last night, giving over the private room to Emma and Rose. He truly had planned to sleep on the floor, but Emma's seduction caught him off guard.

Hellfire, he'd barely put up a fight.

To worsen matters, irritated by his weakness, he'd decided to take her harshly and fast, with no more consideration than a stallion did a mare. Except he hadn't been able to remain aloof and detached. He couldn't take his pleasure without ensuring hers, too. The woman wasn't a whore to be taken lightly, but a noble lady, one he found appealing in far too many ways beyond her supple, alluring body.

Darian traversed the narrow, smelly streets of London, wondering again why Lady Emma de Leon wanted to fornicate with a foreign-born mercenary, a man of peasant stock.

With Darian of Bruges.

God's blood, he couldn't be the only man in the kingdom she desired enough to take to her bed, as she'd said. Apparently she simply hadn't met enough men of her own rank. Whether peasant or noble, all males came similarly equipped and able to put a sword into a sheath. Well, most of them anyway.

And how unreasonable for his stomach to churn at the thought of Emma allowing any other man into her bed. Darian might be her husband, but wouldn't be for long, and so he had no right to feel possessive. While she was his wife, he would take care of her and ensure her sheltered and fed. Afterward, she would again become the responsibility of the king, who could do with his ward as he pleased. Perhaps he'd marry her off to some minor noble who would overlook her family's taint for the price of a dowry.

That was the way the world of the nobility worked and it wasn't his place or his desire to interfere with that world's customs.

He found himself married to a noblewoman only because Emma had interfered in *his* life, and in the five days since that momentous event, he still hadn't figured out why she'd felt compelled to rescue him that ill-fated morning in court.

Wanting him in her bed surely wasn't enough reason for her to risk so much. She might truly believe him innocent of de Salis's murder, but to further lessen her standing with those of high rank, and set aside her opportunity to help Nicole. . . . Something wasn't right.

She *must* have a deeper reason for her actions. He just didn't know what it was. Yet.

The stench of fish slapped him, turning his attention to his whereabouts in time to join what seemed like half of London's populace intent on crossing London Bridge.

Save for a few ferries, the wooden bridge served as the town's only means of crossing the Thames. Shops lined both sides of the bridge, making easy passage at this time of day nigh on impossible.

Darian shouldered his way through the throng, at times catching glimpses of Southwark, where Bishop Henry resided in Winchester Palace and collected fees from the stews he could probably see from his bedchamber window.

Winchester's geese—the harlots of his brothels were sometimes called—had made the bishop a wealthy man.

As did the rents and fees from the wharf. Tall-masted, seaworthy ships vied for space with long, flat river barges. Crusty sailors mingled with harried merchants, none of them with empty arms, both loading or unloading cargo. In came goods from distant lands, out went English wool. Most of the wool went to Darian's native Flanders to return months later as cloth.

The cries of the fishmongers clashed with those of

women selling flowers or apples or meat pies. Gulls and terns flapped and circled overhead, ready to swoop down for the scraps the stray dogs and cats might miss. Beggars raised their cups for alms. Nimble-fingered, sly street urchins harassed the unwary.

Having decided he would begin by finding the informants he'd been drinking with on the night of de Salis's murder, Darian entered the dockside tavern where he'd left Hubert and Gib in the wee hours of that disastrous morn.

His sight adjusted to the dark interior, where instead of fish he smelled sour stew and stale ale, and the pungent odor of too many men packed into too small an enclosed place. Familiar scents, almost welcoming. In such places he belonged.

He moved through the crowd, recognizing a few faces, not seeing the two he sought.

"Darian," a man called softly from a table near the hearth.

Philip.

Black-haired, short of stature, and garbed in brown, Philip blended into his surroundings. If Darian hadn't recognized the voice and turned precisely toward the source, he wasn't sure he would have spotted his fellow mercenary.

Darian slid onto the bench. "William told me you were making inquiries. You should not have. This is my problem to solve."

Philip shrugged a dismissive shoulder. "The earl gave you leave to return?"

The earl would likely be irate when he learned Darian had left Hadone, but that was a problem for later.

"I could not stay away. Have you found Perrin?"

"Nay. He is not in any of his usual hideaways. I even inquired at the Clink. Nothing."

The Clink was no more than a cellar in Winchester Palace, where the bishop's soldiers housed drunkards, debtors, and whores the bishop deemed worthy of confining. That Perrin wasn't there was good news, indeed.

"What *have* you learned?"

Philip smiled. "I have learned how tight-lipped men can be when frightened, that every man has his price, and the more one learns of that morning's events, the more confused one gets."

The first two lessons Darian had learned long ago. "What confuses you?"

"Come with me."

Darian followed Philip out the door and down the street. He didn't ask where they were going, because he had a feeling he knew.

Philip pointed into a narrow space between two buildings. "This is where de Salis's body was found. According to what I hear, a sailor found the body and raised a cry. That would have been shortly after you returned to the barracks."

Darian shook his head. "So I am supposed to have run into de Salis on my way out of the tavern, killed him, and shoved him in here? I would not have killed him in so public a place. Nor would I have left my dagger."

"Aye, well, I am also told Bishop Henry happened to be passing by, saw who'd been killed, and became agitated. Naturally, the bishop's guards hauled de Salis's body away."

The hair on the back of Darian's neck itched. "What

the devil was the bishop doing strolling the streets at that time of morn?"

"No one knows for certain. I talked to no one who will admit to witnessing the murder, or even knowing someone who might shed further light on what happened. Everyone is being very quiet, out of fear, I think. And there is one more confusion. Look around, Darian. See anything unusual?"

The space between the two wooden buildings was barely wide enough to contain a body. All Darian saw were bits of straw, a scrap of old netting, and the ever-present mud. "Nay. Why?"

"If a man was murdered here, one would think there would be blood spilled somewhere."

He saw no dark puddle. No splatters on the buildings' walls.

"In five days the rain might have washed it away. Do you suggest de Salis was killed elsewhere and then put here for someone to find?"

"Probable, I would say."

Darian glanced around, sure that someone on the docks knew more than he was telling. But who?

"I should see if I can find Hubert or Gib. They likely followed me out of the tavern and might have seen something."

Philip took a deeper than normal breath, his eyes narrowing. "It took me two days and much coin to find out who you were spending time with, and where. That is why I happened to be in the tavern. Hubert and Gib have disappeared, too, Darian. No one has seen either of them after they followed you out of the tavern."

A chill seized his spine. "Like Perrin, they must be holed up somewhere. All I have to do is find them."

"Or they are dead."

Or they were dead.

❧

Emma stared at the hound, who insisted she must go out *now*.

"Darian should be here shortly. He would be most displeased if I step outside, even with you to guard me. Can you not wait a bit longer?"

Rose whined in answer.

And Emma knew she might be wrong about Darian's return. He'd stomped out at early light, and it was now nearly time for nooning. Making Rose wait on Darian seemed absurd. Certes, no man in his right mind would come near her with a huge wolfhound at her side. And if the man wasn't in his right mind, Rose would deal with him.

Besides, she would only be out a few minutes and Emma wanted to talk to the innkeeper anyway. Darian might not even know she'd been out of doors.

Still debating, Emma opened the shutters and leaned out to look at the yard below. Two men passed by in earnest conversation, paying no heed to an idle stable lad leaning against a fence post. All seemed very quiet, a good time for a brief outing.

Emma grabbed her cloak and left the room, Rose at her heels.

The innkeeper noticed them immediately. "Thought I told you to keep that hound out of my taproom."

She kept her ire in check. Until Darian found another inn, they needed shelter. "We are merely passing through. Would you, perchance, have parchment, quill, and ink?"

"I can get it."

"Wonderful. I am sure Darian will be happy to pay you for the writing materials and your trouble."

"You are sure he will come back?"

The question took her by surprise. "Certes. Why would he not?"

He snorted. "Never put much faith in a foreigner, and this one is Flemish, one of them mercenaries. I get three or four of them in here at one time, I make sure I get my money first and toss them out at the first sign of trouble."

She could hardly refute the innkeeper's opinion of mercenaries. Tales of their exploits had spread far and wide, of their lack of mercy toward enemies, of pillage and plunder. But for the innkeeper to judge Darian so harshly further pricked her ire.

"I have no doubt Darian will return. He left his horse and dog here, did he not?"

"And ye."

Emma nearly blushed over how low she ranked on the list of what Darian likely considered valuable. But most men were no different. Anything with a monetary value ranked higher than an unasked-for wife.

"And me."

"I can tell yer a noble lady, far too good for the likes of a mercenary. Is there someone nearby who we could send word to come fetch ye, take ye back where ye belong?"

So the innkeeper not only didn't like wolfhounds and mercenaries, he didn't want a noblewoman mucking about his inn, either. She was tempted to tell him she, too, was partly foreign, half Welsh, just to see his reaction. Thankfully, the urge passed quickly.

"No one. You will send the writing materials to my room."

The man grunted, and Emma turned heel and went out the door.

Rose sniffed the ground, then made haste toward the stables. Emma let her go, knowing the hound wouldn't go far and would come when called.

Emma kicked at the hard dirt of the yard, sending a spray of dust over her boots.

Odious innkeeper! How dare he suggest Darian would run off and abandon her? She might be low on his list of valuables, but she knew in her bones that as long as they were married, he would take care of her. Not just because he needed her consent to obtain an annulment. Not even because they made fabulous lovers—which he insisted wouldn't happen again, but she knew it would.

Darian was simply one of those men who could be trusted to keep his word. And the hardened mercenary, who donned a mask of detachment, possessed a big heart, which he tried hard not to show.

One only had to look at Rose for proof. Darian refused to own her, but he cared about the wolfhound.

While the two of them disagreed at times, Emma suspected Darian cared about her, too. Otherwise he wouldn't have, at first, resisted her last night. She wasn't quite sure why he'd been so harsh in the beginning, but his behavior had swiftly gone from rough to tender.

Oh, so tender and considerate. Except he hadn't smiled. If only he had smiled.

Rose bolted from around the stables and headed up the road. She was about to call the hound when she saw Rose's destination.

Darian accepted Rose's greeting with a pat to her head and a frown on his face. The shorter, dark-haired man with him seemed to know the hound, too, so she assumed he must have been at Hadone a time or two and was likely one of the earl's mercenaries. Emma stood still, firmly resisting the urge to greet Darian with as much abandon as the wolfhound.

"Why are you out here?"

Darian's question was harsher than it needed to be. However, he asked out of concern, and she couldn't be too angry over his discomfort.

"Because Rose refused to use the chamber pot."

Darian drolly raised an eyebrow to her comment, while a fully amused smile spread across his companion's face.

The man gave her a courtly bow, then said, "To hear Darian tell it, there is naught Rose cannot do."

Emma couldn't help but smile back as Darian presented her to Philip, who was, as she'd guessed, a fellow mercenary.

Darian handed over a cloth-wrapped meat pie. "I brought this for your nooning. The food here is none too palatable."

Emma gratefully unwrapped the meat-and-gravy-filled pastry. "How is the heft of your purse?"

"Ample. Why?"

"I asked the innkeeper to supply me with writing materials, for which he will likely charge you an outrageous sum. I must send a message to Nicole to let her know we will visit her in a few days, and I need to inform Gwen of everything that has happened."

Now the corner of his mouth twitched with humor as he leaned forward. "Everything?"

Fortunately, she hadn't yet taken a bite of pie or she might have choked. She knew exactly what he referred to, and the wretch had the audacity to tease her about a momentous, very personal event in front of Philip.

"Everything she must know, like of our marriage, and that I gave Earl William the petition to present to King Stephen—that sort of everything. Did you learn aught this morn?"

She took a bite of the warm pie. With her mouth occupied, she couldn't say anything else he might twist to his advantage.

The two men exchanged looks of disappointment.

"Nothing definite," Darian answered. "I came back to check on you and Rose before we resumed our inquiries. Would you be averse to spending another night here?"

Her mouth full, she shook her head and shrugged her shoulders, conveying it mattered naught to her.

"Then we will be going back to Southwark."

She swallowed. "For how long?"

"Not sure."

"If you intend to be out after nightfall, you should take Rose."

He crossed his arms. "Did we not have this argument this morn?"

They had, and Darian was as resolute as before. Except this time she had another piece of reasoning to present.

"Then you will not mind when I take Rose out again. Alone. After nightfall."

"Nay, because I will fetch a rope. Rose goes on one end and you hold on to the other. Understood?"

She understood. She was in for a long afternoon and probably a longer evening. 'Twas a good thing she had letters to write or she might be reduced to combing the tangles out of the wolfhound's hair.

"Lovely lady," Philip commented.

"That she is."

Agreement came easily. Darian saw no harm in acknowledging the lady's beauty, or her intelligence, or her wit. He still didn't know how he'd managed not to laugh out loud at the notion of the hound using the chamber pot.

Or why he hadn't laughed. When was the last time he'd allowed himself more than an amused smile? Too long ago, certes, if he had to look back so far to recollect the occasion.

Unwilling to contemplate his none-too-recent lack of humor, Darian turned his thoughts back to the task at hand, finding Hubert and Gib. They couldn't just disappear. Why was it taking so much longer to get to Southwark from the inn than from Southwark back to Emma—to the inn? Surely they weren't walking slower, were they?

"Too bad you cannot keep her."

Keep Emma? A mercenary with a noble wife? Not an impossibility, but rare. Very rare. Besides, he wanted no wife. Darian liked his life just the way it was.

He grunted. "I need a wife like you need a wife."

"Sometimes I wonder if a wife would not be a pleasant thing to have. A cottage in Flanders. A few little ones to chase. Might be nice."

"Oh, come now. Have you been talking to Thomas? He wants a piece of land in Kent with a plump wife to tend him. There is still a war to be fought, remember?"

"There is, but someday the war will be over."

"Not soon."

"Soon enough to ponder its ending. Given any thought to what you will do afterward?"

Not a single one. "I imagine I will stay in William's service. There is always a need for mercenaries."

"William is losing his sight. He will not be leading soldiers for much longer."

Please, Lord, do not let that happen too soon!

"Then perhaps I will form my own mercenary band. Care to join me?"

Philip chuckled. "Perhaps."

Darian realized that sometime during the morning he'd banished the notion of Philip having aught to do with the theft of his dagger. He'd obviously been laboring on Darian's behalf. Spent a lot of coin, too. Repayment was due, and he would settle that account with more than coin.

Philip deserved his trust. So give it he would. That didn't mean the other mercenaries weren't suspect.

"Where do her sisters live?"

"You cannot have one of her sisters as a wife."

"Funny. I meant to offer myself as a courier for Lady Emma's letters."

Darian stopped walking. "Does not William expect you at Wallingford?"

"Aye. When we are done here, I will certainly make my way to Wallingford. That does not mean I cannot take a roundabout route."

No, it certainly didn't.

"The young one is at Bledloe Abbey. The other . . ." Darian had to think back to court gossip to remember. "The other is rather out of your way. Camelen is somewhere near Shrewsbury, I believe."

"Ah, now I remember. Hugh de Leon's daughter, right?" He whistled low and crossed his arms. "Ye gods, Darian. You are married to the daughter of a Norman baron and a Welsh princess. And you are going to give her up? Have you gone witless?"

A Welsh princess?

Now he wished he'd paid a great deal more heed to court gossip. He'd known of Sir Hugh de Leon, of the knight's allegiance to Empress Maud and his death at Wallingford. He hadn't known the man married a Welsh princess. Did that make Emma royal?

His hands sweat with the notion that he'd bedded royalty.

He tossed those same hands in the air. "Emma is not loot that I can decide to keep or discard. I did not win her, nor did she expect to be trapped into marrying me. We will end the marriage as soon"—as soon as he figured out how to go about obtaining an annulment after consummating the marriage, a consummation he would never in his lifetime forget—"as we are able. Now, might we get on with the task at hand?"

"Certes, Darian. Whatever you say."

Chapter Twelve

The day had been long and disturbing. Darian still had too many questions and too few answers to de Salis's murder. The same could be said about his thoughts of Emma.

He rapped on her door, unable to hold back from checking on her, almost hoping she was asleep and wouldn't answer.

"Who is there?"

Her voice didn't hint of sleepiness. The sun had set hours ago. Apparently she'd waited up for him.

"Darian."

The bolt slid; the latch snicked; the door opened.

Emma stood before him, garbed in her chemise, her bare toes peeking from beneath the hem. Her reddish brown hair hung loose and flowing down around her shoulders. A spark in her wide brown eyes said she was glad to see him, the slight smile on her lips both welcoming and tempting.

He stepped into the room that seemed different than the

night before, though he could see little had changed. Coals glowed in the brazier. The shutters were closed. Lumps bedeviled the mattress under a fern-green woollen coverlet.

In the corner of the room sat a small table and stool that Emma must have requested from the innkeeper. On it rested a bottle of ink, a quill, and two rolled pieces of parchment. Emma's letters to her sisters, no doubt.

"I came to ensure you are well."

She closed the door. "Rose and I passed the day without mishap. Are you going back to Southwark?"

"Not tonight."

She slid the bolt. He tossed his cloak on the bed and reached down to pet the wolfhound, who had bumped up against his leg to gain his attention.

"Any progress?" Emma asked.

"A bit. We learned de Salis visited one of the brothels and laid wagers on a cockfight." The last bothered Darian. If Perrin had lost money to de Salis and couldn't pay, the results could be fatal. "There are two men we have yet to find who could prove useful. Perhaps they will turn up on the morrow."

Emma picked up his cloak and hung it on the peg, covering hers completely, as if he were staying the night. Heaven knew he wanted to, but he didn't dare.

"Philip seems a nice man," she said.

"He can be." Darian waved a hand at the table, struggling to keep that same hand from reaching for Emma. "Philip has offered to act as courier for your letters. Will that do?"

"If you trust him, I have no reason not to. Do you wish food or drink before we retire?"

"Nay." He wasn't staying. In a few minutes he'd leave

for the large room down the hallway. "I know the hour is late, but as long as you are awake, I have a question or two."

She crossed her arms under her bosom, pushing her breasts up and against the thin fabric of her chemise. His mouth went dry with the memory of suckling her dark nipples.

"What about?"

"Philip said you are the daughter of a Norman baron and a Welsh princess. That makes you royalty."

With a self-deprecating smile, she shook her head. "Not really. Oh, my heritage is ancient. Some say the lineage goes back to King Arthur, but—"

"King Arthur?"

Her smile widened. "One would think my heritage would command respect. But since it cannot be proven, it counts for little. True, my mother was the daughter of a Welsh prince, but in England it is my father's blood that makes me noble, and he a minor baron and considered a traitor. Those at court chose to judge me on those merits alone."

Ye gods, if the blood of Arthur Pendragon flowed in her veins . . . she was not only noble but the descendant of Britain's most legendary king.

His ire rose higher than it had earlier this afternoon when contemplating her treatment at court. The king had abominably overstepped when giving her in marriage to a Flemish peasant, subjecting her to the further scorn and pity of her peers.

"Have you no relation on either side with enough power to protest our marriage on your behalf?"

"I have cousins on my father's side who I am sure are reluctant to do aught in my favor. They are allied with

King Stephen and have been appalled by my father's support of Maud. Of my Welsh kin, they have been told of what happened after my father's death and none have come forward to protest our treatment. I look for no aid from anyone."

"Surely your Welsh kin would object to our marriage."

"Perhaps. I gather you have had time to consider how to go about annulling our marriage."

"The matter crossed my mind." And the more he'd thought about it, the angrier he'd become on Emma's behalf. "The king crossed beyond reason when he ordered us to marry. You should not be forced to suffer wedlock to someone so far beneath you in rank."

Emma stared at him hard before asking, "So you believe we can have the marriage set aside because of our difference in rank?"

"Perhaps. If you have no male relative who can vigorously protest the marriage, perhaps Earl William would take up the cause. Emma, why did you come forward in court? This could all have been avoided if you had not lied!"

Emma closed her eyes briefly, wondering why Darian went over this ground again. They'd had this argument before. Why couldn't he accept what she'd told him?

"I did believe you when you told the king and bishop you were innocent, and your emphatic search for the true killer has proven me right. Sweet mercy, Darian, the guards were about to haul you out to the gallows! I could not let them do so!"

"Whyever not? What does the life of one common peasant matter to a lady of royal blood?"

Emma tightened her arms around her midriff to keep from slapping him. "I am not so full of myself that the quality of your blood matters one whit. Noble or peasant, the character of a man is measured by the truthfulness of his word and the honorable nature of his deeds. I saw an honest man accused of a crime he did not commit and sought to save him. Is that not enough?"

"Nay. You could not have truly known I did not kill de Salis. How dare you try to convince me you destroyed your standing with your peers, and set aside your aim to help Nicole, on a whim?"

A whim? How dare he! She'd agonized over the decision.

"The king was ready to let you hang!"

"What matter if a man you have never met or seen before hangs?" He took hold of her upper arms, his warmth seeping through her chemise. His hazel eyes pleaded for the truth. "Why Emma? Why risk all for me?"

He would be appalled, perhaps incensed. Telling the truth might cost her dearly. But she knew he would never believe the reason she'd given, would continue to harangue her for more.

Perhaps the time had come to tell him and let fate have its way. With a great deal of trepidation, she wet her lips.

"Because I saw you . . . in a vision."

His eyes narrowed. "Vision? Like in a dream?"

"I was awake, but entranced."

Darian's hands fell away. He stepped back. "You are a mystic?"

She rubbed at the chill his hands left behind. "I truly wish I could claim to be a mystic and my visions heaven-sent enlightenment. But they are not. I am merely a woman plagued by unholy revelations of people and places."

"So I was part of an unholy revelation, and because of it, you saved me from hanging?"

Not entirely unholy. "I had no choice."

Visibly confused, he sat on the bed. "Tell me about these visions of yours."

She'd never revealed the existence of her visions to anyone but her mother, who'd looked on her with pity, then advised her to tell no one else. Emma had obeyed that command all these years, and disregarding her mother's admonishment didn't come easy.

"I began having them as a child. I discovered that if I stared too long into water, I could see . . . people or places. My mother cautioned me to not invite them and to tell no one of what had been revealed. I am sure she feared for my wits, so she wanted no one else to know. I did as she commanded."

Darian listened intently, not seeming repulsed, so she continued.

"Some of the visions have not yet come to pass. Of those that have, one was of my mother's death in childbirth. I did as my mother ordered and kept the vision to myself. I have wondered ever after if by warning her, she might have taken cautions that would have saved her life."

He shook his head. "You were a child. You cannot be held responsible for your mother's death."

Except the child had possessed the power to interfere and had done naught. Others might excuse the child, but Emma would forever bear the guilt.

"Perhaps my mother would have died anyway, but I will never know if by sharing my knowledge, she might have lived."

He waved a dismissive hand, apparently deciding not to argue further. "Go on."

"From the moment of her death, I decided I would

have no more visions, would never again stare into a pool of water. I had no desire to view anyone else's death, not knowing if I should give warning or no."

"You no longer have visions?"

Not if she could stop them.

"At times I am caught unaware, and one begins to form. If I turn away quickly and concentrate forcefully on other things, the vision dies. Do you remember at Hadone, that first night, when a servant set a washbasin before me? I looked into the water, saw it go bloody, then closed my eyes."

"I thought you suffered the onset of a headache."

"The headaches are a result of halting the visions. If I do not act quickly enough, the ache can last for several days. I was fortunately swift at Hadone, so I did not suffer long."

He rubbed his face, absorbing what she told him. Was he remembering how he'd carried her up the stairs, or their first kiss, which he surely hadn't intended but happened anyway? Her head had ached horribly, but his thoughtfulness and touch had been comforting, his kiss arousing and . . . healing.

The thought brought her up short. No potion or poultice or prayer had ever eased her pain. Yet Darian's kiss had seemed to lessen the ache, allowing her to sleep. Could that be possible?

How foolish! She'd stopped the vision swiftly, that was all.

"Have all your visions come to pass?"

"Not all, as yet. Of some I do not know the meaning. There is a room I have not yet entered, a door I have not yet passed through, a young girl I have not met. I suspect all will come to pass, someday."

"So you expect your visions to come true, as the one of your mother did."

"Aye."

"The vision of me. Did you see me hang?"

Far from it. A smooth-skinned, muscular chest. A glorious smile. A man very much alive.

"Nay. You did not die in the vision."

"Then you did not lie to save me from certain death, as you thought you should have done to save your mother."

Damn visions. How did one explain her dilemma where they were concerned? How angry and fearful they made her feel? How confused and uncertain?

"When I saw you in court that morning, I recognized you as the man in my vision. As matters went from bad to worse, I had to decide if I could live with myself if I did not interfere. That is the horror of the visions, not knowing if I must allow matters to take their course, or if I am expected to intervene to allow the vision to come true. I did nothing to save my mother. In your case I decided that if you were to live, as you did in my vision, then I could not allow them to hang you."

"So your interference had naught to do with your belief in my innocence?"

"I *do* believe you, Darian. I did then, as I do now."

"So what did I do in this vision?"

Emma took a long, steadying breath. She'd been honest with him thus far and foreswore turning coward now. "You became my lover."

"*What?*" He rose from the bed, took a step toward her, then stopped. "In your vision we were lovers?"

"That is likely where I got the notion to tell the king you spent the night with me. I knew we would eventually come together, so I—"

Angrily, he pointed at the bed. "Is that what last night was about? You seduced me to make some dream come true?"

She thought she'd explained clearly. "Not a dream, but a vision that I had when I was but twelve."

His arm lowered, his anger faded somewhat. "Twelve? So long ago?"

"Nigh on ten years now. Imagine my dilemma when I saw the man I knew would become my lover about to be hauled out to have a noose put around his neck. I had to decide what, if anything, I should do. Whether to interfere or no. Are you truly sorry I decided in your favor?"

"Aye. Nay." He tossed his hands in the air. "How were you to know the hanging might not take place? Perhaps a witness would come forward or . . . or the king would change his mind."

King Stephen might be famous for his changeable mind, but she hadn't been willing to take the risk with Darian's life.

"I did not know. And no witness has yet come forward, has he? Darian, the bishop was so intent on his justice, I feared to allow you to leave the royal chamber with his guards."

Darian sat back down on the bed and ran his palms over his face. "This is . . . madness. Impossible. If I told this tale to anyone, they would lock me away . . . which is why I suppose your mother told you not to tell anyone of what you . . . see."

Emma shuddered at the thought of being reviled, locked away. "You believe me?"

"Heaven forefend, I do. I just do not know what to make of it."

"Nothing at all. We go on as we have, carry on as we are meant to." She sat next to him on the mattress. "In my vision we became lovers, that is true. But I also think I was meant to interfere so you would live. I believe you have some destiny to fulfill. Perhaps it has something to do with de Salis, or maybe there is something of import you must do in the future. I do not know, nor do I wish to. All I know is that you are alive to face whatever fate has decreed, and that is enough for me."

He shook his head, his mouth pursed. "So now you expect me to do great deeds in exchange for saving my life? You ask much of me, Emma de Leon."

"I ask nothing of you, Darian of Bruges. You demand enough of yourself for both of us."

He thought that over for a while. "So now your vision is fulfilled. You have done what you saw as your duty. What now?"

The vision wasn't fulfilled. They'd become lovers, but not as she'd foreseen. Darian was upset enough without troubling him further. The vision would come true in time. Withholding a small piece of the truth should not matter overmuch.

"You find de Salis's murderer to clear your name. We visit Nicole to determine her state of mind. I pray Earl William gives my petition to King Stephen and my request for her release is granted. We obtain our annulment and go on with our lives."

"So easy as that?"

"What else can we do but go on?"

He turned to look at her fully. So somber. So weary. "This vision of yours. Any notion of how long we are to remain lovers?"

"For however long we wish to, I would imagine."

Then she kissed him to let him know that she wouldn't mind being his lover for a while longer. And not just to fulfill a vision. Coupling with Darian seemed so natural, so right.

As they eased down on the mattress, she had the distinct feeling Darian was of the same mind.

Darian wanted the night to go on forever, with them tangled in the sheets, his body pressed against Emma's.

He'd meant to sleep elsewhere and ended up in bed with her. Again. And at the moment he couldn't bring himself to care.

Sated and bone weary, he couldn't summon the will to move away from the woman sleeping in his arms.

Her revelations had been so astonishing Darian still wasn't sure he'd absorbed all she told him of her visions—especially her vision of him.

A woman possessed of ancient and distinguished lineage, a Pendragon no less, had put reputation and life at risk to ensure her vision of him came true.

He pushed back several strands of silken hair from her cheek. How beautiful Emma was, inside and out. Of practical nature—most of the time—she was quick to smile and usually easy to talk to.

He couldn't remember the last time he'd talked to a

woman as much as he'd talked to Emma. On the ride to London, he'd revealed more of his past to her than any living being besides Earl William.

Emma had trusted him with the truth this time. As fantastical as her explanation sounded, he couldn't believe she'd contrived the tale.

The visions she suffered bothered her immensely. She claimed the visions weren't heaven-sent enlightenments but unholy revelations, and he could understand why she might consider them thus. How horrible for her to envision her mother's death and not know what to do about it. So Emma had witnessed her mother's death twice—in vision and then reality.

Unbelievable. Except he believed in her visions, just as she'd believed his innocence.

Not that he was an innocent.

What would Emma think of him if told he wasn't merely a mercenary, but an assassin? If de Salis hadn't been murdered on the streets of Southwark, the man would have died a few days later of a silent, secret assassination, of which Darian would have been guilty.

He could almost imagine her horror. Certes, she wouldn't now be pressed skin to skin with him, sleeping peacefully.

He breathed in her enticing scent, deciding Emma didn't need to know the whole truth. Were they in a permanent marriage, he might feel obligated to inform her of precisely how he served William of Ypres, of what he'd done in the earl's service.

Except the marriage wasn't permanent, so he saw no good reason to upset her. Emma believed him to be honest and honorable. The truth fell short of both.

Perhaps, when the time came to apply for the annulment, revealing the repulsive acts he'd committed might prove useful. No right-minded bishop, except perhaps Bishop Henry, would approve of a noblewoman's marriage to an assassin. The pope certainly wouldn't.

But that was for the future.

For now, 'twas probably best to do as Emma suggested and go on as they'd planned.

Too bad she disliked her visions so much that she'd stopped having them. What a boon if she could see de Salis's murderer in a basin of water!

Could she control the visions? Likely not, or she wouldn't fight them so hard, preferring the head pain to knowing what the future held. Had she ever tried to control the visions or merely learned how to halt them?

He shifted slightly to stare up at the ceiling he couldn't see for lack of light. The brazier had gone dark and cold, pitching the room into blackness and allowing a chill to prevail.

Darian knew he should get up and light another brazier full of coals, but he'd slept soundly when colder and Emma wasn't shivering. Besides, getting out of bed meant releasing Emma, and that proved impossible to do.

Her head rested on his shoulder, an arm flung across his chest, her breasts pressed into his side. Her right leg rested between his legs, their thighs pressed together in an intimate embrace.

Never before had he been constrained by such exquisite bindings, and nothing short of the threat of imminent death would compel him to move.

Chapter Thirteen

Two days later, standing in the inn's yard, Emma gave her letters to Philip.

"Are you sure you wish to travel all the way to Camelen? 'Tis far out of your way."

"My lady, I should rather be on the move and visit a part of England I have not seen before than sitting on my . . . than being idle. There is naught as boring than a siege."

She had to smile. "I had the experience of a siege as a girl, but I was on the inside of the castle, with barely a break in my daily activities. We could not go outside the walls, of course, which did not bother me overmuch."

"You suffered no attack, then?"

She laughed lightly. "No more than a few fire arrows over the walls. The weather turned cold and the besiegers went home. My father's enemy never bothered us again."

"A normal siege. Unfortunately, King Stephen is not likely to give up on Wallingford so easily. I will ensure your sisters receive your messages."

"My thanks, Philip. I am sure Gwendolyn will seek assurance of my well-being. Pray let her know I do not lack for anything."

"So I will." Philip turned to Darian. "I wish we had enjoyed better luck. People are still afraid to talk. It might be best if you went back to Hadone for a time and try again in a fortnight or so."

"I will consider it. All I ask is you not inform William of my transgression."

"He will learn of it eventually."

"I prefer to tell him myself."

"As you wish. Fare thee well, my lady. Darian, have a care."

After tucking her letters into his satchel, Philip mounted his horse and left her, Darian, and Rose in the yard to watch him leave.

"I like Philip," she commented.

"Good man."

"You no longer suspect him of stealing your dagger?"

"Nay. He truly has tried to help me. Of the other mercenaries"—he shrugged a shoulder—"I wish I knew for certain who acted against me."

"Are you considering returning to Hadone?"

"I should, I suppose, but I am not yet ready to retreat."

Emma heard both his disappointment and determination. In the past two days, Darian and Philip had learned naught of import and still didn't know the whereabouts of the informants Darian had been with on the night of de Salis's murder. Or of their comrade Perrin's. Emma wasn't sure whose disappearance bothered Darian the most.

"Will you go back to Southwark?"

"For a time, if only to purchase our supper. I have grown fond of a particular vendor's meat pies."

So had she, and if Darian was returning only to purchase supper, she saw no reason why she couldn't accompany him. Oh, to not have to go back to the room for a while . . . the thought was too delicious to resist.

"Take me with you."

His eyebrows immediately rose in surprise, and she recognized his intention to deny her.

"Pray, Darian, if I must sit in that room for another full afternoon, you may return to find me serving ale in the taproom. You are not expecting any danger, are you?"

"Southwark is always a dangerous place."

"What if we take Rose with us? She might certainly welcome a long walk, and if we use the rope, no one would dare come near me."

Darian tilted his head. "You will obey any order I give you without question?"

Right now she would agree to almost anything he asked. "Certes."

He took a long breath before he relented. "I will fetch the rope."

Darian headed for the inn; Emma bent over slightly toward the wolfhound.

"I know you dislike the rope." An understatement, to be sure. "But this is the only way Darian will take us with him. If you try to tug it out of my hands, he may not trust us and insist we remain behind."

She sighed, recognizing the uselessness of trying to reason with a hound to gain the dog's cooperation. Hounds understood commands, but Emma didn't know of one to give to end the tugging.

The first time they'd used the rope, Rose had damn near pulled Emma off her feet. Together they'd learned to stroll through the yard without mishap, but Rose always let Emma know she disliked the restraint.

And true to the hound's feelings, as soon as Darian appeared with rope in hand, Rose began to whine.

"Hush," he told the hound, and the beast immediately obeyed. "Does she always carry on so?"

Every time. "Some."

He looped the rope around Rose's collar. The hound never moved a muscle. Irritated, Emma crossed her arms and stared down at the hound, who'd never accepted the rope from her so easily.

But then, Rose knew her master. While the two of them got along well, Rose knew who she *must* obey.

Darian handed over the other end of the rope, and all along the walk, no tug came from the other end.

As Emma guessed might happen, people took a wide path around them, some staring hard at the restrained wolfhound, knowing the big beast could easily pull the rope out of a woman's hands.

Emma gaped at the crowd on the bridge, and peered into the merchant's stalls. She took a mere glance at the ships in the harbor, cautioning herself to beware the water.

The bustle in the streets lifted her sprits. Through the dominant odor of fish, she caught a whiff of flowers and the aroma of still-crated spices.

They ate meat pies and drank mead.

She watched sailors haul wool onto the ships and carters tug at their oxen to get them moving. A tinker hammered on a kettle's dent. An old woman hawked her apples. Two men loudly bargained over the price of a cask of wine.

"Have you ever seen the like?" Darian asked.

"I have been to London a few times, but never in such an active place as this. I suppose all the noise seems familiar and ordinary to you."

"When were you here last?"

"Several years ago, when Henry was still king. My father thought it time to find me a husband." She smiled at the memory. "You must understand my father thought it would be a matter of showing me about, having some man fall deeply in love with me and asking for my hand. Nothing came of it, so we went home."

He scoffed. "Not precisely how noble marriages are arranged."

"Nay, but that is how my father came to marry my mother. Imagine a Norman baron catching a glimpse of a Welsh princess and pursuing her until she agreed to marry him."

"Sounds like a tale out of a fable."

"I swear it is true."

"I did not say I disbelieve you, but you must admit the tale sounds suspicious. Certes, your father must have had other reasons. . . ." He stared hard down the street, his eyes narrowing. "Stay here. I see someone I need to talk to. Rose, guard."

Within a trice he disappeared into the crowd ahead. Her hand tightened on Rose's rope.

"Come. Let us get out of everyone's way."

Emma moved only a few feet to relax against a building, sure Darian would easily find her when he returned. Rose sat dutifully at her feet, obeying Darian's command.

Briefly, her curiosity took flight, mulling over whom Darian might be talking to, but knowing he would likely tell her later, she soon lost interest. Also sure Darian wouldn't leave her alone on the docks for long, with her mind at ease, she pondered his reaction to the tale of her parents.

She could hardly blame him for doubting. Most noble marriages were arranged affairs. Sometimes the bride and groom didn't meet until they stood facing each other on the church steps. Wealth and power were larger concerns than whether or not the two people liked each other, and she knew of many such marriages.

Her parents had gone about it differently. Their devotion to each other had been deep and unmistakable, obvious enough for a child to see.

She'd never dared hope for such a marriage for herself. Father's single attempt to gain one for her had failed miserably. Afterward, he'd arranged a betrothal, but the lad had died of a fever within weeks of the final arrangements.

It struck her as almost humorous that now she was married, in almost as unusual a circumstance as her parents. Except she'd gained neither love nor security.

She might laugh if the entire affair were not so sad.

Emma glanced down the street. No sign of Darian yet. Her gaze wandered from sailor to street urchin, from crated spices to huge sacks of grain, from the tip of a mast to the tern making slow, sweeping circles.

She watched the tern, flying free and unencumbered, peering downward at the river in search of its next meal. Closer he flew until giving up the hunt and landing on a nearby post.

Emma stared at the bird, and behind it, the wide, sparkling expanse of the river Thames.

∾

Darian could hardly believe his luck. He and Philip had scoured Southwark and turned up no sign of Hubert, Gib, or Perrin. Yet on a simple, though disconcerting stroll down the street, he'd found Hubert.

Even in the shadows of a dark alley, Darian could see the informant had endured a rough few days. The sleeve on his tunic was torn and he didn't wear his usual cap. A fading bruise marred his check and his knuckles were scabbed.

"Where the devil have you been?"

Hubert wiped his nose on his torn sleeve. "Been a guest of the bishop's, and not by choice, I will have ye know."

Then Hubert had spent a few days in the Clink. Philip had inquired of the prison's guards and apparently had been lied to.

"And Gib, too?"

"Gib is dead. Hit his head on a bloomin' rock when they were shovin' us around." He pointed an accusing finger. "This be all yer fault, Darian. If not for ye, they might have left us alone. Ain't safe to be seen with ye, so I will be on my way now."

Darian grabbed hold of Hubert's good sleeve and held tight.

"Why my fault?"

"Did ye see what they did to that knight? Now Gib is dead! Let me go!"

A chill gripped Darian's spine. "Who killed the knight?"

Hubert violently shook his head. "I tell ye and they will slit my throat for sure."

"If you do not tell me, you will not leave this alley! Who killed the knight?"

"I did not see 'em do the deed!"

"But you know. Hubert, give over!"

Hubert's fists clenched, opened, then clenched again. Undaunted, Darian stood his ground until the wildness in the informant's eyes dimmed.

"All I know for certain is the bishop's soldiers caught hold of Gib and me and hauled us over to Winchester Palace. Gib tried to get away and one big guard shoved him and he hit his head and . . . Lord Jesus God, the blood came agushin' out so fast."

"Were they looking for me when they took you?"

"What do ye think! O' course, they were!"

"The knight. His name is Edward de Salis. What do you know about him?"

"He liked the whores. The whores do not like him."

Darian had found the brothel de Salis patronized the night before his murder. One of the whores had admitted the knight had been there, but said nothing about the man's sexual tastes. Given the man's other atrocities, Darian didn't doubt de Salis capable of abusing a harlot.

"How did you escape?"

Hubert jerked his arm; Darian let go of the sleeve.

"They let me go this morn. I came back to gather up me things and hie up to York. Got me a sister there. Ye might want to get yer arse out o' London, too."

Hubert turned to leave.

"How do you know the bishop's guards killed de Salis?"

The informant stopped and turned around, his face twisted in disgust. "They were laughin' over how he squealed like a pig when stuck."

Darian didn't stop Hubert from scurrying out of the alley.

Had the soldiers killed de Salis with the bishop's knowledge and approval? Possibly—except Bishop Henry had been adamantly opposed to the king's approval of the knight's assassination. It didn't make sense for the bishop to order his own guards to kill de Salis first.

Darian now knew who'd killed de Salis, but he still didn't know how his dagger ended up in Bishop Henry's hand, or who had put it there.

And now he couldn't be sure Perrin wasn't in the Clink. If the guards had lied to Philip about Hubert and Gib, they could well have lied about Perrin, too.

Did he dare inquire, or would he find himself locked up, too, for taking the risk, doing neither of them any good?

Answers not forthcoming, Darian stepped out of the alley. Emma must be wondering where he was by now. Damn good thing she'd talked him into bringing the hound along or he wouldn't have been able to go chasing after Hubert.

Of course, he probably shouldn't have brought Emma here to begin with. For a man accustomed to blending into his surroundings, shying notice, he'd made himself rather conspicuous today. Everyone had stared at the man accompanied by an obviously noble woman and a huge wolfhound.

Perhaps Hubert was right about leaving.

But he wasn't going to Hadone. He'd take Emma to Bledloe Abbey to see her sister, and maybe during the journey, he would make sense of this strange connection between Bishop Henry and Edward de Salis.

He found Emma a few feet from where he'd left her, her head bowed and her hands covering her face.

Was she crying? Heaven forefend! Women's tears placed him at a disadvantage because he didn't know how to stop them.

With unsteady hands, he grasped her shoulders. "Emma, what is amiss?"

Her hands slid from her face, and the pain and shine he saw in her eyes nearly buckled his knees. He'd seen her this way once before, at Hadone.

"I looked at the river too long. Stupid of me."

He assumed she'd halted a vision, so now her head hurt.

"Let us get you back to the inn. Can you walk?"

"If I can take your arm."

Darian gladly gave assistance.

Emma held her arms up so Darian could slip her bliaut over her head. He'd insisted it come off so she'd be more comfortable. She'd let him have his way because she didn't have the wherewithal to argue.

Her head felt like a bubble about to burst. Thank heaven the shutters were closed so she didn't have to deal with light.

How stupid of her to become fascinated by sunlight

sparkling on the water. She'd stared too long, too deeply. She knew better.

"At Hadone, Maura brewed a potion for you. If you can tell me what was in it, I will have the innkeeper brew the same."

"Potions never help, only darkness and time."

This ache might take days to subside. She'd seen the beginning of the vision and hadn't stopped it as soon as she ought.

"Sit so I can remove your boots."

Emma complied with the order, wanting nothing more than to pull the coverlet over her head and shut all light and sound out. Become lost in the oblivion of sleep—if sleep would come.

"Willow bark has no effect?"

"Nay."

"This one is worse than the one at Hadone, is it not?"

"It is. My apologies, Darian. I did not mean to inconvenience you."

A tear slid down her cheek, and she cursed her weakness. Crying would only make her eyes red and itchy, doing nothing to ease the pain.

"Hush," he said gently, tugging off her second boot. "Lie back and close your eyes."

Gratefully, she did just that. Darian tucked the coverlet around her, then placed his hand on the side of her head, his fingers making gentle circles at her temple.

Oh, that felt good.

"You saw part of the vision, I gather."

She didn't want to talk about her damn visions, but she didn't want Darian to cease stroking her head, either.

"I fear so. Enough that it was difficult to tear away."

"What did you see?"

Nothing terrifying, and for that she was thankful. Or perhaps she shouldn't be. Had the river turned bloody, she might have halted the vision sooner.

"My sister Gwendolyn. Her firstborn will be a girl."

"Truly?"

She could hear his disbelief.

"Truly."

Emma had seen the baby clearly, sitting on Gwendolyn's lap, mother and daughter smiling lovingly at each other. What bothered her was the pendant the child wore—the gold trefoil pendant Emma had seen sitting beside a scroll in another vision.

Clearly, Gwendolyn's daughter and the pendant were closely bound, but Emma couldn't say why that made her so uneasy. 'Twas merely a piece of jewelry, was it not?

"Will you tell her?"

Tell who what? Oh. He must mean Gwendolyn.

"Gwendolyn does not know about the visions. If I tell her she will bear a girl, she will want to know why I am certain. You see the problem."

"You told me about the visions, why not Gwendolyn?"

Why not, indeed? Darian had believed her and hadn't been repulsed or alarmed, merely curious. But then Darian hadn't witnessed Emma's headaches for many a year. He hadn't been forced to take on added chores Emma couldn't perform because she lay abed. Gwen might well be irate over the secret.

"Perhaps someday. . . . No, do not stop. Ah, I cannot tell you how good that feels."

"Then slide back."

She did. He stretched out on the mattress, and soon his

fingers were again pressed against her temple, working magic.

"If you knew the vision to be pleasant, why did you not let it play out? Then you would not have this headache."

"Because the good can turn to bad in a flash."

She felt him shift, getting comfortable.

"Do they all end badly?"

"Not all."

"Hmmmm."

Emma opened her eyes. Darian lay on his side, propped on an elbow, staring down at her.

"What *hmmmm*?"

"Nothing. Just thinking. How does your head feel?"

Someone had pulled out the piercing dagger, leaving behind the dull thud of a hammer. Darian and his magical fingers.

"Better."

She remembered her foolish thought of the other night. A kiss couldn't be healing. Could it?

She licked her lips. "Kiss me."

His eyebrow shot up. "A strange demand from a sick woman."

"Kiss me."

His lips gently met hers in a kiss that was too short.

"Again."

This time he put some effort into the kiss and Emma could no longer feel the full force of the thud as the wholly female itch between her legs demanded her attention.

How intriguing, and impossible. If a mere kiss could dull the ache, what might happen if . . . Nay, surely coupling wouldn't cure her ailments. But then she'd believed her notion about the kiss nonsense.

"Make love to me."

His fingers stilled. He backed away. "Surely you jest."

"Make love to me, Darian."

"You are ill. Certes, this is no time—"

"'Tis the perfect time. I am always so replete and relaxed afterward that I sleep like a babe, and sleep is what I need. Get undressed. Come to bed."

"If you are certain."

"You waste time."

He rolled off the bed and stripped. Within a few heartbeats he was right where she wanted him. Beside her. Holding her. She melted into his embrace like honey on warm bread.

"I am not sure whether to be flattered or no," he said, a smile to his voice. "I have never been accused of aiding a woman's sleep."

"Well, if you would truly rather not . . ."

"I did not say that. Truth to tell, I am curious. If this works, I may hire out my services as a sleeping potion. Much more enjoyable work than soldiering."

"So long as I have first rights to your services."

She kissed him hard to ensure her rights to whatever powers he might possess.

Darian knew something wasn't right. Walking back from the docks had been torturous for Emma, each step a blow to her resolve not to collapse. He'd carried her up the stairs because he couldn't stand to see her suffer anymore.

And now she wanted sex?

To help her sleep.

That made sense in a strange sort of way, but there was something she wasn't revealing.

Well, he had his secrets, too, and if Emma thought coupling would help her sleep, he'd be a fool to deny her.

Gently but swiftly, he removed her chemise.

Emma's skin was spring soft. Her curves a delight. Her breasts a perfect fit to his hands. After several nights of sleeping together, he now knew where and how she liked to be touched. Every groan, hiss, and murmur confirmed his conjecture. Her eyes remained closed, but her hands were busy. She'd learned him as thoroughly, paying exquisite heed to his male parts.

Her touch aroused him as no other woman's ever had. Her kisses spurred his passion to never-before-experienced heights. Entering her was pure bliss, and watching her come apart beneath him, pulsing around him, sent him on a spiral into ecstasy.

Holding Emma while their breathing returned to normal, Darian knew he was in deep trouble. He didn't want to care about Emma, but he did. Giving her up wouldn't be easy, but give her up he would, for her sake as well as his.

Princesses didn't marry peasants.

Then the princess in his arms sighed, and her breathing evened to a steady rhythm.

Darian nearly laughed out loud at the notion that he had, indeed, put a woman to sleep.

Emma might be asleep, but daylight still seeped between the shutters. He eased out of bed, dressed, and took Rose down the stairs with him.

Rose ran off to sniff at the bushes; Darian strolled into the stable to check on his horse. The poor horse hadn't been out for days and could use a run. With Emma asleep, and naught more to be learned in Southwark, now might be a good time.

"Any interest in selling the horse?"

Darian glanced over his shoulder at the innkeeper. "You wish to purchase my horse?"

"Not me. Some man in here earlier, askin'."

"What man?"

"Did not say. Said he would come back later and speak to ye himself." The innkeeper's nose scrunched when Rose trotted in. "Perhaps he will buy that beast, too. How much longer ye and the lady plannin' on stayin'?"

"The night, at least. Perhaps one more."

He hoped that was all. Emma's headache would surely be gone by then, wouldn't it?

"Cannot say I am sorry to see ye go." The innkeeper waved a hand at the hound. "That one scares the patrons."

Scared the innkeeper, too, but Darian kept the observation to himself, not sorry the sight of the wolfhound made men wary.

Some man inquired about his horse. Apparently not one of the inn's usual patrons or the innkeeper would know his name.

Hubert? Not likely.

A stranger then, inquiring about his horse.

Either that or the bishop's soldiers had learned he'd come to London and now knew his whereabouts.

Chapter Fourteen

Emma woke to the sound of Darian softly calling her name, his hand gently shaking her shoulder. She eased open eyes that would rather remain closed.

He smiled and asked softly, "How is your head?"

"Numb." If she didn't move, the numbness would last for another few hours and then she would be free of the headache's aftermath. "How long have I slept?"

"Most of the afternoon. I loathe waking you, but if you are able to tolerate movement, we should leave."

Darian wanted her to abandon a comfortable bed and leave the inn? The man had surely lost his wits.

"Leave for where?"

"Bledloe Abbey."

"Now?"

"Can you sit up?"

Sit up, she could do. But why? Of all the fool notions! One did *not* begin a journey in late afternoon, particularly a journey that would take them, what? Two days?

"Perhaps on the morn—"

"I will help you."

Surely he couldn't be in earnest. He must be jesting. But Darian proved her wrong when he tossed back the coverlet and grabbed her arm above her elbow to help her rise.

Seated upright and bewildered, Emma dragged her legs over the edge of the mattress to put her feet on the floor. A deep breath didn't blow away the fog in her head. She wasn't alert, but could move about if necessary.

Except she didn't think it necessary.

"If you let me sleep a few hours more—"

"I would like to allow you to sleep away the night, but we must leave as soon as we can."

Granted, she wanted to see Nicole, but did not believe a delay of one more day a bad notion.

"'Tis nearly sunset, Darian. Why now?"

"I fear we have been found out." He reached for the chemise he'd removed from her body and tossed on the floor earlier, before he'd kissed her and eased her pain. "Raise your arms."

She obeyed, wishing he'd be as considerate now as then, kiss her again, perhaps even come to bed for the night and hold her. Instead, he slipped her chemise over her head and tugged it down to cover her nakedness.

"You usually help me out of my garments, not into them," she grumbled.

The wretch smiled. "Believe me, this is an unusual turnabout for me, too. Now your bliaut."

She felt like a babe being dressed, and wanted to protest when she spotted her hose in Darian's hands. She should damn well put them on herself, except she didn't dare bend over, become dizzy, and fall on her face.

Besides, her thoughts kept circling back to something Darian had said.

As he slipped on her hose, she asked the question that finally became clear. "Who has found us out?"

"I am not sure. The innkeeper told me a man inquired about purchasing my horse. Granted, the inquiry could be innocent, but if the man is one of Bishop Henry's guards, I need to get you out of here."

He'd said too much, too fast, little of it making sense except the last part. "What do the bishop's guards want with me?"

Darian tugged on her second boot. "They might take it into their heads to use you to get to me. Give me your hands."

Emma thought she was beginning to understand. Darian believed her in danger, so they were leaving London. Now. All she need do was put one foot in front of the other, get on his horse. . . . Sweet mercy, he wanted her to get on a horse! She put her hands to her head and groaned.

"Emma, I know I ask much of you—"

"That you do. Where is my cloak?"

He tossed it over her shoulders. She managed to tie the strings. He grabbed his satchel from the table and opened the door. Not until then did she miss the hound, who should have been standing beside Darian.

"Where is Rose?"

"Guarding my horse. Ready?"

Not truly, but she managed the trip down the stairs and outside to the stable without mishap. Rose came forward to greet her, the hound's tail wagging in excited anticipation.

Darian backed his already-saddled horse out of the stall.

Disgruntled, she couldn't help but chide. "You were rather confident you could wake me."

"My second choice was to wrap you in the coverlet and carry you out."

Her cheeks warmed. That he would even consider doing such a thing only proved—Emma went still and listened to an insistent, scolding voice from within. His actions proved how urgently he wanted to leave, and Darian wouldn't have rousted her without pressing reason.

The swift tingle up her spine made her look about the yard, wonder if someone was watching them and poised to attack. She saw no one, but that didn't mean no danger lurked in the shadows.

Emma put her hand on Rose's head, taking comfort in the hound's presence, while Darian swiftly tied the satchel to the back of the saddle and swung up.

"If you ride in front of me, you might be more comfortable. Give me your hands."

Gladly, she did as bid, now as eager as he to be gone. He pulled her up to sprawl across his lap, her legs dangling over the left side of the horse.

Definitely a more comfortable position than riding pillion. She was no more than settled when he urged the horse forward. He held her close, her head resting on his shoulder, and now she could feel the tenseness in him she hadn't perceived before.

Still, she felt no fright, confident Darian had all well in hand. Emma closed her eyes to the peal of church bells ringing vespers, and when she next opened them, night had fallen. A mere sliver of moon provided barely enough light to see the road.

"Awake?" Darian asked.

"Almost. Where are we?"

"Several leagues north and west of London. How is your head?"

"Better." Which struck her as strangely humorous. "Did we not already have this conversation?"

"Aye, but that was hours ago."

Several hours, given the lack of light. "Do you intend to ride all night?"

"Not all. Are you comfortable? Need to take a rest?"

"Not as yet."

"You will let me know when you do."

His concern sliced through what little fog remained in her head. What he'd told her earlier now made more sense. For whatever reason, Darian believed the man inquiring about purchasing his horse might be one of Bishop Henry's soldiers. Getting out of the bishop's reach had been one of the reasons William sent Darian to Hadone.

Darian hadn't been concerned about the bishop's men when they'd left Hadone, and a horrible knot began to tighten in her gut.

"Darian, if not for me, you would have stayed in London, would you not?"

"Perhaps, but that is not important right now. Why not try to go back to sleep, get what rest you can?"

Emma closed her eyes, hoping the sway of the horse would again lull her back to oblivion, not wanting to face that Darian had retreated not for his own well-being, but because of her.

She'd become an impediment, a heavy chain that bound his hands and put him at disadvantage. She hadn't the least notion of how to break the links.

Darian awakened from a soldier's sleep—his body resting, but his senses alert—with his back against a tree, Rose's head heavy on his thigh. The morning fog had already begun to lift, hovering a few feet off the ground.

Emma still slept within arm's reach in a patch of long grass, using his saddle as a pillow.

He leaned over to push a cloak's string from near her mouth, still unsure if he'd dragged her from bed for naught.

The man's inquiry might have been just that, nothing more sinister. However, he'd heeded instincts prodding him to leave London, and so here they were, sleeping on the ground.

He'd ridden as long as he dared, until he could barely see the road. They'd traveled slowly, but they'd gone a fair distance by traveling late. Deciding anyone pursuing them would also be wise enough to pull up for the night, he'd given in to arms that ached from holding Emma upright while she slept.

Rose stirred, her head coming up to nudge his elbow. He dug fingers into the shaggy hair behind her ears and scratched vigorously. For a time he savored the simple pleasure of the hound's company.

Rose truly wasn't much trouble, and made for fine

company and a guard for Emma. At some time he would have to take the hound back to Hadone, but right now he enjoyed Rose's companionship.

Rising hurt. Stiff muscles protested movement. A few bends and long stretches eased some of the soreness.

How long dare he allow Emma to sleep? This road between London and Oxford, along the river Thames, was well used during daylight. Not long from now, travelers would begin passing by and the road would be somewhat safer, though brigands were still a worry.

The bishop's soldiers, if indeed they'd followed him, might be along soon, too.

He decided to wake Emma and see how she felt. Depending on whether she still felt poorly or if he could determine if they'd been followed, perhaps they could stop in Bray tonight and continue on to near Oxford on the morrow.

He bent over and grasped Emma's shoulder.

Rose growled low and deep in her throat, the warning freezing his spine for the barest of moments.

He shook Emma, watching her intently, listening for whatever had altered and disturbed the wolfhound. A rustling to his left told him where the intrusion came from, but whether wild beast or human he didn't yet know.

Emma opened her eyes, and he was singularly relieved to see no pain.

Just above a whisper, he said, "Stay where you are, but be alert. We may have a visitor."

"Who?"

"Could be anything from a squirrel to a bear. Or a man." He pulled off his cloak, wanting no encumbrance, and dropped it on the ground beside Emma. "Stay here while I see what is out there that bothers Rose."

Emma sat up, fully awake, her wide eyes expressing concern, but not fear. That was good. The last thing he needed to deal with was a hysterical woman.

"Rose, guard."

Darian strode straight ahead, hoping whatever lurked to his left would stay there until he could come around from the side or behind. When well into the woods, he drew the dagger from his boot and veered left, taking care where he stepped so he made no sound.

He found two men standing statue still, swords in hand but not poised to fight. Soldiers, obviously, and likely in Bishop Henry's service.

With the toss of his dagger, he could kill one soldier where he stood and then quickly dispatch the other. Except the soldiers were probably under orders to take him alive, if they could, and haul him back to the bishop. If he could talk them out of it, perhaps he could spare their lives.

Darian wasn't averse to slitting an evil man's throat without warning, but these two were mere soldiers, following orders. They didn't deserve death unless they meant him harm.

"Looking for me?"

Their swords came up as they spun toward him, their eyes going wide. After a moment of stunned silence, they looked questioningly at one another. At long last, one became bold enough to speak.

"You be Darian of Bruges?"

For an instant he thought about denying his identity, but knew it would do little more than prolong the inevitable.

He nodded. "Who are you?"

"Bishop Henry of Winchester would like a word with you."

"Kindly tell the bishop I must decline his invitation."

"'Tis not an invitation. You are to come with us."

"I take orders from no one other than William of Ypres, so I fear I cannot oblige. Pray give the bishop my regrets."

They rushed forward. Darian flipped his dagger and, with straight and true aim, hit the bold one midchest. With his arms flung wide, the soldier staggered, then dropped, much to the horror of his companion.

Now all he need do was disarm the second soldier and send him on his way.

The soldier looked up from his fallen companion. He scowled, but Darian also saw a lack of confidence.

"Should be easy now," the soldier said. "You ain't got a weapon."

Darian calmly spread out his hands, palms up. "None at all."

The soldier quickened his pace. Darian stood his ground and watched the man's eyes. The sword rose high, primed for a savage blow.

From the distance Darian could hear Rose growl viciously. Damn! There must be more soldiers than these two!

Emma!

The sword sliced through Darian's sleeve, punishing the tunic's owner for his irregular and unpardonable lack of attention.

Emma backed up against the tree.

Rose paced in front of Emma, the hound's feral snarl holding three men at bay.

Three men, one hound. Good odds, if not for the men's weapons. The swords didn't concern Emma as much as the spear. If its wielder judged the hound's movements correctly and accurately let loose that spear . . . the result was too horrible to contemplate.

Rose needed help. The hound couldn't take on all three armed guards at once and survive.

One of the soldiers waved his sword. "Tell the hound to stand down, milady. You come with us peaceful like and no one need get hurt."

Emma seized the chance to stall the soldiers from taking action. "The hound listens only to her master. You must put your weapons away and await his return."

The soldiers looked from one to the other. Through the silence came the piercing cry of a man in horrible pain.

The soldier bearing the spear smiled maliciously. "Sounds like the master ain't comin' back."

Emma swallowed hard, fearing the worst. Ye gods, how many soldiers were there? Had Darian fallen? If he had, she and Rose were doomed, too.

But even as her heart pounded against her ribs, Emma took hope in Rose's continued steady pacing. Had the cry of pain been Darian's, Rose would have reacted differently, wouldn't she?

Emma gathered her bravado. "Or the master is even

now hurrying back to us. Do you truly wish to face both hound and master?"

The soldier who seemed to be the leader turned to the man with the spear. "Kill the hound!"

Horrified, Emma searched the ground for a rock or stick to use as a weapon . . . and spotted the saddle. Calling herself all kinds of a fool for not recognizing the obvious weapon, she bolted toward Darian's horse.

"Stop her!" came the command.

Emma ran faster, praying the spear wasn't headed her way. Or Rose's.

Darian hadn't hobbled the horse. He'd simply looped the reins over the branch of a bush, and the horse was well-enough trained so it thought itself tied.

Rose was barking now, sharply.

Emma forced herself not to glance over her shoulder, to concentrate on mounting the horse. If naught else, she could provide Rose with a distraction by dividing the men's attention.

"'Ware the hound!" one of them ordered.

Emma flipped the reins from the bush. The battle-trained horse snorted and pawed at the ground. Sweet mercy, all she'd ever ridden alone were gentle palfreys! Darian had always ridden this horse with her, or at least held the reins.

Too late for doubts now! Still, her hands shook as she led the horse to a log she used as a mounting block.

One of the men let out a blood-curdling scream. The other two were shouting.

Emma grabbed hold of the mane and leapt, barely making it onto the horse's back.

What she saw from that great height sickened her.

Rose had chosen one of the sword men as her victim. The two grappled on the ground, Rose's massive jaws clamped on the man's shoulder. The other sword man stood back, shouting at the spear's wielder, who sought an opening to kill the hound without killing his fellow soldier.

Emma kicked the horse and charged into the melee; her target, the man with the spear.

Darian jerked the sword from the now-dead soldier's belly, irate over how long he'd taken to disarm and vanquish his opponent.

The cut on his forearm wasn't deep or bleeding heavily, but it burned and the pain had hampered him.

Quickly, he retrieved his dagger from the other soldier's chest, then turned his thoughts and steps to the battle he'd heard but not seen.

Rose had ceased growling. No longer did men shout. Either the wolfhound had emerged victorious or Darian was too late to help her.

Running, breathing heavily, he reasoned that the soldiers wouldn't kill Emma, not if they'd been given orders to take her, too, to Winchester. But they could harm a defenseless, unarmed woman in ways he didn't want to think about.

Darian burst into the clearing. On the edge of his vision, he saw two bloodied soldiers sprawled facedown on the ground. Rose lay near them, also bloodied.

Dead, he judged them all.

Enraged, he sprinted toward the soldier intent on dragging Emma down from the horse. As trained, his horse didn't cooperate—sidestepping, backing up, tossing his head to free the bridle from an enemy's hands. Emma gripped the mane and she pressed her knees in tight to avoid sliding off the horse's bare back. A formidable feat. But she couldn't hold tight much longer.

Darian whistled sharply and the horse instantly went still. Emma's head swiveled toward the sound; the soldier turned around to meet the threat head-on.

Without any thought other than the soldier had dared try to lay hands on Emma, for the second time within minutes, Darian let fly the dagger.

The blade bit deep. The soldier fell where he stood.

Emma stared down at the dead man, then across the expanse of clearing separating them. Anguish twisted her features before she buried her face in the horse's mane.

Her distress was damn near more than he could bear. He should go to her, comfort her, assure her all was now well. Tell her how damn proud of her he was for having the intelligence and courage to use the horse as a weapon.

Except his hands were shaking and guilt clawed at his innards for bungling.

His misjudgment had put her in horrible danger, forced her into a deadly situation. Somehow he had to tell her how sorry he was for not protecting her as he ought.

He'd taken no more than two steps when Emma slid down from the horse's back. Sobbing, she hiked up bloodstained skirts and ran toward him. He managed to drop the sword and brace his legs before she hit him full force.

Silently, he held her while her tears flowed, thankful the blood on her skirts wasn't hers. He didn't even mind her tears, simply because she was alive and able to wet his tunic.

In short order her tenseness eased and the sobs became less harsh and heartrending.

"I am . . . sorry," she said between gulps of air, her forehead pressed against his chest. "I thought if I . . . scattered the men she . . . she might win out. I . . . could not . . . get to her . . . in time."

Darian's throat closed up. He could barely breathe for the arrow of grief piercing his heart.

He'd seen the hound lying near the soldiers. The spear and the blood. But now it finally hit him that the hound he'd ordered to guard Emma had done so to her death.

Darian blinked back the tears threatening to fall, remembering the last time he'd mourned—and the vow he'd taken to never allow himself to care for anyone so much that he would mourn their death.

He'd allowed Rose a place in his heart and now he paid a price. Never again. Not ever again.

He cleared his throat. "Rose killed the soldiers?"

She nodded. "Rose killed one. I . . . your horse . . . we trampled the other."

Sure that Emma had never killed a man before, he tightened his hold, not wanting to think of what that cost her. "You did what you could. 'Tis I who must beg your pardon for not being where I was most needed."

"I heard a man cry out in pain. Are they all . . . gone?"

Darian dearly hoped so. "I need to find their horses to know for sure."

"I am going with you."

A bad idea, but he couldn't deny her because he

couldn't leave Emma alone amidst the carnage. He could no longer tell Rose to guard. Damn. Damn. Damn!

He took another fortifying breath. "Let me get my dagger and then we will go."

Slowly Emma's arms slipped from around him. She took a step back, and through moist and reddened eyes, noticed his arm.

"You are wounded!"

"Not badly enough to warrant concern. It can wait for tending until later."

He retrieved his dagger, wiping it clean on a dry spot on his victim's tunic, deliberately not looking at Rose. He would, later. Maybe bury her so the carrion couldn't have her. Surely he owed her that much for her valor and loyalty.

When he reached Emma's side, she was staring down at her blood-smeared palms. Ye gods, she must have held the reins so tightly they'd sawed off skin.

"Rose would be alive if not for my cowardice," she declared. "The other day, at Hadone. The bloody water in the washbasin." She glanced over at the gruesome scattering of bloodied bodies. "This is the vision I would have seen, had I not stopped it."

"You cannot know what you did not see."

Her hands began to shake.

"I know," she disagreed. "I know!"

Chapter Fifteen

E mma watched Darian toss the third soldier over the back of a horse and could no longer hold her tongue.

"Darian, this is not wise."

His anger still burning hot, he put hands on hips, blood seeping from the wound he hadn't allowed her to tend yet.

"Would you have me bury them?"

Just as he'd buried Rose.

He'd found a small camp shovel in one of the soldier's packs. Ever since, he'd worked feverishly to clear away all signs of their battle with the bishop's soldiers. By himself. All he'd allowed her to do was gather stones to cover the wolfhound's grave.

"You should not have to bury them."

"Then what would you have me do? Ride into the next village and inform whoever is in charge there of several bodies in the forest? I have no intention of spending hours answering the questions of some village official. Do you want to tell anyone how these men died?"

Never would she forget the sight of Rose tearing out a man's throat, or the spear taking the hound's life in turn. Or the sound of bones breaking under the horse's hooves. Or the sight of Darian's dagger protruding from a man's chest.

She might have to live with those memories, but the mere thought of relating them closed her throat.

"Nay" was all she could say.

Having gained the answer he wanted, he nodded sharply. "I prefer no one know we were involved. Granted, we were the victims of their aggression. But we won out, and some might wonder how and speculate, and I prefer not to have my name, or yours, on people's minds and lips."

Neither did she. Once they were done here, she would cover her bloody garments with her cloak—as would Darian—and no one would know what they'd endured this morn.

Except one man. Bishop Henry of Winchester. If Darian carried through with his plan, the bishop would know well before nightfall that the man he'd sent his soldiers out to capture had prevailed. She didn't need a vision to tell her retribution might come in horrific form.

"Darian, I beg you to reconsider. The bishop is a powerful man. Sending his soldiers back to him this way will surely—"

"Enough, Emma!" He slung the fourth soldier over his shoulder. "Go out to the road and see if the way is clear. The sooner done, the sooner we can be on our way."

Emma tossed her hands in frustration. Darian was set

on this course and there was no talking him out of it. As he flung the soldier over the saddle, blood flew from the man's crushed skull to wet the bushes beyond.

Stomach roiling, Emma fled, at first not trying to be quiet. But once away from the sight and coppery aroma of blood, she slowed, and for a moment put her hand on a stout oak for support.

Tears welled up again, and several slid down her cheeks before she dashed the rest away. Crying would do her no good—nor Darian. Nor Rose.

Resolved to playing out her part in what she still considered Darian's unwise plan, Emma made her way through the trees, hoping she went the right way.

How Darian had managed to find a small clearing in the woods between the road and the Thames in the middle of the night, she didn't know. How the bishop's soldiers had managed to find them, she didn't know, either. But what had happened had happened. There was naught she could do to change it.

Could she have prevented the carnage and saved Rose? That mind-bending thought harassed her until she finally saw the road.

Slowly, quietly, she eased out from the cover of the trees. To her left, London. On her right, Oxford, Bledloe Abbey, and Nicole. All seemed so far away.

She saw no one, heard no other sound than a slight breeze playing with leaves, which had begun to turn color and would soon fall.

The restful silence didn't last long enough to suit her. From behind her she heard the plop of horses' hooves on the forest floor. She turned to see Darian leading a line of horses, one tied to the other, bearing gruesome burdens.

Darian tilted his head, his expression questioning. Emma took another look in both directions before waving him forward.

He set the string of horses in motion, leading them a way down the road before swatting the lead horse to keep it moving.

The horses lumbered along as Darian ran back to where she stood. What was done was done, but it still seemed senseless.

"Do you really expect the horses to walk all the way to Winchester Palace without interference or mishap?"

"That would be far too much to ask. One or two of the bodies are likely to fall off." He crossed his arms, also watching the horses climb a slight hill, then disappear from view. "Most people will look at them and cross themselves and leave them alone. However, I am willing to wager some imaginative soul will see a fast way to make some coin and lead the whole lot of them to the bishop in hopes of a reward."

"Or some not so naive soul will dump the bodies and sell the horses."

Darian shrugged. "Either way we are done with them."

How could he be so callous? So hard and unfeeling? Even as she wanted to rail at him, she knew she wouldn't. Had he shown a dram of mercy to the soldiers earlier, she and Darian might be the dead bodies draped over horses.

"I need to wash," he announced. "Coming?"

They walked briskly back to the clearing. Darian scooped up his satchel on the way through, never pausing on his way to the river.

Emma hesitated. She could use a wash, too. Her hands were still bloody, and a dip in cold water might banish the remains of the sting. But to go near the river was a risk. The Thames had caught her once and she didn't want to repeat the experience.

She'd almost decided not to follow Darian; then the clearing suddenly seemed smaller, and men's shouts and Rose's growls again bounced off the trees, accusing her of cowardice, blaming her for their deaths.

Emma hurried after Darian, who'd noticed her absence and waited for her several yards from the river.

"I need to wash, too, but I cannot get too near the river," she stated.

"Give me your hand and close your eyes."

Emma felt as much the babe as she had when he'd put on her hose. But as his fingers entwined with hers, she knew her trust not misplaced. She closed her eyes, allowing him to lead her through the woods and down the slope to the river, the sound of flowing water becoming louder. She halted when he did. Grasping her by the shoulders, he turned her slightly.

"There is a rock behind you, where you can sit and not see much of the river if you look left. Back up a step. There." He took hold of her hands. "Now ease back. Good. You can open your eyes now."

He released her hands and hurried down the slope. She didn't dare watch for fear of becoming entranced by the water. So how was she supposed to wash the blood from her hands, the grit and sweat from her face?

Darian had no such problem, judging by the splashing she heard. Perhaps, if she walked backward down the slope—she'd trip over a rock or fallen branch and end up *in* the river.

Then Darian stood before her, water dripping from his

hair to slide down his bare chest, holding his sodden tunic out for her to take.

Gratefully, she rubbed the soft, cold wool over her face and throat, and washed away the worst of the blood from her hands. They would be raw for a while, but wouldn't bleed, not like Darian's wound.

Darian pulled a short-sleeved tunic from his satchel and tugged it on, leaving his wound exposed.

"Have you an unguent or cloth for bandaging?"

He glanced at his injury. "'Twill heal on its own."

"'Twill continue to bleed if you do not wrap it. If you have no bandaging, cut off the hem of my chemise. That should do for the nonce."

Sighing, he knelt before her, drew his dagger, and lifted her bliaut above her knees to get at the chemise. And she couldn't help but remember the last time he'd knelt before her, helping her dress. That hazy memory seemed a lifetime ago, made more unreal by the sound of his blade slicing through linen.

"We need to replace your bliaut," he said flatly. "Perhaps we can purchase a gown along the way."

Such a mundane concern, but he was right. She would rather not enter the abbey garbed in a bloody gown.

He stuck the dagger in his boot, stood up, and began wrapping the long linen strip around his arm, too loose and jumbled to do any good at all.

Without a thought of why, she bolted off the rock and swatted his hand away, his ineffectual tending pricking her ire. Fiercely, she unwrapped the bandage.

"One would think a man who wields a weapon would know how to wrap an injury! If you intend to stop the blood, then you have to wrap it tighter, like this."

"Emma, I know how—"

"Not that one could tell."

He remained silent while she neatly wrapped and tied off the linen.

"What about your hands?" he asked softly.

She held them up for him to see. "They have stopped bleeding. Your arm has not. My hands will heal long before your arm."

He stared at her as if she'd gone daft. Perhaps she had. All she knew was that her body hurt and her arms ached and she wanted to be quit of this place *now*. She spun to go back to the clearing. Darian clamped a hand on her shoulder.

"Easy, Emma. In a few days the images will fade, the horror will lessen."

She shrugged him off, wanting no comfort. If she let down her guard, she would surely begin sobbing again. "Please, can we just leave?"

Without another word, he obliged her. Soon they were riding out of the clearing as they'd entered it; atop a battle-trained horse, Emma riding across Darian's lap.

Except this time Rose didn't range ahead, enjoying the freedom of scampering along the road and occasionally veering off to investigate some intriguing scent.

Emma desperately tried not to listen, but over and over, the nagging voice she'd heard earlier scolded her for stopping the vision forming in the washbasin.

If she had known they would be attacked, Rose and five soldiers might now be alive.

∽

She'd never slept in a barn. But then, until of late, neither had Emma slept in an inn or on the ground.

Or with a man.

Only some of those new experiences did she wish to banish from her memory.

Rain had forced them to quit the road earlier than she was sure Darian preferred, the handiest shelter a peasant's farm. A few pence gained them a place to sleep, a spare blanket, and, later, a bowl of stew and bread. Unfortunately, the farmer's wife owned no spare gown, so in her bliaut Emma must remain.

She stood near the barn's doorway with the horse while Darian climbed the ladder to the loft, ensuring no mice or birds occupied the space where they would sleep.

The cow in the far corner eyed the horse suspiciously. Swallows flitted in and out of gaps in the walls. Three gray geese couldn't make up their minds over whether they wanted in or out. Several plump brown chickens roosted among the grain sacks. Perched atop a stack of wooden crates a cock watched over his flock. Muddy puddles revealed where the roof wanted for repair.

All and all a warm, cozy place, if somewhat smelly and noisy.

"Looks dry," Darian called down. "Hay seems clean, too."

Good news—and his longest utterance since leaving the clearing. Not that she'd said much, either, both of them keeping their own counsel.

Emma removed her sodden cloak and spread it over the handles of a plow, then pulled down Darian's cloak from where he'd tossed it across his saddle.

She jumped when he reached from behind her to snatch it away.

"I will take care of this. You go rest."

Rest. Be at ease? For that, one need be at peace, an unachievable state of mind just yet. Still, she found a chicken-free sack of grain and sat while Darian hung his cloak on a peg, which also held leather strips, and proceeded to unsaddle his horse.

Emma noted the bandage had held tight and no blood seeped through. Chagrined to realize he might be right about the slightness of his wound, Emma's cheeks warmed over how she'd insisted on bandaging his arm, swatting away his hands because he wrapped the cloth wrongly. Ye gods, how shrewish she must have sounded.

"I beg your pardon, Darian. I did not mean to be so peevish about your wound."

He set his saddle in a dry area near the wall. "Think naught of it. You were overwrought, a not unexpected reaction."

He didn't have to say to what she'd reacted. Damn near every moment of the bloody battle was still too fresh and horrifyingly clear, including sobbing her eyes out against Darian's chest.

"You said the images will fade."

"In time."

"How long?"

He led the horse to the back of the barn. The cow bawled a protest at the intrusion, but seeing neither man nor horse pay any heed, it soon relented to sharing the hay manger.

"Hard to say," Darian finally answered. "Your reaction is not unusual. I know of men who recovered swiftly after their first battle and others who did not." He pointed a finger at her. "The first thing you need do is stop blaming yourself for what happened. If anyone is at fault, I am for not . . . Well, I can think of several things I might have done differently."

A long speech for a man who'd been so silent, and apparently he felt as guilty as she, though for different reasons.

"I cannot help wondering if I had allowed the vision to form if we could have . . . evaded the soldiers."

And Rose would still be alive. Sweet mercy, she couldn't bring herself to say the hound's name aloud.

Darian eased down onto the dirt floor at her feet and leaned against the grain sack next to hers.

"Perhaps, but your visions frighten and confuse you, so you halt them. If you choose not to allow the visions, then you must trust to fate like the rest of us."

Like normal people.

"They are a curse."

"Or a blessing. Or simply part of who you are. Your head punishes you each time you deny a vision, and you have decided the pain is preferable to the confusion. Each of us decides what we can or cannot endure."

Her spine stiffened. "So you think I am wrong to foreswear the visions?"

"I would not presume."

The devil he wouldn't.

"At Hadone, if I had told you that you and I and . . . Rose would be attacked by Bishop Henry's soldiers on the road to Oxford, would you have believed me?"

"Perhaps not then, but when we were in London, had you told me you foresaw trouble along the Oxford road,

I might have heeded the warning. Taken another road, or left earlier." He tossed a dismissive hand. "This is all conjecture, Emma. We will never know what might have been, only what is."

"But you blame me—"

"No more than I blame myself. Had I not let you sleep, or had we ridden later, or had I not stopped precisely where I did, or had Rose heard the soldiers sooner. There are far too many things I could have done differently for me to place any blame on you."

His sincerity rang true, and though her guilt didn't completely disappear, she was glad to know he didn't hold the hound's death against her.

But what truly astounded her was his attitude toward her visions. Besides her mother, she'd told no other soul out of fear of becoming an outcast, reviled and avoided.

She'd certainly learned how to contend with contempt at court and at Hadone when shunned for no other reason than she was her father's daughter.

She'd endured through the worst because of Lady Julia de Vere's unexpected and welcome friendship. And since, she'd sailed swiftly through two headaches because of Darian's tender care.

Or perhaps she'd become a stronger, more confident person since leaving home. Sweet mercy, she would like to believe so.

She'd never questioned Darian's confidence in his abilities. The man always seemed so sure of himself—until now. That he had doubts proved unsettling.

"You were not even sure the man who inquired about purchasing your horse was one of Bishop Henry's men, so could not have known so many would be on us so quickly. You did what you thought best, and I, for one, cannot hold that against you."

He rocked his head from side to side, as if easing tension from his neck. "Would that there were no Bishop Henry, or that he were not so set against mercenaries and for some reason against me in particular."

Odd. That hadn't been her impression at court.

"I did not realize your profession had aught to do with the bishop's anger. I thought him upset because de Salis was a . . . clergyman, or associate, or even a friend."

Darian snickered. "All knew de Salis was a hateful, evil terror of a man. I know of two villages where he and his men burned the huts, killed the men, raped the women, and maimed the children for sport. 'Twas Bishop Henry who ordered the fiend excommunicated several months ago."

A vile man, indeed. And Emma heard echoes of Darian's tale of his own family's demise. A detestable, loathsome beast had been responsible for their deaths, too.

"So Bishop Henry should not have been aggrieved over de Salis's death."

Darian picked up a piece of hay and twirled it between his thumb and forefinger, his brow furrowing.

"Nay, he should not have been," he commented, almost to himself. "The bishop agreed the kingdom would be best off without de Salis, but wanted God to choose the time of his death, not men."

Emma knew he was merely thinking aloud, but this line of thought disturbed her.

"What men?"

He glanced up at her, then away. "I beg pardon, Emma. 'Tis naught of import."

Deep in her bones she knew different.

"What men?"

"Better you do not know. The less involved you are, the less the danger."

"Like this morning?" Becoming alarmed, she pressed on. "Darian, if those soldiers do manage to return to Bishop Henry, he will be after you all the more, and me also because I stood as your witness and thwarted his intent to see you hang! What is it you are not telling me?"

The hay stopped twirling. He bent it in twain. "The morning before de Salis was killed, the king gave the order for his assassination. If de Salis had not died that night, he would have sooner than later."

Assassination!

The king had ordered someone to murder de Salis?

"What man would agree to—"

Emma's stomach flipped so hard she pressed her arms against it, wishing they'd stayed out in the pouring rain, kept riding until they reached Oxford, where they would have been too tired to do aught but sleep.

Sweet mercy, who better to send out to assassinate a troublesome villain than a mercenary? And what better mercenary than the one who sat quietly at her feet, crushing a piece of hay?

"You?"

He tossed the hay aside.

"Aye," he said, confirming her suspicion. "That is what I do, Emma. I execute the worst of the worst. Quickly and cleanly, with no one the wiser, sometimes not even my victim. Most simply vanish without a soul as witness. Had I killed de Salis, his body would not have been found, nor would I have been so witless to leave behind my dagger. Bishop Henry knows this, yet he accused me before the king and others."

And she'd stepped into the muddle, believing Darian guiltless—among other reasons. Ye gods. At least she'd been right to believe his plea of innocence. He hadn't killed de Salis, but he would have obeyed the king's order, as he'd apparently done in the past.

How dare the king and bishop turn on the man to whom they'd given such appalling duty!

"You were betrayed! The very men who ordered you to assassinate de Salis accused you of doing the very thing they had ordered! Perhaps you should change allegiance, Darian. Empress Maud would not force you to accept such dreadful duty."

He stared up at her, then said with a sad smile, "Only you."

"What?"

He rose, took a swipe at the dust on his arse, then crossed his arms. "I assure you the empress has her own assassins, so she has no need of me. Nor does anyone force me to be an assassin. I believe some men deserve death and am most pleased to send them to hell."

Horrified, she had no answer.

"You need not fear me, Emma, unless you have maimed a child of late."

Absurdly, she shook her head.

"I thought not."

He grabbed a nearby bucket and strode out of the barn into the pouring rain.

Emma groaned and hung her head. This couldn't be happening. The Darian she knew couldn't be that hard-hearted and brutal. True, he'd proved this morn he could be ruthless in battle. But he'd been fighting men who'd attacked them, defending himself and her, not mercilessly killing someone because it pleased him to send a man, however deserving, to hell.

What had happened to the sometimes humorous, of-tentimes restless and annoying, but most times patient and kind man she'd come to know? Where was the gen-tle, considerate lover?

How could two so different men occupy the same body?

The gloriously smiling lover in her vision turned out to be a cold-blooded assassin. If ever she'd needed proof that her visions were devil-sent, this was it.

Chapter Sixteen

N ice place," Darian commented.

Sitting on a bench in Mother Abbess's small but nicely appointed office, hands clasped on her lap to keep from fretting, Emma looked up at where Darian stood by the open-shuttered window overlooking the yard below.

Today, he seemed no different than the Darian of Bruges she'd come to know before learning about Darian the assassin.

She'd pondered his revelation most of last eve and into the night, up in the hayloft, where she'd slept alone. She'd both condemned and excused him, and still wasn't sure of her feelings on his profession.

This morn, as they'd ridden toward Oxford, her preoccupation with Darian had given over to her concern for Nicole.

Darian didn't need her, Nicole might, and Emma hoped that at long last she could do right by someone.

"The abbey does seem nice, though not quite what I expected," she admitted.

"You have never been here?"

"When Gwendolyn and I were asked to choose an abbey for Nicole, we chose Bledloe because Mother Abbess has a reputation for merciful firmness."

"You knew nothing else of the abbey?"

"Only that it was south of Oxford. Sedwick, Camelen's steward, escorted Nicole here, and he told Gwen he thought we had made a wise decision, so that eased our minds a bit."

So had Nicole's first letter. In later missives, though, both Emma and Gwen had noticed the same oddity—a decided lack of spirit and resignation to a fate she'd once railed against.

"What did you expect?" he asked.

"The only abbeys I had ever seen were Westminster and Shrewsbury. I imagined all abbeys as huge, imposing edifices of stone."

Built of wood, Bledloe Abbey was neither dark nor dreary. High, elegant arches graced the passageway they'd been ushered through, and round-topped windows of clear glass allowed in light. From the moment she'd stepped through the doorway, she sensed serenity, a place where the world of men and their sinful behavior and wars dare not intrude.

Emma wished for a bit more serenity now, but knew she wouldn't relax until Mother Abbess, who'd been very kind, returned with Nicole. Unable to sit any longer, Emma rose and walked over to stand at the window next to Darian.

Only a day ago, she'd thrown herself in his arms, sobbing unceasingly, seeking comfort from overbearing distress. Today, she was merely impatient, a bit nervous, and too confused to obtain assurance in her husband's embrace.

Besides, to have the abbess and Nicole walk in and find her and Darian in each other's arms amounted to inexcusably inappropriate behavior in an abbey full of innocent, celibate women.

Hurried footsteps and a child's excited voice alerted Emma her wait was almost over. Nicole burst into the room, a huge grin lighting her face.

She has grown! How can that be?

"Emma! You came so soon!"

With tears in her eyes, Emma opened her arms in time to catch her little sister on a leap.

Hugs and kisses ensued, and though she could hear Darian chuckle, Emma paid him no heed. Let him laugh. She had Nicole to hug and exclaim over, and for a time her world seemed without care or woe, only joy.

Emma finally let the girl go to hold her out at arm's length to get a good look at her.

Garbed in a black robe in the style of the nuns, her uncovered dark hair shiny and pulled back in a braid, Nicole looked older, if not wiser.

"Oh, dear, you have grown," Emma moaned the observation, eliciting light laughter from both Nicole and the abbess.

"I have. Sister Amelia had to let down the hem of my robe a fortnight ago." Then Nicole frowned and waved a hand toward the stain on Emma's bliaut. "But what of this? And your hands are raw. Are you hurt?"

"Nay. We had a mishap on the road, is all. Naught for

you to worry over." Emma finally remembered her manners. "Nicole, I should like you to meet Darian of Bruges. 'Twas his friend Philip who delivered my letter to you."

Nicole dipped into a curtsy, and to Emma's amazement, Darian smiled politely and executed a bow worthy of a courtier.

"I am pleased to finally meet you, Nicole. Your sister has talked of nothing but you the entire way."

"Is it your blood on Emma's gown?"

Darian glanced down at the white bandaging he hadn't removed from his arm. "A bit, perhaps, but as she said, our injuries are slight and of no consequence."

The round-faced Mother Abbess stepped forward. "Lady Emma, I know you wish time alone with Nicole, and I am sure she wants to show you the cloister and kitchen garden."

"Oh, aye! May I, Mother Abbess?"

"Certes. I shall even excuse you from afternoon prayers—this once only."

"My thanks. Come, Emma. We have a truly lovely garden."

"I am sure you do," Emma said, ruffling the girl's hair before asking Darian, "Coming?"

His polite smile remained in place, but Emma detected a slight stiffening.

"Truth to tell, I was about to ask a boon of Mother Abbess," he declared. "Lady Emma has waited long for this visit with her sister, and our travels have not been without hardship. She is in need of rest and would enjoy spending Michaelmas with Nicole. If it is agreeable, I should like to leave her in your care for a few days."

Stunned, Emma could only stare at him.

She'd imagined this visit as no more than a few hours and then . . . Sweet mercy, she'd never given a thought to afterward. To where she would go. Whether with or without Darian.

"Her Ladyship is most welcome to stay," the abbess answered. "We have humble guest chambers, where I am sure she would be most comfortable. She and Nicole can spend time together, and I would dearly love to visit with her, too."

"Well, then, I shall leave you to get on with it. Fare thee well, ladies."

Oh, no. He wasn't getting out the door without some explanation of why he intended to leave her here—and for how long he considered a *few* days.

She stepped into his path of retreat. "Where are you going?"

"Wallingford. I will be gone four days, five at most."

She took the last to mean he intended to come back for her within a reasonable time. Relief threatened to weaken her knees as she acknowledged she'd feared he might not come back for her at all.

Nor should she be surprised he would take this opportunity to see Earl William and his fellow mercenaries. He could easily make Wallingford within a few hours.

Except he could have given her warning.

"I see. I shall look for your return in four days, then."

His stiff smile eased somewhat. "Perhaps five. Have a nice visit, my lady."

Reluctantly, she eased out of his way. Perhaps this was best. 'Twould give her time to sort out her thoughts and feelings. Ye gods, Darian was only halfway down the passageway and she missed him already.

Then the thought struck her that she had business at Wallingford, too!

"Darian, wait!"

As fast as she could manage, and still retain a mote of dignity, Emma strode down the hall.

"Perhaps I should come with you. I gave Earl William the charge of presenting my petition to King Stephen and I should like to know if he has done so yet. If you give me but a few hours with Nicole, we can—"

"Nay. *You* are to go *no* closer than this abbey to Wallingford. A siege camp is no place for a lady."

She wished he would cease reminding her of her rank. Her name on his lips sounded so much better, especially when they stood this close. Despite being in this place of chastity, she felt the pull of his body on hers.

She lowered her voice, well aware the abbess and Nicole stood in the doorway watching and listening.

"With you I would be safe."

He raised an eyebrow sardonically and answered in kind. "Look down at the blood on your bliaut and then tell me how safe you were yester morn."

"That was different. The bishop's soldiers were intent on capturing us. There would be no such danger in the camp."

He sighed, and just as she thought he might relent, as he'd surrendered to her pleas before, he reached for her hand and brought it to his lips.

"Not this time, Emma. Visit with your sister. I shall ask William about the petition, and I give you my word I will come back for you."

If naught else, Darian always kept his word, and this

time pressing him would do no good. This time he intended to protect her by leaving her behind.

Emma swallowed hard. "Three days."

"Michaelmas is in three days. Spend it with your sister and I will try to come the day after."

Darian released her hand and strode down the long passageway to the door at the far end.

Not until the door closed behind him, did Emma square her shoulders and turn around. As she'd suspected, in the doorway stood the abbess and Nicole. Her sister looked a bit confused. The abbess, however, wasn't confused at all, and Emma foresaw a long, possibly uncomfortable visit with the abbess, a visit she intended to put off as long as possible.

She held out her hand. "Come, Nicole, show me the cloister."

"Oh, pray, not yet," the abbess said, her hand clamping onto Nicole's shoulder. "Since you are staying, let us see you settled first. Nicole, your sister looks of a size with Sister Agnes. Go ask her, nicely and gently, please, if Emma might borrow her spare robe so our laundress can repair your sister's garments. Have her bring the robes to the guest chambers along with some unguent. Then hie off to the kitchen and inform Sister Enid that we require several buckets of hot water for a bath. Can you remember all that?"

"Certes, Mother Abbess. But when can I show Emma the gardens?"

"You think the gardens will not be there later, or on the morrow? Patience, child, patience."

Nicole gave such an aggrieved sigh that Emma was forced to hide her smile behind her hand. She and Gwen had worried for naught. Nicole hadn't changed one whit, despite the odd tone of her letters.

"I can remember. Robes, unguent, hot water."

Nicole scampered down an adjoining passageway and Emma struggled to control her laughter.

The abbess came toward her, grinning, shaking her head. "Nicole will likely reach the chambers before we do." Her grin faded into a soft smile. "Let me see your hands, child."

Emma held out what she hadn't truly thought to hide, placing them in the abbess's smooth, soft but not weak hands.

"A mishap on the road, hmm?"

"Burns from a horse's reins."

"I see. They should heal nicely with time and unguent. Come, a hot bath and comb and fresh clothing will do you good."

Thankful the abbess had decided to delay her questions, Emma gave herself up to the care of the woman she guessed mothered everyone in her chapter house. Including Nicole.

But as they passed the door through which Darian had fled the nunnery for the more familiar surroundings of a siege camp, she couldn't help but hope that four days would pass quickly.

The following morning, Emma attended chapel with the nuns. Garbed in robes she'd never imagined wearing, she murmured the Latin prayers, but foreswore joining in the chants, preferring to let the glorious, uplifting voices of the nuns do them justice.

Watching Nicole join in the rites, Emma noted the girl *had* changed, though not to the extreme she and Gwen had feared. Though still spirited, she could now stand quietly, her head bowed in respectful prayer or silent reflection, a thing Nicole had never managed during services in Camelen's chapel or the village church.

Perhaps Nicole flourished because of Mother Abbess's firmness, or she responded to the tutelage of the women of all ages who dedicated themselves to God's work. Whichever, Nicole had managed to fit in at Bledloe Abbey as Emma hadn't been able to do at court.

The abbess led the procession from chapel into the refectory. Nicole, along with a few of the younger novices, set fragrant bread and aromatic cheese on the long tables. Emma was about to take a seat at the low end of one of those tables when the abbess waved her to bench next to her.

Even here, rank was given its due.

After a prayer to thank the Lord for the meal set before them, all observed the clerical custom of silence during meals as a time to reflect.

This much time devoted to inner reflection was all well and good for the nuns; Emma wanted no part of examining her problems this morn. She wished the meal would be over quickly so she could seek a distraction, something to occupy her thoughts so she wouldn't miss Darian so much.

A small hand landed on her shoulder. Nicole mouthed the word "Come." Emma glanced over at the abbess, who smiled and nodded her permission to leave table.

Hand in hand, Emma and Nicole escaped.

Emma squeezed Nicole's hand. "I beg pardon for falling asleep so early last eve."

"I admit I was disappointed, but when you were in your bath, I could see how tired you were. And as Mother Abbess reminded me, the gardens are yet here this morn. Emma, who is Darian of Bruges?"

She'd hoped Nicole wouldn't ask about Darian because she wasn't sure how much to tell her little sister. The girl deserved a measure of honesty, but Emma shied from revealing all. She'd not set a good example for the girl.

"Darian and I were wed about a sennight ago. Neither of us expected King Stephen to demand we—"

Nicole abruptly halted, her eyes opening wide in dismay. "You were wed and did not invite me to stand witness?"

How like Nicole to think first of how events affected her personally. But then, most children did the same.

"The wedding happened too quickly for us to invite guests. I would have preferred to have both you and Gwendolyn present, but your attendance was not possible."

Nicole glanced at their clasped hands. "You wear no ring."

"Not as yet."

"Why not?"

Emma suspected Darian didn't plan to obey the king's order to provide her with a ring, considering it a waste of funds to purchase jewelry for a woman who would be his wife for so short a time.

In truth, she'd given no thought to the lack until now,

and it seemed foolish for her finger to suddenly feel s naked when it had never borne the weight of a ring.

"Did I not tell you all happened in great haste? Come were you not about to show me the cloister?"

To Emma's relief, Nicole accepted the diversion and led them into the centermost area of the abbey, a large garden open to the sky, enclosed on all four sides by the abbey's buildings.

Divided into quarters by paths, each area contained a abundance of plants, bushes, and trees. Scattered along the paths were benches, where the nuns could spend time meditating, or reading, or simply enjoying the beauty and solemnity of the garden.

Nicole knew the name of every plant, and Emma lis tened to a long litany of names before Nicole picked grape from the vines clinging to the north wall.

"These are lovely, and ready for picking. Here, is it no sweet?"

Emma ate the offering. "Delicious."

Nicole pointed toward the south wall. "The apples and pears are near ready, too."

Emma dutifully exclaimed over the size and abun dance of ripening fruit.

"Would you like an apple? They are quite delicious."

Emma almost said yes, but not far from the apple tree water bubbled in a pretty marble fountain. Best to avoid the lovely fountain.

"What I would rather do is sit a moment." Emma tugged Nicole over to a bench. "Now, I wish to know how you fare."

"Quite well."

"No complaints?"

"None."

Having raised Nicole from birth, Emma knew a lie from a truth.

"So you are utterly content and are considering taking vows?"

"Nay!"

"Whyever not? Mother Abbess is kindly, and your meals are provided, and you have this lovely cloister."

Nicole finally pouted. "I should rather not be awakened in the middle of the night to go down to prayer."

"Ah."

"And two of the Sisters snore so loudly they keep all in the dormitory awake for those few hours we can sleep. The nuns live by the sundial. A time for this, a time for that. And it seems that when I am interested in doing this, it is time for that."

"Such as?"

Nicole's eyes brightened to sparkling. "I have a way with plants, or so Sister Enid says. The kitchen garden is my favorite place in the whole abbey, and I love picking and chopping and mixing the herbs!"

"You like to cook?"

"Heaven forefend! 'Tis the medicinal uses I study." Nicole turned their clasped hands palms up, then ran a finger over Emma's healing wound. "The unguent we used on your hand contains hound's-tongue, very soothing for bruises and burns. Lavender added to a bath eases the spirit. Saffron is used to cure fevers and balance the humors."

Emma smiled. "I did not know that about saffron."

"Well, you should, because I think saffron might help you. Do you still have headaches?"

Emma remembered the last headache Nicole had witnessed. The pain in her head had sharpened the pain in her heart when told of her father's and brother's death. She'd somehow managed to endure through the vigil and burial rites without falling on her face. Barely.

"I do get headaches, but the past two have not been so severe."

"I have a packet for you, in the infirmary. 'Tis a mix of willow bark, saffron, and tansy. The next time you have a headache, make a tea of it and let me know if the mixture helps. If not, I will mix you another, perhaps add more tansy."

Sweet mercy! Now Emma knew why Nicole took an interest in medicinal herbs. Her little sister strove to find a cure for headaches. How utterly sweet of her, and how unnecessary because Emma knew the cure.

If she never again looked into a pool, river, lake, fountain, or washbasin, she would never again suffer a headache. Unfortunately, no matter what precautions she took, sometimes she became entranced.

Of course, if she allowed the vision to play out, she wouldn't suffer, either. But she wasn't yet ready to allow the visions, even knowing she might have saved Rose.

Coward, a little voice whispered. Wise, her defenses countered.

Either way, Emma didn't dare tell all that to her little sister, nor would she hamper the child's quest. Perhaps Nicole's mixture could cure someone else, if not the sister whom she yearned to help.

"I would be honored to try your mixture."

Nicole leapt from the bench. "We can go to the infirmary and—oh, no. I fear we must wait."

Mother Abbess strolled down the path toward them.

Nicole sighed. "'Tis time for lessons. Today, I must practice my numbers. I prefer writing."

"You are late, Nicole," the abbess scolded gently.

"I am going," she said, then bent down for a hug. "I shall find you before sext, and we can visit the infirmary while everyone is reading before dinner."

"I look forward to it."

Nicole walked off at what Emma judged a sluggish pace. But then, Nicole had never liked numbers.

The abbess took the seat Nicole had vacated. "I gather Nicole told you of her surprise for you."

"You mean the herb mixture to cure my headaches? I must say, I am surprised she would take an interest."

"Did so from the first. Nicole endures the lessons and chores and what she views as endless prayer in return for the hours she is allowed in the infirmary. At times I think her smiles do more to ease our ailing Sisters than the poultices and potions."

"Nicole has a bright smile, and it does me good to see it again. Gwendolyn and I were most concerned about her, and I am delighted to see we worried for naught."

"Why the worry?"

Emma smiled, thinking their fears rather foolish now. "Her letters did not read as if written by Nicole. The girl's spirit seemed dulled, and we feared she had become despondent."

"Oh, dear," the abbess said, chagrined. "I fear it my fault. While teaching her to be sparse with her words and mindful of the cost of parchment, I may have stifled her."

Emma put a hand on the abbess's arm. "Whatever the reason, I now know our concerns unwarranted. Nicole is content, and for that, I thank you. We did right to send her to you."

The abbess gave an appreciative nod. "'Tis not all my doing. Nicole's contentment comes from finding a purpose here, and she is welcome to pursue her interest in medicinal herbs for as long as she remains with us."

Emma worried her bottom lip. "My petition to allow her to return to Camelen may have recently been presented to the king. After seeing how she flourishes, I wonder if remaining here for a time would not be best for her."

"Nicole speaks of you and Gwendolyn often. She loves and misses you both. All three of you have suffered much these past months."

Emma rubbed her palms on the woollen robe. "Times have not been the best. However, Gwendolyn is now happy with her role as wife and lady of Camelen, and Nicole has, as you say, found a purpose. Perhaps our lives are beginning to turn right again."

"But not for you as yet. I can be a very good listener, if you care to talk."

So Mother Abbess hadn't come to the cloister merely to shoo Nicole off to lessons. While airing her burdens might make her feel better, Emma feared shocking the abbess.

"The tale is rather sordid."

The abbess waved a dismissive hand. "I can spare you some of the tale. Lady Julia is at present visiting her uncle in Oxford, for Michaelmas. Several days ago, when the earl came to present us with gifts, Lady Julia and I spent some time on the bench under the pear tree. I swan, I heard more of court gossip than I wished to!"

Julia! Now *she* would be the one to tell a tale of woe!

"Is Julia still in Oxford? I would dearly love to visit with her."

"Likely. I can find out by day's end, if you wish. So you see, I am aware of how you were treated at court, and what transpired in the king's chamber."

Then the abbess surely knew of Darian's being accused of murder, of how Emma had stood witness, and of their marriage.

"I thank you for not telling Nicole."

"'Twas not my tale to tell, but yours. Nor will anything you tell me leave this cloister, if you do not wish it." She smiled. "Julia is not so circumspect."

"That she is not, but I like her all the same."

"So do I. I also happen to be impressed with your Darian, and I had not expected to be, given your tryst in the queen's solar."

There were some things Emma would never tell anyone, but she could give this woman of the cloth more of the truth than others.

"The tryst never happened. I . . . lied when I told the king that Darian had spent the night with me."

The abbess's eyes went wide. "You lied?"

"The bishop accused Darian of murdering Edward de Salis, and I believed Darian when he declared his innocence. No one else would come to his defense. When the king judged him guilty and ordered the guards to take him away and alert the hangman, I had to halt the injustice. So I lied."

"My word! You were that sure of his innocence you committed a sin for his benefit?"

She'd committed worse sins with Darian, which she wasn't about to confess.

"Darian proved me right, and ever since has been ferreting out the true murderer. Philip, the man who delivered my letter to Nicole, has been aiding that effort."

"One lie has brought you much grief."

The abbess didn't know how much. "But the lie saved Darian from hanging, preventing a grave injustice. I would do it again."

"What upset Julia most was the king's forcing you to marry so far beneath you. A woman of your heritage should not be made to suffer such insult."

The statement brought Emma up short. But then, the abbess, as were most of those who rose to authority in the Church, was likely of noble birth. Kindly or not, the nun considered the marriage between noble and commoner disgraceful.

As did Darian. She heard his wish for deliverance every time he called her "lady" or "princess."

"We intend to have the marriage annulled when possible."

"On what grounds?"

A very good question, one Emma sidestepped. "The problem is not grounds, but Bishop Henry. He is not inclined to favor Darian, nor is he pleased with me for standing witness, and if he ever finds out I lied—and he will when Darian exposes de Salis's true murderer—well, I cannot see any hope of our petition arriving in Rome."

"Quite a muddle."

A muddle, indeed. Especially when one considered how badly Bishop Henry wanted to get his hands on Darian.

The abbess rose from the bench. "Your situation intrigues me. I am sure we possess some writings on the subject in our library, and I know an abbot and an archbishop who are well versed in procedural matters. I am not sure we can discover a solution before you leave us, but would you be averse to my making inquiries on your behalf? Without using your name, of course. Though by the way news travels, they may guess on whose behalf I seek answers."

Emma took a long breath. Before her stood a woman who might be able to help end her marriage to Darian. He would certainly be pleased if someone could tell him how to do so.

Sorrow akin to grief clenched her heart. She'd known all along their marriage would be short-lived, that one day they would part and never again cross paths. That day had always seemed far off. No longer.

Though so many people had expressed disapproval of a woman of her rank marrying a commoner, she realized she wouldn't mind being married to a commoner—if that man could be Darian.

Even as her heart cried out for more time, she told the abbess, "Darian and I would be grateful for your guidance."

Chapter Seventeen

Darian stared down at the river from the wall walk of Crowmarsh, the timber fortress the king had ordered built across the Thames from Wallingford Castle. From here, one could see far up and down the river and observe any enemy troops attempting to either enter or leave Wallingford.

Crowmarsh wasn't the only siege location, of course. Groups of tents surrounded Wallingford, sheltering hundreds of troops. At the moment many of them huddled around campfires. Some engaged in weapons practice. All of them were bored.

No one had gone into or come out of Wallingford Castle for months and many people believed Brian fitz Count had stocked enough supplies to last through winter and well into spring.

Darian thought it a waste to commit so many soldiers and so much coin to what seemed an unending venture, but he understood the king's reasons. The rebel stronghold closest to London, Wallingford was a thorn in the royal paw and wanted plucking. If the castle fell, the blow to the empress's cause would be near fatal. Except that blow wouldn't happen anytime soon. The stalemate would continue, no progress made.

Just as he'd reached a stalemate in his own life. He'd not only made no progress, but might have made his situation worse.

Clearing his name of the murder had become an obsession, leading him to commit several errors—which Earl William had forcefully pointed out yester noon.

Disobeying the order to stay at Hadone had topped the earl's litany of sins committed, and as Darian informed him of further transgressions—taking Emma and Rose to London with him, exposing his presence too openly in Southwark—William's anger and disappointment resulted in a ruthless tongue-lashing.

Only from Earl William would Darian have withstood the severe reprimand without giving a defense, especially a reprimand so deserved. He'd put Emma's life at risk and lost Rose—and ye gods, how he missed them both.

Who would have ever believed he would miss the hound's nose nudging his elbow for a pat on the head, or a treat, or to toss a stick? How many times had he waved her off or ignored her? Now he'd give a pretty penny to have her back.

As much as he missed the hound, he missed Emma so very much more. They'd been apart for less than a full day and already he longed to peer into her doe-brown eyes, hear the lilt of her voice, bask in her calm patience, and revel in her uninhibited passion. A singular woman,

Emma, and he couldn't decide which of her many qualities and mannerisms delighted him the most.

He could do nothing for the wolfhound who'd served him so loyally, but he *must* untangle Emma from the coil of his problems.

To sever their marriage, they might be required to expose the lie she'd told in court. With her lie revealed, he damn well might hang because he had only Hubert's word—not a *trustworthy* witness—that the bishop's guards had murdered de Salis.

Hubert had gone to York, or so he'd said. Finding the informant again might not be easy, and even if he did find Hubert, hauling him before the king would do little good.

Knowing who had committed the deed and proving it were coils of a different sort.

Which meant he must return to Southwark.

So what did he do with Emma while he prowled Southwark? Leave her at Bledloe Abbey? Take her home to Camelen? He highly doubted she'd be willing to go back to either Westminster Palace or Hadone.

Or he could purchase a small manor, perhaps in Kent, where she might be content to reside until after all was settled. He could visit Emma from time to time to ensure the household supplied, speak to her of events and people having nothing to do with the war or murderers, and spend the nights snuggled together in a soft bed, their limbs entangled in sleep after a lusty, blissful coupling.

Yearning bloomed in his soul and burst through him, the attack so robust he couldn't mount a defense to halt its advance.

To think that a few days ago, he'd shuddered when Thomas spoke wistfully of such an arrangement. A comfortable home; a waiting, willing wife. Why did it now sound wonderful and reasonable if the wife could be Emma?

He scoffed at the ridiculous notion. No noblewoman would settle for such a life. No princess should be asked to live in a humble abode, there to await infrequent visits from her mercenary husband.

So why couldn't he banish the sight of Emma standing in a cottage's doorway, smiling as she greeted him with a warm, inviting kiss?

Footsteps on the plank stairway preceded Earl William's arrival on the wall walk, and even as he braced for another lecture, Darian thanked the Fates for timely intervention from his impossible longings.

The earl leaned against one of the pike-tipped logs of the palisade, his attention focused on the castle across the river.

"Armand said you were up here. Looking for a way to get into Wallingford?"

Darian heard the merest hint of William's anger. Striving to keep the peace, he followed the earl's lead.

"I can think of no way that has not already been tried. Fitz Count has repelled every effort."

"Maud has no chance of winning without Brian fitz Count. His staunch support of her is of no benefit to him, and yet he remains loyal. Were that all the *king's* supporters so steadfastly loyal."

William's admiration for a formidable, honorable enemy didn't surprise Darian.

"If the king wins, what happens to fitz Count?"

"If he hopes to keep his lands, Brian had best consider again pledging his loyalty to the king. An intelligent man bends with the wind. What I need to know is which way you are bending."

Darian knew William wasn't worried about him defecting to Empress Maud.

"My loyalty is still to you, William."

"Yet you disobeyed my orders. Nigh on a fortnight ago, I would have sworn to all and sundry you would be the last to do so, no matter the provocation. Yet here you stand, and I am proven wrong."

Darian couldn't deny the obvious. "I should not have, I know that now."

William nodded an acknowledgement. "I have watched you grow from a frightened child into a man any father would be proud to call his son. Since Bishop Henry hauled de Salis's body into the king's chamber, you have changed yet again, and whether that change is good or bad, I cannot determine. Only you can say what is best for you."

He knew what the earl wanted to hear, and truly, no matter the clarity and appeal of Darian's useless yearnings and unwanted emotions, there was really no other answer.

"Best for me would be to expose de Salis's murderer, obtain an annulment, and then resume my usual duties," he stated. "William, after Philip left, I found Hubert. The bishop's men seized him and Gib on the morn of de Salis's murder."

To the earl's raised eyebrow, Darian went on to tell him of Gib's death and Hubert's incarceration in the Clink, of Philip's inquiring at the Clink about not only the two informants but Perrin, and of his suspicion the guards had lied about holding all three men.

"Philip and I believe Perrin ran afoul of de Salis, perhaps over a wager at a cockfight and somehow got tossed in the Clink. He could still be in there, or gone the way of Gib."

William shook his head in disgust. "If the bishop were holding Perrin, he should have notified me. But apparently Bishop Henry has decided to harass my band. Perrin was easy prey because of his gambling. You, he tried to hang for a murder he ordered his guards to commit. God's blood, if he persists I will have to find a way to deal with him."

The earl stood silent for a moment, then said, "Philip should return from Camelen in a few days. Before we accuse the king's brother of ordering a murder, I want to hear exactly what the Clink's guards told him."

Darian had promised Emma to return to Bledloe Abbey on the day after Michaelmas. If he must wait for Philip, he would break that promise.

Truth to tell, he probably shouldn't go back to the abbey at all. Emma would be safe there, whether pleased with her residence or not. She'd see his absence as abandonment, and perhaps that wasn't so bad, either.

The less he must deal with Emma, the more distance and time between them, the easier for him to dismiss foolish notions about snug cottages, welcoming kisses, and blissful couplings.

Except he would go back, if only because he'd given Emma his word. He might be late, but he'd keep his word.

"I have naught better to do than await Philip."

"Splendid. Between times, you can resume your duties. There are two captains who seem to believe the villages hereabouts are open to looting. Go inform them they are mistaken."

"What of Perrin?"

The earl took a long breath. "If he is still alive, we

should get him out. Tell Marc and Armand what you have told me, then send them to Southwark to see what they can learn. They will likely be back before Philip gets here. Now I am off for an audience with the king."

Darian could think of numerous reasons for the audience, but only one that interested him. "Has the king read Lady Emma's petition?"

"I gave it to him the day I arrived and he has not yet made a decision."

"One would think the disposition of a child a rather easy decision to make."

"I will nudge him. You go nowhere near the king."

Vividly remembering what occurred the last time he'd entered the royal presence, Darian knew that was one order he would have no trouble obeying.

∽

At midafternoon on the second day after Michaelmas, Emma glanced out the window of Mother Abbess's office and tried not to fret.

"Come sit," Lady Julia de Vere commanded gently. "Darian will come when he comes."

"I merely enjoy the sunshine," Emma countered, doubting either Julia or Mother Abbess believed her.

"Lady Julia is correct, child. Waiting on a man is frustrating at least, fruitless at most," the abbess stated, a view Emma wasn't sure she shared, but decided not to comment.

"What have you found, Mother Abbess?"

From a stack of rolled parchments on her desk, testimony to the abbess's pursuit of information on annulments, she chose a scroll to pick up and wave.

"The Church fathers are most insistent a man do his duty to his wife. If Darian abandons you, there is no sound reason for the marriage to continue."

Emma sat down in the chair beside Julia's. "Darian will be back. If not today, then tomorrow, or as soon as he is able."

Mother Abbess sighed. "You are quite sure?"

To believe otherwise would toss her into despair. She had to believe Darian had been delayed for good reason—not because he planned to abandon her.

"Darian keeps his word."

The abbess picked up yet another scroll. "Consanguinity seems the most often cited reason for the granting of an annulment. Might you and Darian be related within the proscribed seven degrees?"

Julia laughed. "Their relation to each other would be truly remarkable, Mother Abbess. For a Flemish peasant to be related to a Norman-Welsh noble, they would have to trace their heritage back nigh onto Adam and Eve."

"So I feared," the abbess said, then to Emma's amusement, she blushed. "Might your Darian be impotent?"

The Church took a dim view of marriage in general, considering the creation of children the only reason why men and women might be permitted to have sexual intimacy. Heaven help a couple if they took pleasure in the marriage bed, the enjoyment of lusty tumbles considered a venial sin.

With as straight a face as she could manage, Emma answered, "I fear Darian has no physical impediment on that score."

"Well, if you are so certain, then we may assume the marriage consummated?"

Emma's amusement fled as her own cheeks grew warm. "We may."

The abbess tossed the scroll aside. "Then we are left with only the matter of consent. I assume the king asked you both for your consent."

Emma remembered the moment vividly. "He did, and we both gave our consent. Grudgingly, but we gave consent."

The abbess's eyes narrowed. "How grudgingly?"

"If I remember correctly, I said, 'Only because you order me to' and Darian said, 'If you insist.'"

The abbess huffed. "That is hardly freely given consent!"

"They were about to hang Darian. We had no choice."

"What woman is truly given a choice?" Julia grumbled. "I swan, few women would dare defy whatever marriage is arranged for her, especially when ordered by the king. The quality of consent is not a consideration."

"Perhaps," the abbess said, "but the Church frowns upon forced marriages."

"Bishop Henry was present when Darian and I exchanged vows, such as they were, and did not question the quality of our consent."

"I cannot say why the bishop did not, but no matter. I would say the very nature of your marriage to Darian gives you grounds for annulment."

So simple an answer. Maybe.

"To whom must we apply?"

The abbess smiled slyly. "Truly, you could petition any bishop, but were I you, I would go to Theobald of Bec, archbishop of Canterbury."

"Why Canterbury?"

The abbess's smile widened. "For many a year, Bishop Henry held the position of papal legate, which placed Winchester over Canterbury, which has always been the traditional head of the Church here in England. When Pope Innocent II died, Henry lost the position. Archbishop Theobald went to Rome to ask Pope Celestine II for the appointment to legate and was refused. Both bishops now await a decision from Pope Eugene III as to which man, if either, will be granted the honor and power. Believe me, Theobald would be most happy to tweak Henry's nose in any fashion, even if it is simply nullifying a marriage Henry blessed."

Julia clapped her hands. "Oh, how perfect! Only think, Emma, you can have your annulment and have a bit of revenge on Bishop Henry at the same time."

Perfect, Emma thought dully. Her marriage had begun because of Bishop Henry and might end because of him, too. She wished she'd never heard of Henry, bishop of Winchester!

Julia bounced out of her chair. "Now that all is settled, I must go. My uncle expects me to return to my duties as the king's hostage, so I shall be leaving on the morrow."

Mother Abbess received the first farewell hug. "Have a care, Julia, and tell your uncle I expect him to behave so naught will discomfit you."

Julia giggled. "I shall certainly tell him of your expectation. Oh, Emma. I am sorry we did not have more time to visit. Perhaps the next time we see each other, nothing of import will hinder us from a longer talk. Pray remember, I wish to help in any way I can."

Emma gratefully accepted Julia's embrace. They'd spent most of the afternoon together and Julia still hadn't said all she wanted to, even though she'd spent nigh on an hour exclaiming her delight over the possibility of the annulment. Though thoroughly spoiled and ever mindful of her rank, Julia de Vere's friendship was warm, and her desire to help sincere.

"I will remember. Pleasant journey."

With Julia gone and Mother Abbess off to return all those scrolls of parchment to the library, Emma wandered into the cloister, very aware of why Nicole loved it so.

Scented by the plants and open to the sky, dotted by benches and statues, the cloister was designed to help a troubled soul forget the woes of the kingdom beyond the abbey's high curtain walls.

Except Emma couldn't forget. Darian was out there. Still at Wallingford? On the road to the abbey? Or had something happened to delay him? And she couldn't help but worry over what Bishop Henry might do if someone presented him with his slain soldiers.

Sweet mercy, she believed Darian would keep his word. But the longer apart, the more she missed him— and worried.

She reached up and picked an apple, realized she hadn't wandered to this corner of the cloister before, and spotted the reason why.

The fountain.

A saint she couldn't name, carved of white marble, presided over the small pool at his feet. Water gently trickled down the rocks behind him, the sound soothing. Enticing.

The pool might show her answers to her questions.

Oh, no. She would not resort to such measures. For all

she knew, the pool would show her a room she'd not yet been in, or a person she'd not yet met.

But she'd never truly attempted to control what she saw, had always accepted that the water would show her what it would. If she concentrated on a place, or a person, or a question, might the water reveal true answers?

What folly! But how intriguing. Dare she try? Was she willing to accept a horrific vision for no better reason than to satisfy her curiosity? She hadn't been willing at Hadone. If she hadn't turned coward, Rose might still be alive.

And her last vision, that of Gwendolyn and her babe, hadn't been frightening. And perhaps Darian was right when he'd said that by denying the visions, she denied a part of herself.

Terrified, chiding herself for cowardice, Emma put the apple on a bench, filled her head with Darian's beloved face, and stepped up to the pool.

The trickling water sent gentle ripples over the surface, but she saw her reflection clearly, and soon the beloved face she yearned to see appeared.

Darian sat cross-legged in the dirt, one of five men in a circle. She recognized Thomas and Armand, members of his mercenary band. All were laughing, except Darian, who wore a furtive smile. Then he tossed a pair of dice into the middle of the circle and his smile widened into a glorious grin.

Heart pounding, captivated by Darian's grin, Emma knelt down to have a better look. Darian looked so happy, an emotion she'd never seen in him before. Smiles, certes, but not like this. Not glorious.

What she wouldn't give to be with him at this moment,

to reach out, to touch his mouth—the water rippled and Darian disappeared.

Emma blinked, realizing she'd put a single finger into the pool to touch Darian's lips, halting the vision. She closed her eyes, waiting for the pain to pierce the back of her skull and burst through her head.

Other than slight dizziness, nothing happened.

She stood up, opened her eyes, and stared at the statue. The dizziness abated. She felt no pain, no hurt of any kind.

Sweet mercy, she'd invited a vision and saw what she wished to see! Darian.

Playing dice. Grinning at his fellow mercenaries. Happy with them as he'd never been with her. And obviously in no hurry to leave their company.

Apparently Darian didn't miss her as much as she missed him. He experienced no longings, no sadness, no sense of obligation to return to her as quickly as she wanted him to return.

Emma plopped down on the bench, grabbed the apple and took a full, satisfying bite, taking her rising ire out on a hapless piece of fruit. Here she'd been miserable and he—the wretch—was happily playing at dice, enjoying himself, and from the grin on his face he was winning.

Emma groaned, becoming aware she couldn't take Darian to task for dallying at Wallingford or he would know she'd seen him in a vision—had spied on him.

She swallowed, the apple hitting her stomach with a thud.

Well, she hadn't *intended* to spy, only test whether or not she could control a vision, and now she wasn't proud of her accomplishment. 'Twas devious and ignoble to observe others when they weren't aware of being watched.

Just because she missed Darian wasn't an acceptable excuse for her behavior.

If she told Darian of what she saw, he might be angry, and God's truth, she didn't wish to argue with him anymore. All she wanted was for him to come fetch her because she missed him so much because she . . . loved him.

Denial flared and died all within a heartbeat. Joy flamed, and she basked in the sensation of a glowing heart and jubilant soul. She loved Darian, and the elation was almost too much to bear.

Too quickly, the elation also faded.

Loving Darian might be considered greater folly than testing her visions.

She loved a husband who wanted quit of their marriage. She loved a mercenary who'd admitted to assassinations. She loved a man who didn't miss her enough to leave his dice game—if, indeed, he were tossing dice.

Had the vision shown her what Darian was doing now, or an event to take place in the future? Perhaps he didn't dally at Wallingford. Maybe Darian was even now on his way.

The brief flash of hope died when she acknowledged she knew that wasn't true. Just as she'd *known* the bloody water in the washbasin at Hadone had been a foretelling of the battle with the bishop's soldiers, she *knew* the fountain's pool showed her what Darian did this very moment.

How very odd to realize she might be learning about how her visions worked, too.

Still, she shouldn't have given in to temptation, should have walked past the fountain without peering into the water. Then she wouldn't now feel so forsaken and miserable.

Except if not for Darian, she might never have found the courage to purposely gaze into the water. She might never have known the bliss of loving a man with her whole heart and soul.

No matter what the future held, she'd taken risks and felt hardier for the experiences. Still, if Darian didn't come to fetch her—soon—she might not be quick to recover.

❧

"The damn guard lied to me!" Philip tossed his hand in the air. "On my oath, I will boil that guard's balls!"

"So long as you allow me to cut them off first." Furious, Darian glanced around at the three other men in Earl William's sumptuous tent, gathered to discuss what action to take against Bishop Henry. "My lord, we shall need your kind permission."

William shook his head. "'Tis not the guard's balls that deserve boiling. He followed orders, likely given by Bishop Henry, and if you disturb Henry's balls, the king might take offense."

Marc huffed. "Well, the guards lied to Armand and me, too. They audaciously claimed they knew neither Hubert nor Gib. If they lied about the informants, then their claim that no one named Perrin resided in the Clink might also be a lie."

"It well might," William allowed. "However, where the bishop is concerned, we must use caution. He can be dangerous." The earl rubbed at his chin. "Oh, he dislikes mercenaries with a passion and would delight in having every one of you sent back to Flanders, but he knows the king would not stand for it. Stephen needs us. The more

I think about it, the more I believe you men are not his true targets. I am. But Henry cannot attack me directly because I enjoy Stephen's patronage, so he attempts to discredit me through all of you."

Marc whistled low; Philip groaned.

Darian thought the earl's reasoning both sensible and somehow sad.

"He resents you so much?"

William nodded. "Bishop Henry is unreasonably jealous of all who have influence with King Stephen. Of late, Henry's hold on Stephen has slipped and Henry seeks to raise himself in his brother's esteem. He will do what he believes he must to once again be Stephen's most trusted advisor."

Powerful men abhorred a loss of power, and struck harshly at all whom they perceived as enemies.

"So when Perrin fell into Henry's hands, likely over a gambling debt, the bishop held him to make it appear he deserted. Edward de Salis also fell into his hands, likely on the same evening, and the bishop devised a plan to blame me for his murder—to discredit you for lack of control over your band."

"So it seems to me."

"But that means Henry, or one of his minions, convinced one of us to steal my dagger and hand it over to him as evidence against me."

"Convinced, or coerced. Right now, I am more concerned with what Henry has planned for the future."

"William, we need to know who took the dagger."

"And we will find out. Did any of you learn why de Salis was in Southwark? I find it strange he was there at so convenient a time for Henry?"

Marc raised his hands, palms up. "To visit the stews? Wager on the cockfights? Why else does a knight prowl about Southwark?"

William crossed his arms. "De Salis hails from near York. I should think he could find those entertainments closer to home."

"Bishop Henry excommunicated de Salis," Philip stated. "Perhaps de Salis came to ask the bishop to rescind the order."

"Not likely. From what we know of de Salis, he would not care about Henry's ruling to begin with."

Though Darian listened, he paced, his instincts screaming that he knew of another connection between the two men. "A whore told me de Salis had spent his last night on earth with her, but I had the feeling she knew more about de Salis she was afraid to tell. Philip, when we first met up, you mentioned noting that people were frightened to talk about de Salis. Could he have been in Southwark longer than one night?"

"Possible."

Darian ran a hand through his hair. "William, when we stood in the king's antechamber, we spoke of Henry's opposition to doing away with de Salis. I voiced the opinion Henry would not be so complacent if his villages were being burned. Could de Salis have gone to Southwark to treat with Bishop Henry for just such an agreement?"

Philip's eyes went wide. "Henry in league with de Salis? The king would toss a fit!"

"Just so," William agreed. "Henry could have treated for an agreement to protect his holdings, or de Salis offered to leave the bishop's holdings in peace in exchange for payment."

One thing still confused Darian. "Then why did Henry argue so hard against doing away with the man?"

William had a ready answer. "So he could use de Salis as a means to hang you, discredit me, and still appear to all and sundry as a righteous man of the cloth."

Darian clenched his fists. "Not to all. Whoever took my dagger *must* have known how it might be used."

"Not necessarily. I have some thoughts on the matter, but prefer to confirm my conjecture first. Philip, Marc, you will tell no one of what we discussed here. No one. Understood? Darian, stay a moment yet."

Philip and Marc recognized the earl's dismissal and left the tent, leaving Darian alone with the earl.

"Are you going to tell me of your conjecture?" Darian asked.

"I believe if you think on it, you will come to the same conclusion as I, but that is not why I wanted to speak with you. The king has decided to refuse Lady Emma's petition. Pray tell her ladyship I am sorry I cannot send her better news."

Darian's heart fell. "Did the king give a reason?"

All the while William explained the king's plan for Nicole, Darian's anger rose to near overflowing, the unfairness to the girl, and possibly Emma, appalling. And there was naught he could do but warn them.

Chapter Eighteen

Emma knew if she ran the length of the passageway, she would set a bad example for Nicole, scandalize Mother Abbess, and allow Darian to see how glad she was to see him.

His standing in the passageway answered every prayer she'd murmured since looking into the fountain two days ago. Since realizing she'd fallen in love with her husband.

That revelation had hurled her emotions into a whirlwind, tossing them up and pitching them down, rocking her so violently she felt she'd lost all sense of balance.

Her pace quickened, leaving Mother Abbess and Nicole to follow in her wake. She couldn't fling herself into his arms, but she did have to touch him to gain an anchor. So as she approached him, she smiled and held out her hands.

His answering smile warmed her clear through, and with palms pressed to palms, Emma's inner calm returned. Maybe Darian had missed her, too, despite his lingering overlong at Wallingford.

"You are late by two days."

"Unavoidable. You look rested."

"There is little else to do here. How went your talk with Earl William?"

He glanced down the passageway, where she could hear Mother Abbess and Nicole coming closer. His smile went sad.

So softly she strained to hear, he said, "I will tell you all later, but I fear I bring more bad news than good." He squeezed her hands. "Emma, the king denied your petition."

She wasn't surprised, but the news wasn't easy to accept. Emma bit down on her bottom lip to hold back the tears, her failure to secure Nicole's freedom squeezing her heart.

"Do you know why?"

He nodded, then looked past her again. "Mother Abbess, might we beg the use of your office for a private moment?"

"Certes."

Nicole came to stand at Emma's side.

"Is aught amiss?" the girl asked.

Emma let go of Darian's hands, and pulled Nicole to her side. "I fear there is, dearest, and since it concerns both you and Mother Abbess, we might as well all hear it at the same time."

Once seated in the abbess's office, Emma pulled Nicole onto her lap. "You will remember the day we both left home, I gave you my oath to petition the king for your release from Bledloe Abbey, so you could return home to Camelen."

Nicole nodded, and Emma wished to the heavens above she need not dash the glimmer of hope in the girl's eyes.

"I fear the king has denied us, dearest."

Hope faded into resignation. "He fears I will try to kill Alberic, does he not?"

"Nay," Darian said. "'Tis your lineage and the king's remorse that keep you here. When your father was killed and King Stephen gave your father's lands to Alberic of Chester, he ordered Alberic to marry one of you. He chose Gwendolyn. Emma was sent to court, and the king is now regretting his hasty decision to marry her off to me. I fear, Nicole, you are the only de Leon sister over whom he still retains control."

Emma grew wary. "What does the king want of Nicole?"

"He told Earl William that once this dispute with Maud is over, he fears trouble in Wales. A bargain of marriage to a female in the line of Pendragon might persuade a Welsh prince from rebellion, even sway a prince to the king's side. He has allowed you and Gwendolyn to slip from his grasp and intends to hold fast to Nicole."

That the king intended to use a little girl as a political pawn wasn't surprising, but to realize that girl might be Nicole disturbed Emma greatly.

"She is all of ten!"

"Emma, there is no immediate danger of the king marrying her off. The Welsh have not taken sides in this war, preferring to allow Stephen and Maud to wreak havoc on each other. And truly, this war could drag on for many years because neither side is strong enough to defeat the other, and Stephen and Maud refuse to budge from their positions each time they negotiate."

All true, but at the moment Emma didn't care about the damn war.

"But what harm for Nicole to go home to Camelen? Why must she remain here?"

And she knew the answer even before Darian said, "Because Camelen is too close to Wales. Some enterprising prince may take it into his head to seize her before she can be of use to King Stephen."

Nicole slipped off Emma's lap and faced Darian. "Have I no say in the matter?"

Darian put a hand on Nicole's shoulder. "I fear not right now, little one. Much depends on the outcome of this war. Your fate will depend upon who sits on England's throne when next there is trouble with Wales."

"Then I must stay at Bledloe Abbey until . . . until the king decides who it pleases him I must marry."

"So he says. Does that upset you overmuch?"

Nicole tilted her head. "Nay, truly it does not."

Emma supposed she should be glad Nicole took the news so well, but the whole thing still made her angry. "Perhaps, in a few months, I can again petition the king and—"

"Nay, Lady Emma, do not," Mother Abbess interrupted. "Do nothing to remind King Stephen that Nicole is available for his use. If he intends Nicole for a Welsh prince, then he may put her out of his mind until that opportunity arises. As Darian says, much depends upon the war's outcome, and the Welsh response to whoever occupies the English throne."

Emma was tempted to race into the cloister, peer into the water in the fountain, and demand to know who would lay final claim to the throne.

But then, given the nature of her visions, she might only be more confused and angry than she was now.

Emma held out her arms and Nicole slipped into them. "Ah, dearest, I wish I knew what was best."

"No decision needs be made immediately," Darian said, his voice soothing. "If Nicole is amenable, perhaps this is the safest place for her to reside. She is well out of the reach of Welsh raiders and the king has too many other matters to settle to give Nicole much thought. What say you, Nicole?"

Emma felt her little sister's sigh.

"I truly have no choice, do I?"

Mother Abbess pushed up from her desk. "Perhaps you will someday, but for now, your choice is whether to accompany me to the chapel for prayer or hie off to the infirmary."

Nicole's head popped off Emma's shoulder. "The infirmary!"

"I thought as much. If you hurry, you can relieve Sister Enid so she might attend chapel."

"As you say, Mother Abbess."

"Walk."

"How can I hurry—"

Mother Abbess pointed to the door, and with another sigh, Nicole obeyed.

The abbess shuffled out from behind her desk and patted Emma on the shoulder. "Worry not for Nicole for the nonce. The girl is both bright and resilient, and we shall help her weather the storm. Darian, men are not allowed to take meals or sleep within our walls, but there is a small priest's house, currently unoccupied, a half-league south of here." The nun fetched a key from a peg near the door and handed it to Darian. "You may spend the night there, if it suits you."

Darian twirled the key in his fingers. "I am sure it will do me nicely, Mother Abbess. A roof over my head is always welcome."

"Emma, I shall see you at supper," the abbess ordered, then left her office.

Her emotions in upheaval, Emma could only stare at the door, numb, not knowing if she should feel angry or sad, relieved or resigned.

"Nicole took the news well," Darian commented.

"Better than I, I believe."

"Since there is naught else you can do, might I suggest you fetch your cloak. You can help me decide if the priest's hut is worthy of housing my exalted personage."

He teased, of course. The priest's hut was likely a lovely, well-kept cottage where a bishop could spend the night in comfort. Still, the walk Darian proposed sounded wonderful, and they had so many other things to talk about.

"I will meet you at the gate."

Darian set a slow pace. Now that he was in Emma's solitary company again, he wasn't in any hurry to give it up.

"Did you have a nice visit with Nicole?"

"We had some wonderful talks."

"So your mind is more at ease?"

She sighed. "It was until you brought news of the king's intentions."

"Apparently, when the king reached Wallingford, the earl of Chester berated him for allowing you to marry. I do not think the king had decided on either your fate or Nicole's until Chester pointed out how valuable you two could be when dealing with the Welsh. If we obtain an annulment, I fear the same fate for you."

Emma merely shrugged a shoulder. "Kings use their wards to make alliances. If my father had not wanted a love match for me, he would have done the same for himself."

She spoke true, and he still hated how Emma might be used. He detested the thought of Emma being given in marriage to any man, a Welsh prince or no. Emma was *his* wife, damn it! Even if not for much longer, a few days or possibly weeks. But right now, she was still his!

"Unfair to the woman."

"I doubt the men are much happier. Imagine being given a woman, being told you must take her to wife . . . but then you do, do you not? Fortunately for you, we intend to bring our marriage to an end."

Obtaining an annulment would free them both from this marriage, which neither of them had wanted. But only he would be free to go on with life as he chose. Emma should have the same freedom!

"I also had a few enlightening talks with Mother Abbess," she continued. "She feels we should present the archbishop of Canterbury with our petition for annulment, citing forced consent as our reason. Hard feelings exist between Canterbury and Winchester, so the archbishop of Canterbury might be open to annulling a marriage blessed by the bishop of Winchester. So our marriage begins with a blessing from Henry and ends with a bit of revenge for his blessing. Is that not sweet?"

She didn't sound pleased in the least, and he dared feel a spark of hope for the plan that had come into his head while on the ride from Wallingford to Bledloe Abbey.

His palms sweaty, he suggested, "Perhaps we should not annul our marriage."

She stopped and stared at him with those wide brown eyes he'd missed becoming lost in. "Why?"

Because I love you. Fearful of her response, he instead gave her a sensible reason.

"You could do whatever you wanted, live wherever you please without worry over becoming snared in the king's machinations."

She still stared, peering inside him too deeply. He looked away before she could reach his heart, his very soul, and learn his secrets.

'Twouldn't do for Emma to know of his selfishness. 'Twould be disastrous for him to reveal how much he loved her.

He'd wrestled with the emotion ever since realizing why the king's plans infuriated him. Why snug cottages and welcoming kisses appealed. Why he wanted to keep Emma for himself.

Perhaps his affection for a wolfhound had weakened his defenses, but Emma had somehow found a key to the lock and flung the door wide open.

"Do I understand rightly that you are willing to sacrifice your freedom so I could not be forced to marry a Welsh prince?"

Somehow his noble offer no longer sounded so noble. "Aye."

For what seemed an eternity, she stared off into the distance, and the longer her silence, the tighter the coil in his stomach.

Finally, she said softly, "I appreciate your offer, but fear I must refuse."

The kick to his gut set him in motion again, the distress too deep that for several steps he couldn't think much less talk. She walked silently beside him, not offering a reason for refusing, and sweet mercy he didn't want to hear from her lips what he already knew.

Noblewomen did *not* marry commoners. Descendants of the legendary house of Pendragon did not bind themselves to Flemish peasants. So he would give Emma what she wanted and pray to God some Welsh prince made her happy.

Hoping his voice wouldn't reveal his distress, Darian managed to say, "Then we should make for Canterbury."

"Earl William will not mind?"

"He gives me leave to settle our affairs."

"I suppose we should be grateful for his understanding."

Darian decided Emma didn't need to know everything that had happened at Wallingford, especially how harshly William had reacted to his disobedience.

"'Twill take some time for me to regain Earl William's full respect and trust."

And were he to be completely honest, his trust in his fellow mercenaries had been shaken, too. Even while they'd eaten together, gone out on patrol, shook dice, he'd wondered which one had taken his dagger out of his pack.

All the while at Wallingford, he'd kept his boots on with the dagger securely tucked inside.

Had any of them noticed? He would wager they all did.

"Earl William will not take long to again give you his trust," she stated with more confidence than he felt. "You are a man of your word, Darian. He knows this. He is also aware of your sense of honor and duty. I predict 'twill take little time for him to realize you are all that you were before I meddled in your life."

Emma had no idea of what her meddling cost him. "You meddled me out of a noose. Have I thanked you for that yet?"

Emma smiled. "Not as yet. Oh, my, I expected the priest's hut to be nice, but not *this* nice."

The hut was actually a small manor built of stone nestled amidst a small copse of trees. Oak doors graced the entrance, and white shutters elegantly covered the windows.

Darian put key to lock and lifted the latch, opening the door to a graciously appointed room. A large table sat in the center of the plank floor, surrounded by four armed, beautifully carved chairs. Beside the stone hearth sat a full woodbox. Against the far wall was a large bed, the thick mattress covered in deep blue velvet to match the drapes on the rods supported by four thick corner posters.

"If this is the accommodation a priest enjoys, perhaps I should consider taking vows!"

Emma laughed as she looked around. "It is nice, is it not? Large but not grandiose, sizable but yet snug and inviting. You should be very comfortable here for the night."

Snug cottages and welcoming smiles. Impossible yearnings.

Darian tossed the key on the table. "Better than a tent."

"I should think so," she commented, then tilted her head. "You slept in a tent at Wallingford?"

"On a folded-up blanket, listening to Thomas snore. At least tonight I will have quiet—and heat."

"But will you not miss the company? Having someone with whom to share your meals or . . . toss dice with?"

He'd prefer to share his meals with her. "Tossing dice helps pass the time on a rainy night. Not much else to do when trapped in a tent."

"Do you often win?"

"Not against Thomas, which is why I rarely let him talk me into playing. Why?"

"Merely curious."

Wondering why the devil she should be curious about his dicing habits, Darian scrunched down at the hearth and began to pull wood from the box, arranging it for a fire. Behind him, Emma pulled out a chair and sat down.

"Darian, when we apply for the annulment, if I must admit to lying about your being with me the night of de Salis's murder, your neck might end up in that noose."

"I think not," he said, and finished building and lighting the fire while he told her of the conclusions he and William had reached.

With the tale over and the fire burning brightly, he dusted his hands and turned around to find her frowning deeply.

Hoping to reassure her, he said, "If William confirms his suspicion over who took my dagger, and we can prove

Bishop Henry's men killed de Salis, I need fear no noose."

"That has been the key all along, has it not? To learn who took your dagger?"

"Aye, which means I should have focused on my fellow mercenaries instead of on de Salis. Problem was, I did not want one of them to be involved."

"There is also the matter of the bishop's dead soldiers. If any of the men we . . . disposed of in the clearing were returned to Winchester Palace, Bishop Henry may find a way to punish you for those deaths."

"He is welcome to try, but for those deaths I have a trustworthy witness to what transpired. You. Now, if you are ready, I will walk you back to the abbey gate. The abbess expects you for supper."

She glanced at the door. "I do not believe I am ready."

He'd seen that look in her eyes before, at Hadone, just before she'd begged him to take her with him to London, fearful he might leave her behind.

"I will be here on the morn, Emma. My horse is in the abbey's stables. You can sleep in his stall, if you wish, to ensure I do not leave for Canterbury without you."

She waved a dismissive hand. "That did not concern me. 'Tis just that I would rather spend the night here, with you."

And there he went, flying up to heaven again.

"Likely Mother Abbess would come marching out here herself to drag you back inside."

"Well, we *are* married." Emma got up and sauntered toward him. "Mother Abbess was also the one to point out to me that the Church does not approve of men who keep themselves from their wives, so she has no right to keep me from you."

She moved with the grace of a swan, her hands clasped behind her back, her bosom firm and high and enticing.

He had no intention of resisting temptation if the woman persisted. Hellfire, if Emma had accepted his offer to remain married, he'd have had her in the bed and on her back by now. So why did he feel obligated to remind Emma she dallied with a man who couldn't compare to a Welsh prince?

"We will not be husband and wife much longer. Canterbury is only four days away."

Four days left to wish for that which he couldn't have, to long for a life that couldn't be.

She didn't stop until she pressed up against him, her arms snaking around his waist, her eyes filled with desire.

"Then we have four days. You are still my husband in the eyes of the Church and king. I missed you, Darian. I missed you so very much."

What could he do except enfold her, kiss a mouth ripe for his kiss. Over and over, he dipped into her sweet mouth, his passion rising, indulging in a fantasy he had no business entertaining.

She'd missed him, but not for the reason he might have hoped. She wanted him, not out of love but because she'd missed the pleasure he could give her.

And, damn, if that was all she wanted from him, then he'd make the coupling so memorable she would forever compare all other men to him and find them wanting.

Breathing raggedly, he removed her circlet and veil. "How much time have we before you must return for supper?"

She tugged the laces of his tunic. "Enough, if you hurry."

He pulled off her bliaut and chemise as one. "I do not like hurrying with you. You are a morsel to be savored, not a quick tidbit."

Her smile turned saucy. "I might like being a tidbit."

Darian toed off his boots; Emma eased her beautiful bare arse onto a chair to remove hers, then slowly, sensually, slid her fingers down her legs to remove her hose.

He couldn't get out of his breeches fast enough to suit him, his male parts aching and his penis so hard it hurt.

Her approving inspection increased the pressure in his loins. Morsel to be savored or no, he wasn't going to last long if he didn't rein in his nigh out-of-control desire.

Darian had almost regained domination over his passion when Emma stood up, all creamy skin and luscious curves, all his for the next little while.

She stared at the male part he strove to restrain. "I was right when I informed Mother Abbess of your prowess."

Though stunned, he inflated, just a bit. "You talked to Mother Abbess of our affair?"

She padded toward him, the fire's light flickering over her skin in an alluring swirl of light and shadow.

"One of the grounds for annulment is male impotence." She wrapped her warm, cunning hands around his penis. "'Twas necessary to assure her you suffered no physical impairments. Indeed, were I to describe to her how long, and thick, and firm your phallus is, she would likely envy me its use."

He cupped her breasts, which fit his hands perfectly, so willing to answer her siren's call he turned a deaf ear to all but the sound of her voice and the silkiness of her skin beneath his fingertips.

"Too bad for the abbess, then, because I want no one but you." Then she squeezed him gently, the pressure sublime. "Have a care, Emma, or you will be a mere crumb instead of a tidbit."

She whispered, "Missed me, did you?"

"Can you not feel how much?"

In answer she opened her hand and swirled a fingertip around the tip. "Not wholly as yet."

"Then allow me to show you."

He swept her up and crossed the floor to toss her onto the blue velvet coverlet. The woman slithered back to the middle of the bed, her smile seductive.

Emma had refused his offer to remain married, but for at least four more days, she was his wife. This woman he would love forever would share what days and nights were left to them. How did one crowd a lifetime of memories into a mere four days?

With enthusiasm. Without regrets.

"You are no tidbit, Emma. You are the whole damn banquet."

"Then come feast."

Darian accepted the invitation with a feral growl, making her giggle until he pounced onto the bed and smothered her amusement with consuming kisses.

Emma mewed her approval, the small sound increasing his appetite. But knowing the final course worth the wait, Darian hushed his cravings, refusing to gorge.

He took his time to sip at and savor her mouth, to enjoy the sweet taste and revel in how hungrily she kissed him back. Without need for words, with venerable caresses and reverent touches, he worshiped her body from breasts to calves, until the lady refused to any longer endure his homage.

Darian gave Emma what she loudly begged for, hoping none of the nuns lurked outside the hut. Then he feasted in powerful, lengthy strokes, making good her claim of his potency. Was there any grander sight than Emma reaching her bliss and coming apart? Nothing in his experience could compare.

Her pulses gave him permission to give in to his screaming need, and joined to the hilt, he surrendered.

Spent and replete, determined not to dwell on the morrow or the days to come, Darian drew Emma into his embrace and defied fate to tear her out of his arms.

Emma missed supper. Morning came too early.

And the most direct and safest route to Canterbury ran through the heart of Southwark. They would have to pass Bishop Henry's palace to cross over the London Bridge.

Chapter Nineteen

Late in the afternoon on the second day of their journey, Darian pulled the horse over to the side of the road.

Surprised and wary, Emma asked, "Is aught amiss?"

"Nay, just a last rest before we reach London."

Emma slid off Darian's horse, doing her utmost to hide her nervousness.

She'd managed to part from Nicole without becoming overset. Passing by the spot on the road where they'd been attacked and buried the wolfhound, Emma had kept her ire under control.

Spending her days and nights with Darian had proven delightful until his offer to forgo the annulment drifted through her thoughts and she wondered if she'd been wrong to refuse him.

Sweet mercy, she would have agreed in a trice if he'd given any sign that he *wanted* to remain married, that he didn't offer out of a sense of obligation or duty. She didn't want to be the cause for which he sacrificed his freedom.

She might love him, but he apparently hadn't fallen in love with her. The marriage wasn't meant to be, and while the knowledge distressed her, she'd managed to hide her emotions.

But now, as they neared Southwark, she was having trouble keeping her hands from shaking and her heart from pounding.

Darian dropped lightly to the ground and looked her over, something he'd done several times before to her delight. This time, however, no enticement or appreciation sparked his inspection.

"I beg pardon, Emma, but only a blind man could mistake you for a peasant."

She glanced down at the rough-weave gray gown she now wore.

They'd slept in yet another barn last night, and the farmer's wife delightedly traded one of her old gowns and mantle for Emma's topaz bliaut and gauzy veil. The new owner hadn't minded the faint traces of blood the laundress at the abbey hadn't been able to remove. The rough-weave gown was warm and comfortable as long as she wore it over her chemise to protect her skin.

Emma considered the trade a good one.

"Perhaps, but I should not draw undue attention. A pity we cannot make your horse less noticeable."

"People are more accustomed to seeing horses on the streets of Southwark than a noblewoman, particularly at this time of day."

Darian had timed their arrival, believing the safest time to pass through Southwark was just before nightfall, when the shops were closing and most everyone was more concerned in gaining a safe haven for the night than in other people's business. When the bishop's guards who patrolled the streets should be more interested in their supper and evening entertainments than closely inspecting whoever wished to cross London Bridge.

His plan sounded reasonable, and since she had no other plan to offer—other than abandoning the trip to Canterbury—she hadn't voiced an objection.

He reached beneath her cloak's hood and tugged forward the mantle that covered her hair. By the time he was done wrapping and tucking, she could barely see, much less breathe.

She grabbed his wrists to halt further arranging. "I cannot breathe."

"What?"

Emma pulled the mantle away from her nose and mouth. "I need to breathe."

"Oh. Beg pardon."

"Pardon granted. I am not the one Bishop Henry is most anxious to dangle from a rope. You should hide *your* face."

He smiled. "Not hardly. You remember all I told you."

They'd gone over the plans twice and her memory wasn't faulty. But his fussing with her mantle said he worried for her safety. She worried, too. If they were caught, Bishop Henry might do away with them both, especially if he'd taken umbrage over Darian brazenly sending his dead soldiers back to him.

To assure him, she repeated his instructions. "We ride up the street as if we belonged, at a steady, unhurried pace. I will look no one in the eye, if I need not, but I should watch for patrols. Once over the bridge we will ride through London and out the east gate, then find another barn in which to spend the night."

"One more thing." He tucked a finger under her raised chin. "Show no fear. Always assume your enemies can smell it."

Here she thought she'd done an excellent job of hiding her fear from Darian. The man missed little where she was concerned, always seemed to know what she needed, and when, and then provided.

She might love him, but loving him was like trying to hold the wind in a fist. The closer they got to Canterbury, the more he would slip through her fingers because she couldn't bring herself to agree to his offer.

He glanced west, where the setting sun would hail the end of day if the clouds didn't conceal it. "A hard rain would be welcome. Patrols dislike getting wet as much as ordinary folk."

In their dark clothing, with the hoods of their cloaks covering their heads, they might look like ordinary folk if they weren't atop a horse. But the horse was also a weapon they couldn't afford to leave behind.

"Then I shall pray for a nasty storm!"

"Nothing in excess, please. I need to see, too." He swung up into the saddle and reached for her hand. "Ride pillion. I want you behind me."

Emma preferred riding in front of him, but could see the sense in his request. He needed to observe what was going on in front of them without hindrance, and his hands must be without encumbrance. She truly hoped he found naught amiss and need not draw his dagger.

Settled behind Darian, all she could do was clutch his cloak and pray. As the minutes passed, the sky darkened, casting welcome shadows over the whole land. The rain came just as the buildings of Southwark came into view, but fell too lightly to chase anyone inside.

Unable to see completely around Darian, she could observe only what was to the sides. On her left were the wharfs and stews, the warehouses and coaching inns. On the right, the bishop of Winchester's palace.

Straight ahead would be London Bridge.

She might as well have kept the mantle over her nose and mouth because now she couldn't breathe anyway. The horse's hooves hit the road too loudly. Too many people looked their way.

Still, they made steady progress. Emma forced herself to breathe and chastised herself for worrying overmuch. Darian's plan seemed to be working nicely.

Darian slowed down and softly said, "Guards."

So much for eased fears.

Two men leaned against a building, paying little heed to anyone on the street as they talked to each other. Emma easily recognized their livery as that of the bishop. The sight of it pricked her ire.

"Do we go on?"

"Straight on to the bridge."

They passed the bishop's soldiers without mishap. She took a deep gulp of air.

"Nearly there, Emma. Hold on."

She could see the bridge. A few more moments and they'd be safely out of the bishop's liberty.

"You there, on the horse! Halt!"

Emma's stomach flipped. Darian quickened the pace as much as he dared on the busy street, expertly veering around a lumbering ox cart, then a group of sailors.

On the edge of her vision, she caught sight of a bishop's guard running toward them. And then another.

"Darian, on the right," she warned him, unsuccessful at hiding her rising panic.

"The left, too. Something is amiss, Emma. These guards should be out patrolling the streets, not loitering near the palace."

To make her nightmare complete, four guards, with spears at the ready, came off the bridge.

Too many to fight. Surrounded.

Darian slowed to a halt and sighed deeply. "I believe we are about to accept the bishop's invitation to view the innards of his palace."

Emma closed her eyes and prayed Bishop Henry was elsewhere, like his main residence—Wolvesey Castle in the city of Winchester, several leagues west.

"Come down," a guard ordered, directed at her.

"Back up and give the lady room," Darian commanded. "Should she land on your spear, the bishop will not be pleased."

The guard hesitated, but then obeyed. "Easy now. Keep yer hands outside yer cloak."

Emma almost wished she had a weapon. Almost. She slid off and stepped to the side to give Darian room to dismount. But before he could, the guard with the spear lunged at Darian.

She screamed, and for her trouble, she suffered a harsh, dirty paw over her mouth. Thankfully, the spear stopped short of Darian's leg.

"Hand yer dagger over first. No tricks, now."

Darian flipped his cloak back and slowly reached

down and retrieved the dagger. He released it to drop in the dirt.

The guard kicked the dagger sideways. "Here ye go, Captain. His Eminence will sure be glad to see it again."

"That he will. Come down, Darian, gently. Hate to have you bleed all over the palace floors."

Darian did as bid, his hands in clear sight. "Unhand the lady. She is no threat to you."

"Nor are you any longer," the captain bragged. "Let her go and let us get them inside. There may be a bonus in this for all of us."

Released, Emma took Darian's outstretched hand, seeing no sign he was worried in the least. That was probably good. She was scared enough for the both of them.

৩৯

Henry, bishop of Winchester, dined in sumptuous surroundings so ostentatious Darian couldn't help but gape. He'd heard rumors of the wealth Bishop Henry commanded from the stews and merchants and wharfs of Southwark. Now he knew the rumors true.

At least a dozen elegantly garbed servants were arrayed behind the bishop at a respectful distance. Each held a bowl or platter heaped with food, or a washbasin and towels, or flagons that likely held fine wine. All awaited the command of the man seated in a thronelike chair, dining alone at the most pretentious table Darian had ever seen.

With Emma's hand clasped firmly in his, Darian followed their armed escort to the foot of the long table while the patrol's captain traversed the length to place the lion-headed dagger within the bishop's reach.

Bishop Henry, just because he could, Darian supposed, took his time to acknowledge the captain and pick up the dagger.

"Darian of Bruges," he said flatly. "Your audacity amazes me."

"How so, Your Eminence?"

For his audacity, Emma squeezed his hand—hard.

But now he had the bishop's full attention, narrowed eyes and furrowed brow and all.

"First you lie to the king in his chambers and allow this farce of a marriage. Then you and Philip brazenly poke into my affairs in Southwark. Were that not enough, you killed five soldiers who meant you no harm. And now you have the gall to pass through my liberty?"

Darian had done all those things—in a fashion—except one, the most important one at the moment. "I did not lie to King Stephen. I did not kill Edward de Salis, as you know very well."

The bishop sighed. "De Salis was found with his throat slit, your dagger beside him. I see no reason to doubt the evidence, no matter Lady Emma's confession."

"Then you might wish to speak to your captains about what they do in your name and then do not inform you."

"Are you accusing one of my men of disloyalty?" the bishop asked, his tone taking on a hard edge.

"Most certainly not. I am sure they are all as steadfast in their loyalty to you as you are to the king."

The insult sliced as cleanly as would his dagger. The bishop reddened at the reminder that he'd once abandoned his brother's cause in favor of Maud's. Not that the bishop had been given much choice, or so he'd claimed later to Stephen. However, Stephen hadn't been pleased.

The bishop waved an angry hand at his captain. "Take them down to the Clink until the mercenary learns to respect his betters."

Beside him, Emma drew in a sharp breath. This time Darian squeezed *her* hand, hoping to reassure her and tell her to remain silent at the same time.

"We appreciate your offer of hospitality, Your Eminence, but I fear you have no choice but to release us."

"Ha! Neither you nor Lady Emma will see the light of day for a very long time, if ever."

Darian shrugged a shoulder. "Then you will need to answer to the king for my and the lady's disappearance."

Bishop Henry broke into wicked laughter, giving Darian pause. "You think my brother cares what happens to either of you?"

Maybe not, but William cared, and Emma's sister Gwendolyn cared, and perhaps between the two of them, they could convince King Stephen to care.

"He most certainly cares what happens to Lady Emma. You see, we are on our way to Canterbury—"

"So said the rumors at court." Bishop Henry finally looked at Emma. "You should be more careful in whom you confide, my lady. Some women simply have no head for what to keep secret and what not."

Emma spit out a vile oath Darian didn't think a lady should know. "Julia de Vere. She knew we might go to Canterbury. That is why there were so many guards at the bridge. They were watching for us. I beg pardon, Darian. I should have told you Julia was aware of what we might do."

"Precisely." The bishop gloated. "I appreciate your arrival in timely fashion."

Darian sighed inwardly. He hadn't expected an ambush, and Emma looked so forlorn he couldn't hold her responsible.

"No matter," he told Emma. "We will still be on our way to Canterbury come morn, all because the good bishop prefers to sit on his arse in his comfortable palace instead of attending his brother at Wallingford."

"You dare!"

To get them safely out of Winchester Palace, Darian knew he had to boldly dare the bluff he'd begun.

"Were you at Wallingford, you would know that Earl William knows how Edward de Salis was killed, and by whom, and is at this moment investigating why de Salis was in Southwark to begin with. Tell me, was it you who invited de Salis to negotiate a treaty, or did he invite himself?"

Bishop Henry came up out of his chair. "Preposterous!"

"Your first mistake was to let Hubert out of the Clink. He overheard one of your guards say that de Salis squealed like a pig when stuck. Once we knew who killed de Salis, the rest fell into place rather easily."

The captain paled, but Henry actually relaxed.

"If William believes the king will trust the word of a lowly worm over mine, he is mistaken."

"Then you should not have held Hubert for several days to be certain his words would not be heard by the king, nor should your guards have lied to Philip and Marc about his having been held. Marc already knew otherwise, so the guard's lies only confirmed our supposition."

Henry glanced tellingly at the captain and Darian prayed he was also right about the rest of his conjecture. William had told him he could figure it out with some thought, and everything he'd learned mulled around in his head until he concluded only one person could have given Bishop Henry the dagger.

"Your second mistake was to involve Perrin. Too many people saw him and de Salis together at a cockfight. Perrin must have lost a goodly sum he could not immediately make good on and ended up in your cellar. Whatever you offered Perrin to steal my dagger must have covered the wager, and then some. I do hope he is still alive and in the Clink, or Earl William will be very unhappy."

The bishop puffed in ire. "Your Earl William is not long for his command, mark my words. Nor have I heard anything that convinces me I should not hang you and the lady right now."

Darian's heart thumped against his ribs, and only his training kept the stink of his fear from leaking out.

"Hang me, if you will, but should Lady Emma disappear, the king will be *most* upset."

"Over a traitor's daughter? I think not."

Darian took a deep breath. "Were you at Wallingford, you would know the earl of Chester has reminded King Stephen of how valuable a princess of Wales, a descendant of Pendragon, might be in future dealings with the Welsh. You know we are on our way to Canterbury to annul our marriage, which will return Lady Emma to King Stephen's wardship, which at this moment he very much desires. If aught untoward happens to her, the king will want to know why, and how and by whom. You may be hard-pressed to explain why several people saw her enter your palace and never come out."

The bishop merely stared at him, his eyes widening in both shock and dismay.

Darian held out his free hand, feeling victory within

his grasp. "You may as well give me my dagger and horse and release us. And Perrin, too. Holding us will only cause you further grief."

Bishop Henry pounded his fist on the table, rattling the plates and knocking over a goblet of ruby-colored wine.

"Stephen takes advice from Chester? The fool! He *knows* the man is not to be trusted. Captain, lock up these two and make ready for Wallingford on the morn."

His silk robes billowing out around him, the bishop stalked out of the room through a tall, ornately carved side door.

Stunned, Darian stared after him.

"I thought your reasoning sounded good," Emma said, too calmly for the situation.

Sound, but apparently not reasonable enough for Henry, bishop of Winchester, whose jealousy of Chester had overcome the man's good sense. Which was what Darian had hoped for, but not with this result.

As the guards ushered them out, Darian took a long look at his dagger on the bishop's table. This was the second time he'd lost it to Bishop Henry, and he very much feared he wouldn't get it back this time.

At least Emma didn't appear distressed, which made no sense. They were headed for the cellar beneath the palace, a prison called the Clink, and only heaven knew who and what they'd find down there.

"Why are you so calm?"

In answer she glanced around at the guards, then smiled up at him. "Do not fret, Darian. All will be well."

And only heaven knew why her smile and reassurance made him trust she might be right.

Chapter Twenty

The rose-crested door.

Emma had seen the door and the passage beyond in a vision, and the moment she spotted it in the bishop's hall had known what it meant. *This is the way out.*

Their capture had been frightening, the consequences too horrible to contemplate until she'd recognized the door and *knew* all would be well once she and Darian passed through it. And they would. She didn't know when or how, only that they would somehow reach safety through the rose-bedecked door.

Naturally, she would inform Darian, but not while they were surrounded by the bishop's guards, who now led them down the stairs into the large, earthen cellar known as the Clink. Emma wrapped her mantle across her nose and mouth, but still the stench nearly overwhelmed her.

The cellar was dimly lit by torches on either side of the stairs, allowing just enough light to see her way down the center aisle between two walls of iron bars. One cell for the women, the other for the men.

Keys jangled. Gates clanged and squealed. Soon she and Darian were locked on opposite sides of the room. Thankfully, they shouldn't be apart long.

Emma briefly glanced at the three women in the cell. All of them sat on the dirt floor, none of them dressed in better than tattered rags. Drunkards? Whores? Not particularly caring to know why the women were in the cell, she turned away to watch Darian make a closer inspection of the men.

She winced when he bent over a man curled up in the corner, picked him up by the front of his tunic, and then pinned him against the wall.

"You sorry son of a bitch! Were I not in so good of a mood, I would shake the life right out of you."

"Have mercy, Darian! I have been in this place for far too long, and not one moment has been pleasant."

Emma couldn't see the man's face, but realized he must be Perrin.

"You damn near got me hung!"

"Whatever for?"

"The murder of Edward de Salis."

"De Salis is dead?"

Darian let go of Perrin and stepped back, his hands clenched. "Murdered. Some believe I slit his throat."

"Did you?"

Darian tossed his hands in the air. "Nay! The bishop used the dagger you stole to frame me for the murder. Why the devil did you give it to him?"

Even from across the room, Emma heard Perrin's sigh.

"Bishop Henry told me he admired your dagger and

would give me five pounds and forgive all of my gambling debts if I gave him your dagger. With the coin, I knew I could purchase a dagger to replace yours and no one would ever know."

"You did not think I would notice the difference in the daggers?"

"The deal was too good to pass up. Never did it occur to me the bishop would lie."

Darian scoffed. "I gather you did not receive your five pounds."

"Nay, and he tossed me in here anyway. Does Earl William know Bishop Henry accuses you of murder?"

"Bishop Henry made the accusation in the royal chambers in front of the king and Earl William. He also knows who stole the dagger."

Perrin groaned. "The earl will have my balls in a bowl."

"Aye, well, first we must get out of here."

Darian turned around and came to the gate of the men's cell. "Why did you tell me not to fret?"

Emma pulled her mantle away from her mouth. "If you can get us back into the bishop's hall, I can guide us out of the palace. I know what lies beyond those tall oak doors."

Darian's eyes narrowed. "You have been in the palace before?"

How did she tell him she'd seen the rose-bedecked door and the passageway beyond it without giving her secrets away to Perrin? "Once, as I hope never to envision it again."

Darian's eyebrows shot up; then he nodded, telling her

he understood. His small hand signal brought Perrin to the iron bars.

Tall and gaunt, dark-haired and unshaven, Perrin leaned against the bars. His clothing was dirt-caked and his skin pale. Weeks of enduring Bishop Henry's hospitality had taken a toll.

"How much of the palace have you seen?" Darian asked of his fellow mercenary.

"Not much. The hall, this cell, a bit of the yard."

"Wonderful." Darian rubbed at his forehead. "I suppose our first step is to get the guards' attention, then overpower them."

"They will return, likely twice more before dawn," Perrin said. "They bring several people in each night."

"So all we need do is be ready for them when they bring in another group of drunkards. When do they let them go?"

Perrin gave a burst of laughter. "When they are of a mind."

Darian leaned on the bars. "We need a plan."

"'Ere now," a gray-haired man said, "if yer escapin', ye got to takes me with ye."

"And me," another demanded.

One of the women sidled up next to Emma. "I would not mind gettin' out o' this hole in the ground."

Darian bowed his head, and Emma felt his misery. Getting the three of them out of the palace would be risky enough without having to escort several drunkards and whores with them.

Darian's head came up and he announced, "Perrin and I will overpower the guards. If everyone remains quiet and leaves us be, anyone who wants to walk out of here may do so. However, escaping may be to your detriment, so consider carefully before you decide to leave."

"Sounds fair to me," declared the gray-haired man. With mischief in his eyes, he added, "Most o' us knows these halls and walls better than we ought to. You keep that gate from closin' and those of us who are of a mind can find our way out."

During the grunts of agreement, Emma wondered how many of the current prisoners would suffer future consequences for having escaped. If they were caught, the guards certainly wouldn't be gentle with them.

But the prisoners were all beyond the age of reason, and each could make up his or her mind. Emma wished them all well and hoped they didn't hinder her own escape.

Darian and Perrin talked quietly, likely deciding on how best to overpower the guards.

The woman at her side nudged her elbow and whispered, "The sandy-haired one. He yers, dearie?"

Not for much longer. Not after they petitioned for an annulment. But the curious woman didn't need to know that Darian would soon be unwed. For now, Darian was hers.

"My husband."

The woman sighed. "A pity. Would not mind givin' that one a tumble. Might not even charge him."

Emma blushed, realizing she was speaking to one of Winchester's geese. A whore of the stews. A woman who sold her body to earn her living.

Embarrassment quickly gave over to curiosity, and the oddest sense of pride in the woman's admiration of Darian.

Emma knew a lady should back away in disgust, but there was truly nowhere to go. And heaven help her, she couldn't help but smile at the whore.

"I shall pass along your compliment, though I shall also strive to ensure he has no need for your services."

The whore chuckled. "If all wives were so clever, I would starve. Come sit. Not much for us to do 'cept wait."

Wait and hope that when the guards returned, Darian and Perrin's plan would work.

Seated in the far corner of the windowless cellar, Darian had no idea what time of the night it might be, just knew he'd remained awake for what felt like hours while the others slept.

In the women's cell Emma dozed lightly. Too often those doe-brown eyes had sought him out, and not once had he seen a hint of anger that because of him she shared a dank, dirty cell with whores.

Once more, he hadn't taken care of Emma as he ought. No princess should suffer the indignity of a night spent in the Clink, curled up on a dirt floor with the rabble of Southwark for company.

She should be furious. Instead, Emma calmly accepted that he would get her out of the cell and they would escape and all would be well. Such faith humbled him.

But then, Emma didn't rely solely on his abilities. Apparently at some time in the past, she'd seen the bishop's palace in a vision, or at least the door in the hall and what lay beyond it.

He'd never placed his trust in a vision before, and while it felt strange, his instincts told him such trust wasn't misplaced. He had to trust in Emma, as she trusted in him. He didn't doubt her belief that she knew an escape route, hadn't even questioned the cell's inhabitants, who apparently knew of other ways out.

Where Emma led, he would follow. Straight into hell, if that's where fate took them.

Lord above, he'd fallen hard for the woman, and setting her free of him would be a difficult task. Living without her would be pure hell, indeed.

When Darian finally heard footsteps on the stairs, he nudged Perrin, who instantly awakened and without words understood he was now supposed to be dead.

Silently, Darian hurried toward the bars.

Two guards noisily brought down three men, one of them so drunk one of the guards practically carried him. Perfect.

The clamor woke almost everyone, and to Darian's relief, none of the men got up or seemed about to warn the guards.

Across the room Emma stirred, but didn't make any threatening or otherwise suspicious moves, either.

The guard not holding up the drunk drew his short sword from his scabbard and fetched the large key from the hook. "Everyone stay put, now. Ain't mornin' yet, just got us some new guests."

The gate swung open and the guard shoved the more sober of the drunkards into the cell. The other guard entered to dump his burden a few feet from the gate.

"You have a dead one in the back," Darian said. "He is beginning to stink."

"Ah, hell," the guard at the gate grumbled, and waved his sword at his comrade. "Go have a look."

In preparation the prisoners had left a wide circle around Perrin. Darian tensed. The guard kicked Perrin, who grabbed hold of the guard's leg and knocked him off balance.

Darian took advantage of the armed guard's shock and leapt for the gate. A solid punch to the guard's jaw took him down. Within a trice, Darian dragged the unconscious guard over to the far corner of the cell, where Perrin stood over his victim.

Darian noted how swiftly the cell emptied of prisoners, the sobered men quietly and hastily making their way up the stairway. He also knew the guards could rouse at any moment, and the need to hurry quickened his own steps.

He found the key in the dirt outside the cell, where the armed guard had dropped it when he went down.

Perrin picked up the guard's sword. "Not the best quality, but 'twill do. There should be more weapons in the armory at the top of the stairs."

Darian locked the guards into the cell. "Will there be guards in the armory?"

"Likely not. They are supposed to be out patrolling the streets, and the servants should be asleep. Our way should be clear."

With a relieved nod, Darian opened the women's cell, anxious to have Emma in his arms again. Her bright smile reflected both pride and relief. He pulled her close for a brief hug, vowing he would claim a less hurried one later. Hand in hand, they left the cell.

All three of the other women had also escaped the cell.

Two had already scampered up the stairs. One seemed content to linger.

She put a hand on Perrin's arm. "My thanks, kind sirs, fer yer good deed. Ye ever in need of a tumble, ye come see Molly."

Emma squeezed his hand, as if warning him he'd best not accept the offer. Darian had to smile, rather liking the sign of possessiveness.

Perrin smiled, too, but at Molly. "Our thanks for the offer, Molly, but first we must all get out safely. Do you know a way out?"

Molly waved a dismissive hand. "This place has more ins and outs than a mole has holes. Want me to show ye one?"

Perrin looked to Darian.

Trusting in Emma's vision, he shook his head. "We have a bit of business with the bishop first. We will find our own way out, Molly. You have a care getting past the guards."

"Aye, well, you have a care in yer business with the bishop that ye do not end up back down here!"

Darian handed Molly the key. "If you happen to hear we met ill fortune, come get us out."

Her gap-toothed smile widened, and the whore dropped the key into her gown and patted the ample breast where the key landed. "A bargain. God go with ye."

Molly sped up the stairs.

"You know a way out?" Perrin asked.

"We must get back to the hall," Darian answered. "Armory first. I need a dagger."

If Perrin noticed that Darian held on to Emma's hand on their way up the stairs, all the time they spent in the armory, and down the passageway to the bishop's hall, he said nothing. Nor did Darian care what Perrin thought. Emma didn't object, and Darian didn't intend to release her until they were well out of harm's way.

In the hall Emma pointed to the tall oak doors through which the bishop had passed earlier. "Through there."

Darian glanced toward the table, which had been cleared—save for one bright, shiny object. His dagger! Darian didn't question his good fortune, just snatched it up on his way through the room.

Once past the rose-decorated door, Emma again pointed, this time down the passageway to another door. "Every lord has a secret way out of his castle to a postern gate. This is Bishop Henry's."

"Do you know where it leads?"

"Nay, only that we must pass through it."

"Then we shall."

Darian grabbed a torch from a wall sconce; Perrin opened the door.

Reluctantly, Darian let go of Emma's hand to cautiously lead them down a long flight of stairs, the light from the torch allowing him to see only a few feet ahead. At the bottom of the stairway was an earthen tunnel, and Darian glanced back at Emma and Perrin, wondering if they, too, noted the air stale from disuse. No fresh air had invaded this tunnel in a very long time, and despite the assurance of Emma's vision, Darian prayed there was a door at the end of it.

Silently, with his head ducked to clear the roof of the narrow tunnel, he picked up the pace and soon felt the slight strain in his calves from an uphill tilt to the floor. Judging by the long trek, they were far from the palace when Darian spotted the door he sought, hoping no lock proved a hindrance.

He handed the torch back to Emma. "Stay here while I see where we are."

The door groaned, but it opened, and Darian eased out.

Freedom had never smelled so good. By the sliver of moon, he glanced around, again grateful for good fortune.

He went back into the tunnel, took back the torch, and doused it in the dirt. "It appears we are at the very south end of the palace grounds. The livery is to the left. What say, Perrin? Go for horses?"

"Lead on."

Darian grabbed hold of Emma's hand and swiftly led them the few steps to where they entered the stables. To his delight, his horse occupied one of the stalls, the saddle and his satchel resting nearby.

Hands on hips, Perrin glanced around. "The postern gate must be close."

That made sense to Darian. He was almost ready to begin saddling up when the thought struck him that taking his horse might be a bad idea.

"Perrin, is your horse still in the stables at Westminster?"

"Should be. Why?"

"Emma and I can get to the other side of the Thames more secretly if we are not on horseback. You take mine, I will use yours, and we can trade when we next meet up."

As they'd surmised, the postern gate wasn't far from the stables, and the guard, sleeping beside it, was so easily tied up and gagged that Darian began to fidget over how easily they were making their escape. Still, not one to overly question good fortune when it came his way, he closed the postern gate behind them, hoping to never again cross paths with Bishop Henry.

With his satchel in one hand, his other arm draped over Emma's shoulders, Darian watched Perrin ride west on his way to Wallingford.

"Will William accept Perrin back into the band?" Emma asked.

"I suspect he will, but that is between Perrin and William."

She slipped an arm around his waist and rested her head against his shoulder, her weariness overcoming the strength she'd shown all day.

He gave her a squeeze. "Let us find a place to catch a few hours' sleep. On the morn, I believe we shall forgo the bridge and find a ferry to take us across the river."

"By morn, the bishop's guards will know we have escaped and will be searching for us."

"Then we will have a care not to let them find us." He looked down into her worried eyes. "You did well, Emma. If not for your vision of the door, we would not have escaped so easily."

The compliment earned him a sleepy smile. "Perhaps, but we are not out of danger yet."

"Nay, but I vow, we will sleep in a bed in Rochester tomorrow night."

And the night after that, they would be in Canterbury. Darian turned Emma toward the river to find a secluded spot along the bank, where they could wait for the dawn, determined not to think about what would happen in Canterbury.

❧

True to his word, Darian found a lovely inn in
Rochester, and Emma eyed the bed in the private room
with both gratitude and trepidation.

Tonight might well be her last night with Darian, and
she could barely look at him for fear of bursting into tears.

This morn, they'd caught a ferry easily enough and
found Perrin's horse right where it should be. The ride to
Rochester hadn't proven a strain, except for growing distance between them. They'd ridden for leagues pressed
close together with barely a word spoken between them.

Darian was still very quiet as he lit the charcoal in the
brazier, and Emma struggled to find something to say to
lighten the mood. If this was her last night with Darian,
she wanted to spend it in laughter and loving, not ponder-
ing what she'd done wrong.

"Perhaps we should spend an added night on our journey to Canterbury. You are becoming more proficient at
choosing inns."

With the brazier beginning to glow, he rose up slowly,
a soft smile on his face. "Am I? Good, because I have been
giving thought to . . . after. I am assuming you do not wish
to stay in Canterbury. Where do you want to go?"

"Home."

The answer came out without thought, and Emma realized why. 'Twas truly her only safe haven, a place of
comfort if not serenity. Among people who loved her.
And if the king wished her to reside somewhere else, then
he could damn well take time from the war to deal with
her.

And joy of joys, she couldn't possibly travel all that way on her own. She needed an escort, and just as she'd reasoned at Hadone that 'twas sensible to enlist Darian's aid in getting to Bledloe Abbey, so did that reasoning seem sensible now.

"Would you be willing to take me to Camelen?"

"Certes."

Wonderful! Tonight would not be her last night with Darian, no matter what happened in Canterbury, which brightened her spirits considerably. Except for one thing.

"Must we go through London?"

He shook his head emphatically. "Nay. We can go to Dover and take a ship to Southampton—unless being on the water would be overly taxing for you."

"Better I risk a vision than again pass by Winchester Palace. But what of you . . . after? Will you return to Earl William's service?"

He sat down on the bed, his clasped hands dangling between his knees. "'Tis all I know how to do, though 'twill not be the same as before. I damaged William's faith in me, and I am not sure I can regain it."

Knowing how much he admired William, and how much the earl had done for Darian over the years, Emma understood his sorrow. She sat down next to him on the bed, not sure if he needed compassion or a distraction.

She decided on the latter. "Have you given thought to doing something else?"

"Such as?"

Emma shrugged a shoulder, having no suggestion in mind. "What do mercenaries do when they are no longer mercenaries?"

He gazed off into the distance, beyond the walls of the

inn. "Thomas wants to purchase land in Kent, build a cottage, and find himself a plump wife to cook his meals and share his bed. Philip thinks that a good plan, too, only he would go back to Flanders."

A wife and cottage. She swallowed hard against the heartbreak that someday a very fortunate woman might share Darian's life until death did they part. Perhaps in Flanders.

"Will you go back to Flanders?"

"There is naught for me in Flanders anymore. But I may have no choice when the war is over. The Flemish in England are here by the king's leave. When we are no longer needed for his army, he may well send us all home. 'Twould certainly make Bishop Henry happy, and I can think of few others who would miss us."

Bishop Henry could go to the devil!

"I would miss you!"

He stared at her hard, setting her insides to churning and her heart to thumping.

"How much would you miss me?"

"Very much."

"But not enough to remain married to me."

Her thumping heart ached so much, the tears began to flow. She'd refused him once, with good reason, and those reasons hadn't changed. He sought to protect her from the king's machinations, out of a sense of duty. Not because he wanted *her* as his wife.

"Oh, Darian, if only—"

He put a finger on her lips, hushing her refusal. "When Thomas and Philip spoke of cottages and wives, I began thinking the arrangement sounded wonderful, but only if *you* were the wife standing in the doorway to welcome me home. I love you, Emma, and would never ask you to—"

Emma grabbed his hand and pulled it away from her mouth, her tears falling faster now, but for a joy-filled reason!

Darian loved her! 'Twas all she'd needed to hear.

"Ask," she commanded.

"But you are a princess. A cottage would never do—"

"A cottage would do me fine!" How could the man be so stubborn! "Have pity, Darian! I love you, too! Ask!"

His eyes went wide with surprise, and the hint of a smile tugged at the corners of his mouth. "You do? You love me?"

Emma never got the chance to answer. Darian's mouth possessed hers, his kiss a mix of elation and demand. They fell onto the mattress and celebrated with kiss after kiss, leaving Emma breathless and dizzy.

"This is not wise," Darian said with no conviction in his tone, only relief. "Princesses do not marry commoners."

"Since this one already did, I see no reason to discuss it further. We have dealt well enough together so far, have we not?"

His smile spread wider. Mischief glinted in his eyes. "In some ways, better than others," he teased.

"In one way, best of all. You still have not asked."

In a movement quick and lithe, Darian rose from the bed and shucked his tunic.

Emma held her breath as her vision became reality. Naked from the waist up, his smile glorious, Darian held out his hand in invitation, just as she'd envisioned him doing so many years ago.

"Will you be my wife, Emma? Share my life, whatever that life might be?"

Emma took Darian's hand and joyously stepped into the vision she'd begun to doubt would ever happen. She hadn't understood his declaration of love had to come first. With understanding came a serenity and ecstasy so sublime her eyes filled with tears.

"Gladly, my lord. I know not what that life might be, but I cannot envision my life without you."

"Pray do not ever try."

"Never," she promised, and sealed their fate with a kiss.

Epilogue

The decision to visit Camelen was easily made. The decision to tell Gwendolyn about her visions and how badly she'd handled them had caused Emma many a sleepless night—without reason, as it turned out.

Gwendolyn had taken the news very well, indeed, and didn't seem upset over the burdens she'd assumed whenever Emma suffered one of her headaches.

But now, sitting shoulder to shoulder with Gwendolyn on the edge of the bed in the lord's bedchamber, Emma learned she wasn't the only sister who had kept secrets from childhood on.

In her newly ring-bedecked hand, Emma held a scroll tied with a scarlet ribbon, and in the other hand rested a trefoil-shaped gold pendant. Both objects she'd seen in her visions. In one vision they'd sat on a table. In the other a little girl, who Emma knew would be Gwen's daughter, had worn the pendant.

Emma glanced at her sister, whose pregnancy was now

beginning to show, and who glowed with happiness in her marriage to Alberic and with the impending birth. Emma hadn't yet decided whether to tell Gwen she would give birth to a daughter.

The decision could wait. First Emma wanted to know why Gwendolyn hadn't told her about these ancient artifacts and of their significance.

"Mother gave these to you before she died?"

Gwen nodded. "Hours before, with little explanation of their power and no instruction on their use. With Alberic's help, I have since learned how the magic works."

"Magic?"

With barely a pause for breath, Gwendolyn told Emma of the ancient spell written on the parchment. Of the ring Alberic now wore—which apparently couldn't be removed from his hand—and the trefoil pendant, both necessary to the working of the spell.

A spell handed down through the ages from mother to daughter to granddaughter in an unbroken line of matriarchal inheritance to the descendants of Pendragon. A spell entrusted to them by Merlin the Sorcerer. A spell to recall King Arthur from Avalon at the time of England's most dire need.

Emma gaped at Gwendolyn. "Recall King Arthur?"

Gwen sighed. "I know this must sound impossible, but I swear, Emma, it is true. Unroll the scroll and tell me what you see."

Emma saw words she couldn't read, though they looked oddly familiar.

"Ancient Welsh, perhaps?"

Gwen smiled. "Then you see the same language I do, perhaps because we are sisters and Mother could have passed the scroll to either of us. When Alberic looks at the scroll, he sees mostly Welsh. Rhys the Bard sees the language of the Moors. So you see, there are guards in place so no one can read the spell who is not meant to."

It took Emma a moment to absorb that the words on the scroll appeared in different languages to different people.

"Can you read it?"

"A few words only. As can Alberic. The phrases he can read appear to him in Norman French."

Emma stared at the scroll. "I see no Norman French."

Gwendolyn laughed lightly. "Because you are not meant to read the spell, Emma. I am, as will my daughter after me. I always wondered why Mother gave the artifacts to me, not you. Perhaps because you were already burdened with the visions?"

Which explained much, especially the vision of Gwen's daughter wearing the trefoil pendant. Emma suddenly knew what she was supposed to tell her sister, though she didn't know why, or if it was important for Gwen to know.

'Struth, now that Emma had decided to accept future visions she couldn't avoid, those from the past became clearer, their meaning understandable. Sweet mercy, she'd spent so many wasted days in bed with headaches she shouldn't have suffered.

"You must give your daughter the pendant when she is very young, Gwen."

"I intend to. I shall also explain both the spell and the responsibility to keep it secret and safe. I do not want her to suffer the torments of doubt and confusion I did."

Emma knew well how doubt and confusion tormented

the mind and hurt the heart. Visions had caused Emma's torment; ancient magic had caused Gwendolyn's. And they'd suffered alone because their mother had told both of them to keep silent.

Emma shook her head at their blind obedience. "We should have shared our secrets earlier. Neither of us would have suffered so much if we had talked of our fears."

"I tried to talk to Father about mine, but it hurt him so much to speak of Mother that I ceased."

"After Mother died, I could not bring myself to tell him I had envisioned her death." Emma sighed. "Ah, Gwen, how young and hopeless we were."

Gwen took the scroll and pendant and placed them in their velvet pouch. "Perhaps we were, but no longer. I am happy and content." She winked. "I believe you are, too. Your Darian is both handsome and attentive. And our husbands seem to get on well. I would say that is cause for celebration."

So would Emma, if not for Nicole.

"Does it seem selfish for us to celebrate our happiness when Nicole still lingers in Bledloe Abbey?"

Gwen frowned. "Did you not say she seemed satisfied to reside with the nuns for a time?"

Until the time came when the king decided on the fate of his ward, Nicole would be safe and well cared for at Bledloe Abbey. But Emma had another concern.

"Aye, so she seems. Gwen, you are the guardian of an ancient, magical spell. I have visions, which some would deem magical. 'Twould be reasonable to expect Nicole to possess some magical quality, too, would it not?"

Gwen thought that over. "I should think Nicole would

have told one of us if she experienced something she deemed unusual."

"Perhaps not. We kept our secrets from each other for a very long time."

"From each other, but not from our parents, who then *ordered* us to keep our secrets. You by Mother, me by Father. Would Nicole have told Father if she experienced oddities? Or perhaps William?"

Gwen's brow scrunched. "I doubt she told Father. But our brother?" She shrugged. "Nicole followed William around like a devoted pup, and he doted on her. 'Tis possible, I suppose. Do you believe we should ask Nicole?"

Emma didn't know if, by asking, she would be doing the girl a disservice or not.

"Perhaps we should wait to see if Nicole brings up the subject, and then decide how to deal with it." Emma tossed a hand in the air, remembering how they'd futilely worried over the tone of Nicole's letters. "And perhaps we again worry over naught. 'Twould not be the first time!"

A rap on the door preceded Alberic's entrance into the bedchamber, Darian behind him, his smile bright. Oh, how she loved his smile!

Alberic tossed an arm over Gwendolyn's shoulders. "You two have been up here since supper, shamefully neglecting your husbands, who have decided such conduct must cease."

Gwendolyn beamed at her husband's teasing. "Poor dears."

Emma crossed the room to take Darian's upraised hand. "We did not mean to neglect you, merely lost all sense of time while we talked."

"So we assumed," Darian said. "Finished?"

Not hardly, but in the days ahead, she would have time for more such talks with Gwendolyn while Darian went to speak to Earl William at Wallingford. Having decided to leave the earl's service, Darian felt honor-bound to inform the earl himself.

"For now."

"Then we bid thee good night, my lord, my lady."

Darian pulled her out into the passageway and closed the bedchamber door behind them. A few steps away was the bedchamber Emma, Gwendolyn, and Nicole had once shared, which she and Darian would occupy for one more night before Darian left on the morn.

His packed satchel lay on the floor at the foot of the bed. His cloak hung on a peg near the door. Emma intended to take all night to say fare thee well.

Her thumb glided along the gold band she'd quickly become accustomed to wearing. It suited her perfectly, as did the man who'd given it to her. She would miss Darian, but assured of his love and their commitment to each other, she couldn't begrudge him a few days apart.

"You neglected to tell me of the extent of your dowry."

Darian's comment caught her off guard.

"Is that what you and Alberic talked about?"

"'Twould seem my princess is not without means."

Good to hear!

"I did not tell you because I was not sure Alberic would honor my father's intentions. Alberic is willing to give up a portion of Camelen?"

With a gleam in his eyes, Darian placed his warm palms against her cheeks. "Alberic and I came to a bargain. In return for my oaths of fealty and homage, he grants your dowry. The portion I am interested in is a holding he speaks of not far south of here. Apparently the manor house is large enough to hold us, several children, and a servant or two besides."

Emma grasped fistfuls of his tunic, able to envision them there without the aid of a pool of water. "I know the place, and the manor is as lovely as anywhere in the kingdom. But Darian, be very sure you wish to settle in one place, or to serve Alberic as his vassal. I should hate for you to one day realize such a life was not what you desire."

He lowered his head until their foreheads touched. "Alberic is a decent, honorable man I can serve in good conscience. Becoming his vassal will be no hardship whatever. Granted, for most of my life, I vowed I would never want a home or family for fear of losing all. Then I met you, and now I can think of nothing I want more. If you want something different, tell me now."

"I want for you to be happy in your choice."

"And I you."

She'd sealed her fate when she refused to allow a king to hang a mercenary, and what an excellent choice that had been.

"Then I say we spend the rest of the night on the matter of producing children to fill our manor."

And so they did.

ABOUT THE AUTHOR

SHARI ANTON's secretarial career ended when she took a creative writing class and found she possessed some talent for writing fiction. The author of several highly acclaimed historical novels, she now works in her home office, where she can take unlimited coffee breaks. Shari and her husband live in southeastern Wisconsin, where they have two grown children and do their best to spoil their two adorable little grandsons. You can write to her at P.O. Box 510611, New Berlin, WI 53151-0611, or visit her Web site at www.sharianton.com.

THE MAGIC
DOESN'T STOP HERE!

∽

Turn the page
for a preview of
Shari Anton's next novel,

Sunset Magic

the third book in her
enchanting trilogy.

Available in mass market Fall 2007.

Chapter One

R hodri ap Dafydd skillfully wielded two weapons in the service of Connor ap Maelgwn, chieftain of Glenvair.

During supper, to lift the gloom wrought by the latest bad news from England, Rhodri had played his harp and sung the praises of the Welsh princes who, after years of fighting, had driven most of the Anglo-Normans from Welsh lands.

Tonight, he sat cross-legged on the hard-packed earthen floor, within the central fire pit's flickering glow, sliding a whetstone along the edge of his sword, preparing for another battle he hoped wouldn't come.

Connor paced a path in the dirt and tapped the rolled parchment containing the bad news against his leg. "If it is true that King Stephen's heir is dead, he may succumb to his magnate's pleas to bargain for peace. England at peace always means trouble for Wales. Better they should continue to fight amongst themselves and leave us be."

"Agreed," Rhodri said, remembering a time when England had been at peace under King Henry. Wales had suffered mightily.

Rhodri had been all of ten when King Henry died and Stephen of Blois, Henry's nephew, had seized the English throne. Empress Maud, Henry's daughter, objected by raising an army and challenging Stephen for the right to rule England. Now Maud's son, Henry Plantagenet, who some said was as forceful and ambitious as the grandsire he'd been named for, was poised to succeed where his mother had failed for eighteen long years.

"Wales must unite," Connor declared. "If we do not, we may perish."

A knot formed in Rhodri's gut. During his apprenticeship to a chaired bard, he'd learned the history of Wales all the way back to ancient times. Rarely had the Welsh princes banded together under one leader to stave off invasions.

"Each of the princes has his ambitions for expanding his own lands. For them to unite for a common cause might require a miracle. Have you one at the ready?"

Connor sighed and eased down onto a nearby stool, placing his deeply wrinkled hands on his knees. White hair revealed his advanced years; a furrowed brow bespoke a troubled mind. Still, vigor and intelligence lit the chieftain's amber eyes, belying any belief that his mind might wither with age.

"No ready miracles," Connor admitted. "However, we may have time to conjure one. Most likely, Stephen will be forced to name Henry Plantagenet as his heir, so the lad will have to wait until Stephen dies to claim England's crown."

Rhodri inwardly scoffed. He could name several sons and nephews who'd sent fathers, uncles, and brothers to their graves before their natural end. Youth tended to impatience when the prize was within reach.

Henry Plantagenet, duke of Normandy and Aquitaine, count of Anjou, Touraine, and Maine, wasn't known for his patience.

Nor were the Marcher earls. They'd lost most of their royally granted land in Wales over the past few years, and they eagerly awaited the chance to reclaim those lands and punish the native princes for their audacity in believing Wales should be ruled by the Welsh.

Knowing his irritation caused his mind to wander from his task, Rhodri set aside his whetstone and sword.

"If peace comes to England, the earls of the March will once again turn their thoughts toward us. With the aid of Prince Madog of Powys, we will defend Glenvair as we have always done."

"That we will," Connor stated firmly, then leaned forward, elbows on knees. "I am of a mind, however, to try to gain an advantage." He waved the rolled parchment. "Though my niece is always kind enough to send us whatever news she hears of affairs in England, I wish to heaven above that when Gwendolyn and her sisters were orphaned, I had gone to Camelen to fetch them and bring them to Glenvair. That mistake must now be made right."

Rhodri didn't see how Connor could do aught now for his long-dead sister's girls. He well remembered the day Connor received word that his Norman brother-by-marriage, Sir Hugh de Leon, along with his son, William, had lost their lives fighting for the Empress Maud, and that the three surviving girls had been made wards of King Stephen.

Gwendolyn had been forced to marry Alberic, the bastard son of the earl of Chester, one of the most hated of the Marcher lords. Emma had been sent to King Stephen's court, where she'd been forced to marry Darian of Bruges, a Flemish mercenary. Nicole had been given to the Church and, as far as Rhodri knew, still resided in Bledloe Abbey.

"The girls were out of your reach then, as they are now."

"Gwendolyn and Emma, perhaps, but not Nicole. Stephen holds her captive in Bledloe Abbey. He intends to wed her to a Welsh prince to forge an alliance with the English crown, driving a wedge between the princes. We must remove that weapon from Stephen's armory and use it to our own advantage."

That meant stealing Nicole out of Bledloe Abbey, near Oxford, in the heart of England. A raid that far into enemy territory might prove disastrous.

Connor ap Maelgwn was a cunning chieftain, a ferocious soldier, and an honorable man. How much was he willing to risk to wrest his youngest niece from English control?

"Kidnapping Nicole might be considered an act of war. And what of her sisters? Surely, Gwendolyn and Emma will not approve of your scheme, and their husbands would make formidable opponents."

Connor took a long breath. "I am hopeful that, for a time, England's lords will be more concerned with the fate of the crown than with other matters. As for Nicole's sisters, I believe they can be convinced my motives are not selfish. Our family's heritage must be preserved. The tree of Pendragon *must* bear a Welsh branch to remain strong."

Pendragon. The bloodline of the revered King Arthur.

Rhodri knew every word of the ancient legends and could sing the tales of Arthur's conquests and his downfall. But even though he had the right to call Connor his uncle, Rhodri couldn't claim the bloodline. His widowed father had married into the family, taking one of Connor's sisters as his second wife several years after Rhodri's birth.

He'd always felt like a blade of grass within the mighty oak's shade, close in kinship but not a twig on the tree. His name wouldn't be recorded as a descendant of Pendragon, but there were other ways to ensure one's name was remembered through time. 'Twas one of the reasons he'd become a bard. All he needed was the chance to advance in his profession.

But that was for the future. Right now, he must do his utmost to counsel Connor.

"You cannot march a band of Welsh across half of England without drawing attention. The raid would fail."

"True, which is why I propose to send one man."

From the way his uncle looked at him, Rhodri knew who he intended to send. The prospect both excited and disturbed him. He was honored by Connor's faith and trust in him, but he foresaw problems. He wasn't one of Nicole's favorite people, as Connor well knew.

"You want *me* to kidnap Nicole out of Bledloe Abbey and bring her to Glenvair?"

"Better if Nicole comes of her own free will. Talk to

her, Rhodri. Convince her that coming to Wales is the best course."

"She does not like me. She may not listen."

"Nicole was no more than a handful of years old when she was last here. Surely she can now be reasoned with. And if reasoning fails, bring her anyway. Her fate is too important to leave to chance."

Connor rose and ambled off, leaving Rhodri to ponder how he might accomplish this task.

Talk to her, Connor had said. Would an appeal to Nicole's sense of duty to her Pendragon heritage work? Perhaps, if she felt a sense of duty. Problem was, the Nicole he remembered cared only for her own concerns. A princess who struck out when she didn't get what she wanted.

Rhodri ap Dafydd rubbed his leg, remembering the last time he'd tried to convince Nicole de Leon to do something she didn't care to do, fearing this time she might do far worse than kick his shin and get him into more trouble than before.

Your time here is done, Nicole. Come out.

Nicole de Leon bolted upright on her narrow cot. Her eyes snapped open to see only the night-shrouded dormitory, not the owner of the voice from beyond the grave that had awakened her.

Why, she silently asked . . . and received no answer. Her brother William never answered her questions, merely gave orders he expected her to follow.

Even as sorrow for his plight flooded her, so did ire

that William had seen fit to disturb her sleep. Again. Other spirits weren't so inconsiderate. But then, William hadn't been overly considerate in life, and death hadn't wrought a change.

Nicole deeply breathed in the familiar scents of woolen robes hanging on their pegs, and of the burning night candle near the doorway. A glance over the cots revealed she hadn't disturbed the nuns who would soon rise for matins and begin yet another day of prayer, meditation, and service in God's name.

For eight years Bledloe Abbey had been her home, these nuns her gentle companions and patient teachers. William wanted her to leave them behind. For where? To do what?

Silence reigned.

Calmer now, but knowing she wouldn't go back to sleep, Nicole silently rose and slipped on her black robe over the linen chemise that protected her skin from the prickly wool. With her bedding straightened, hose and boots in hand, she padded her way to the infirmary where she knew Mother Abbess would be awake.

Mother Abbess rarely slept these days, too aware the heavenly reward she'd spent her life working toward was about to become reality.

Soon now, dear, soon!

This voice, too, came from beyond the grave. Sister Enid's soft, excited greeting as Nicole entered the herb-scented, tranquil infirmary made her smile.

Sister Enid had left mortal life behind a few days after Beltane. In life, the nun had considered the care of Mother Abbess her life's work, and so her spirit lingered to see her duty completed. The two old and dear friends would pass through the veil between this life and the next together.

Would that William would pass through that veil, find peace, and cease pestering her with orders she refused to obey. She'd done so once, the first time William had spoken to her, taking advantage of her youth and grief over his death. Nicole thanked the Lord every day that she hadn't possessed the skill or strength to murder her now brother-by-marriage, Alberic, and that he'd long since forgiven her for trying to stab him with William's dagger.

And now William wanted her to leave Bledloe Abbey, for no other purpose than his selfish, unwarranted need for revenge against Alberic, no doubt. Nicole lowered onto the stool beside Mother Abbess's cot, resolved to ignore her brother's latest command, just as she'd ignored so many of his other demands.

"What brings you here so early?" Mother Abbess asked, the clarity of her voice belying both her advanced age and failing health.

As Sister Enid said, Mother Abbess would soon die. Still, the abbess looked no different this morn than she had last eve—frail and withered, her thin hair as white as fresh snow. In her gnarled hands she held prayer beads worn from years of use. Her green eyes, however, still often saw too much.

To hide the full truth, Nicole bent over to put on her black short hose and boots.

"I woke and did not wish to disturb the others. So I came to see how you fare."

"Harrumph. We must usually pull you from your cot of a morn. What spoils your slumber?"

Nicole smiled. "Perhaps I have at long last become accustomed to waking before the bell is rung."

Mother Abbess chuckled at the lie. "When sheep take wing." Then she sobered. "What ails you, child?"

Nicole grappled for something troublesome the old nun might accept in answer, and easily found one that had floated in and out of her thoughts for several days now.

"Prince Eustace's death, and how his loss will affect King Stephen and the war."

Mother Abbess's fingers slid from one bead to the next, seeking solace and wisdom in the prayer that had sustained her all her life.

"You fear King Stephen may now remember you are here."

Bluntly put. Apparently, Mother Abbess also had been mulling what possible actions the king could take upon the loss of his heir. Nicole didn't care if Stephen eventually lost his throne or not, but as his ward, she cared very much whether or not he would use her in an attempt to gain a desired alliance.

"I cannot say I am of a mind to marry a Welsh prince."

"You have always known the day might come. You also know how to avoid the king's machinations."

Nicole fingered the ends of her brown, waist-length braid. She could cut her hair short, cover it with a veil, and utter vows. She recoiled as she always did when she considered becoming a nun and spending her entire life in Bledloe Abbey.

"You well know I have no calling to the Lord's service. 'Twould be no less than I deserved if God struck me deaf and blind the moment I uttered insincere vows."

"Then perhaps you should consult your sisters. They would come if you summoned them."

Emma and Gwendolyn would certainly make every effort, but they had husbands and children and estates to care for. And certes, at ten and eight, Nicole felt she shouldn't burden her beloved sisters if she could work out her problems on her own.

And, certes, no problem yet existed. King Stephen hadn't yet decreed whom she should marry. Worrying over it would do her no good, and Nicole wanted no distractions from what she saw as her immediate and more important task. Caring for Mother Abbess.

"I will consult Emma and Gwendolyn when the proper time comes," she said, more to ease the furrows on the abbess's brow than to quell her own misgivings. "Are you in pain? Need you a potion?"

"These old bones ache from disuse, but the pain reminds me there is life inside me yet. Go ready for prayer. The bell will ring soon."

Though she preferred to remain in the infirmary, brewing potions and mixing unguents, she would attend morning prayers, if only out of love for Mother Abbess.

Nicole rose from the stool and kissed her friend and mentor's thin-skinned forehead, wondering if she should tell the abbess of the joyous reunion with Sister Enid awaiting her on the other side of life.

She would, she decided, but not until the very end when the abbess had no time left for questions and lectures.

Sister Enid, Nicole was sure, would let her know when that time was upon them.

"I will bring your morning repast after matins. Is there aught particular you would like?"

Another shift of fingers, another bead to hold between thumb and forefinger. Another prayer offered up to some good purpose.

"Nay. My hunger now is not for victuals. Ask the sisters to pray that I might see our Lord's face sooner than later."

The abbess had thoroughly accepted her impending death. Nicole wasn't in that much of a hurry.

"I will do no such thing. Our Lord will take you when He wills and not a moment before. Have pity on those of us you leave behind, dearest Abbess. We shall be like lost ships in a storm-tossed sea without you to guide us home."

The nun chuckled. "Oh, life will continue without me, and each of you will find your way."

"Rudderless, wind-deprived, becalmed ships, I tell you."

Mother Abbess's hand rose, and Nicole took the hand that had gently but firmly guided a headstrong girl into womanhood.

"The way is never easy, Nicole de Leon. Remember this. When times seem the most confusing, point your bow to either sunrise or sunset and follow your heart."

Appealing images—in opposite directions.

And neither course guaranteed a welcoming shoreline or safe haven.

THE DISH

Where authors give you the inside scoop!

♥ ♥ ♥ ♥ ♥ ♥ ♥ ♥ ♥ ♥ ♥ ♥ ♥ ♥ ♥

*From the desks of Shari Anton
and Paula Quinn*

Dear Readers:

From intimate visions to dancing warriors to King Arthur, Shari Anton and Paula Quinn dish in this author-to-author interview.

Shari Anton: Paula, how nice to see your **LORD OF SEDUCTION** (on sale now) on the bookstore shelves with my **TWILIGHT MAGIC** (on sale now) this December! Double the medieval fun! You really must tell me about your story.

Paula Quinn: Well, Shari, Tanon Risande is a prim and proper lady of the realm. Her predictable little world is turned upside down with the arrival of a fierce Welsh prince, Gareth ab Owain, who has come to claim her as his bride. Tanon has no intention of submitting to such a rough warrior, but Gareth is determined to prove to her that he is no savage. He will use far more persuasive methods to lure this lady willingly into his arms . . . and into his bed.

Is your couple as seemingly mismatched as mine?

Shari Anton: Of course! Lady Emma de Leon is about to present a petition to King Stephen when Darian of Bruges is accused of murder. She recognizes Darian as the man she once saw in a very intimate vision, so she's compelled to save him by giving him an alibi, claiming they spent the previous night together. The king then insists they marry. Emma had planned on the bedding, but not the wedding, especially to an ungrateful Flemish mercenary who wants no wife! The last thing Darian wants is to be the man of Emma's dreams, but ignoring Emma's charms and rebuffing her advances prove futile.

Prince Gareth sounds like a true **LORD OF SEDUCTION**! What aspect of him will intrigue readers most?

Paula Quinn: My favorite thing about Gareth is that he learned to fight by dancing. Yes, this warrior dances like nobody's business! I also love that he goes barefoot and wears torcs. There's something very feral about it. He's extremely confident without being arrogant (although Tanon would disagree).

You've added a paranormal element to **TWILIGHT MAGIC**. How fascinating that Emma has visions!

Shari Anton: Poor Emma doesn't like having them. Lucky for my story Emma saw Darian in a vision before she learned how to halt them! And scattered throughout my Magic trilogy is the legend of King Arthur.

So between us we have Norman ladies, a Welsh prince, a Flemish mercenary, torcs and dancing, visions and intrigue. Wow! I'd say Warner Forever readers are in for a real treat this month.

Paula Quinn: Agreed!

Sincerely,

Shari Anton   Paula Quinn

TWILIGHT MAGIC   LORD OF SEDUCTION
www.sharianton.com   www.paulaquinn.com